I0607158

A Time
of
Their Own

by

Linda LaRoque

A Wild Rose Press Bouquet

A Time of Their Own

A Law of Her Own, COPYRIGHT © 2014 by Linda LaRoque
A Marshal of Her Own, COPYRIGHT © 2014 by Linda LaRoque
A Love of His Own, COPYRIGHT © 2014 by Linda LaRoque

Contact Information: info@thewildrosepress.com
Cover Art by *Diana Carlile*

The Wild Rose Press, Inc.
PO Box 708
Adams Basin, NY 14410-0708
Visit us at www.thewildrosepress.com
Publishing History:
First Cactus Rose Edition, 2014
Print ISBN 978-1-62830-417-6
Digital ISBN 978-1-62830-440-4
Published in the United States of America

She gazed up at him and he looked his fill—the smooth skin, clear blue eyes, and full pink lips. Lips he didn't doubt would be quite enjoyable to taste. He breathed in her scent and felt his groin tighten in response to the clean womanly smell. If she wore perfumed powder, she'd used it sparingly.

He lifted his hand toward her hair, but sought her eyes before he touched the blond tresses. She didn't shrink back in fear. Like corn silk, the strands slid through his fingers.

"Have you seen enough, Mr. Reardon?"

"Well, can't say I wouldn't like to see more."

"You'll have to wait for that until after the ceremony."

He chuckled. "I can wait." His fingers dropped from her hair, his knuckles brushed down her cheek. "Why are you doing this, Miss Dawson?"

"You're an innocent man. I'm here in a strange place, a strange time, and I need you to help me. Will that suffice until after the ceremony, when I can explain things further?"

"Yes, if you're sure about this."

"I'm sure."

"It's not often a man gets engaged and marries all in one day. I think a kiss might be in order. And I want to hear you say my name, Charity."

"I agree, Turner, a kiss would definitely seal the deal."

Hands at her waist, Turner lowered his head and softly touched his lips to hers. She didn't back away, so he pulled her closer, crushing her softness to his hard length. She moaned and her arms went around his neck. *Oh, God, she was sweet.*

Praise for Linda LaRoque

A LAW OF HER OWN

"A well thought out, well written story…With her descriptions of the life and time, Mrs. LaRoque paints a wonderful picture of Texas in the 1800's."

~Fallen Angel Reviews

"LaRoque's characters come alive in a fast-paced western romance you will want to finish in one read. There is realism to the story that only a few time travel authors can bring to the page."

~Night Own Romance

"The research…was phenomenal. I certainly never expected the twists and turns that led to the characters becoming involved with one another let alone what led to the capture of the true murderer."

~Simply Romance Reviews

A MARSHAL OF HER OWN

"Ms. LaRoque brings her characters to life with vivid descriptions and effortlessly weaves humor with drama…a visually creative, touching and uplifting romance. I highly recommend this book."

~You Gotta Read Reviews

"Dessa wasn't the only person swept back in time through the pages of this incredible tale…Ms. La Roque does a marvelous job of bringing both the past and present characters to life in their different settings."

~Long and Short Reviews (Book of the Year 2012)

A LOVE OF HIS OWN

"It was great to revisit with old friends from the first two books in the series…. I can assure you, you won't be disappointed."

~Romancing the Book

A Law
of
Her Own

by

Linda LaRoque

Dedication

In loving memory of my mother, Rose.
She would have enjoyed this story as she did life.
Remembering her laughter makes me smile.

Chapter One

New York, June 14, 2008

"Daddy. I'm quitting."

There, she'd done it. Charity Dawson had been telling her father for the five years she'd worked in his law firm she didn't want to practice corporate law.

Her father's face reddened, and he rose from his chair. He strode around the massive mahogany desk. "Now, honey, you're just tired and need a vacation."

Her dream was to be a public defender. She'd had her fill of rich clients needing legal loopholes for their lack of honesty on income tax returns or lawsuits in which they were clearly at fault.

"No, Daddy, I need a life change."

She walked toward him, arms outstretched, intent on kissing him goodbye. He stepped back.

Hands at her sides, she whispered, "Goodbye, Daddy. I love you."

Then she turned and walked from the silent office. The door closing behind her sounded like the lid dropping on her coffin.

****

Texas, June 15, 2008

The morning after her arrival in Austin, Charity arranged to rent a car at her hotel for the short drive to the cabin fifteen miles west of Fredericksburg. She'd slept late, so by the time she made travel arrangements and ate an early lunch, it was just after noon. Unable to resist the lure of the shops in Fredericksburg, she stopped in the small German town and strolled through the great selection of merchandise.

By late afternoon she was back in her car, headed west to the cabin she'd rented. The owner had given her good directions, so she had no problem finding it. She pulled in the drive, got out, and stood for a minute admiring the view. It was a lovely place, made of rough hewn logs. The roof was tin and extended out over a wooden porch held up with cedar posts. Colorful pink and yellow flowers lined the walkway to and across the front of the house.

To one side stood an old footed cast iron bathtub, filled with lavender, Gerbera daisies, and a short green ground cover. It sat regally under a nearly dead mesquite tree. On the opposite side large boulders served as the backdrop for a cactus garden. The prickly pear cactus was in bloom. Its orange and yellow blossoms were an odd comparison to the steer skull on display. Oak trees, some small, others large and dominating, surrounded the perimeter of the house and as far as she could see.

She smiled in pleasure. The dwelling exuded rest, peace, and quiet. It was just what she needed to gather her defenses and decide what to do.

The key was right where she'd been told it'd be— under the ugly cast iron frog by the step. She opened the door, peeked around inside, then went back for her luggage. Though she'd tried to pack lightly, she'd come with three large bags. Lugging them up the narrow, steep stairway was a chore. She left them on the landing and went downstairs to close the front door.

Standing in the living area, she surveyed her surroundings. Quaint was the only way she could describe the small house. A stuffed sofa and chair, a desk, and a built-in bookshelf were the only furniture in the room other than a couple of end tables and standing lamps. She loved it and couldn't wait to see the rest of the lodge.

In the kitchen, a wooden table dominated the center of the small room. A vase of silk roses placed in the center added additional color to the blue-and-white tablecloth. A breakfront with a variety of colorful dishes covered one wall.

She gazed at the vintage appliances—an old gas stove and one of those refrigerators with the rounded sides. A yellow sticky note on its door caught her eye. *Laid in a few groceries for you to make do until you can get to the grocers.*

How nice of them.

On the counter sat a loaf of bread, a box of crackers, and a bottle of Bordeaux wine. She opened the icebox to add the items she'd bought in town and found eggs, milk, cheese, fresh fruit, and butter, just what she needed after her long trip from New York. She was hungry, but a hot bath and her pajamas would come first.

She hurried up the stairs to find the bathroom with its old claw foot tub. Turning on the hot water, she let it warm, adjusting it with the cold before putting in the stopper. A variety of bath salts sat on a small table. She selected one—lavender—sprinkled it liberally in the water, and ran to get a change of clothes.

There was only one bedroom. It had a double bed

with a cast iron headboard, an oak chest, and wallpaper with large cabbage roses. In any other house, the paper would have been garish, but it fit the cabin and furnishings perfectly.

She heaved a suitcase onto the bed and retrieved clean underwear, her pajamas, and her comfy flip-flops. Stepping out of her sandals, she stripped off her light gray slacks and pink blouse, tossing them on the bed. They were too wrinkled to wear again. Her lacy pink bra and bikini panties joined the stack. With her fresh clothes in her arms, she padded barefoot to the bathroom.

The tub was almost full, so she turned off the tap. Thick Egyptian cotton towels and washcloths were neatly stacked in the cabinet. A variety of fresh bars of scented soaps filled a straw basket. After smelling a few, she picked one that smelled like the lavender bath salts she'd added earlier. She selected a towel and washcloth and set the items on the toilet seat.

The water was hot. Cautiously, she eased one leg after the other into the fragrant water. Then she slowly sank, bit by bit, until her butt landed on the tub bottom. With a sigh, she gradually leaned back and immersed her arms and shoulders. Steam rose from the water, bringing with it the heavenly scent of lavender. She breathed in the fragrance and allowed the warmth to ease her tense muscles.

Her cell phone rang, and she ignored it. She'd call them back. Thirty minutes later she stepped from the tub and dried with the thick towel. Her blond hair, cut to fall just below her chin, had curled from the moist heat. She selected one of the body lotions from the cabinet and spread it generously on her body. The aroma of the thick cream wasn't strong, yet it exuded a subtle scent that was pleasant to the senses.

Dressed in her pajamas and sandals, she hung the towel up to dry and rinsed the tub with the dirty washcloth before adding it to the rack. Now for food. Nope, she better check to see who called first. She opened the cell phone to see Daddy's name and number. *Please, Lord. I hope it's not a scathing message.* Keying in the numbers, she waited for his message.

She jerked her ear away from the phone as his voice boomed across the airwaves. "Why the hell haven't you called me, young lady? Don't you know I'm sitting here, worrying, wondering if you made it okay?" He paused for a minute. Voice gruff, he added, "I'm sorry, Charity. I didn't realize you were so unhappy. Ah, shit, I did too but was too damn selfish to do anything about it. Things will be different when you get home, I promise. Call me. I love you, baby."

****

After her breakfast of eggs and toast, wearing her sandals and still in her pajamas, Charity took her coffee to the back porch. She'd not noticed when she drove in yesterday, but just thirty feet from the cabin was a pond, tank, or whatever they were called in Texas. Dirt was built up around the sides. She strolled out to a large oak that grew out over the pond, casting a shadow on the sunlit water. The water was clear, so much so that through it she could see every indention in the mud below, tadpoles and small fish catching bugs as they landed on the surface.

There was nothing groomed about the yard out back. Oh, the grass and weeds had been mowed, but the ground was littered with small fallen oak leaves. Even so, it was picturesque and didn't detract from the cabin's beauty at all.

She refilled her coffee cup and left the back porch to walk along the path around the small tank. Her sandals slid on some of the loose rocks, and she fought to gain her balance before falling. Next time out she'd wear tennis shoes, or at least something with a closed toe. Behind the berm ran a creek. A small wooden bridge made access to the other side easy. She sidestepped down the embankment and stopped at the bridge to peer at a small clearing completely shaded by large trees on the other side. In this weather, it might be the perfect place to sit outside on a blanket in the shade and read. At the airport, she'd bought several paperback novels—an interesting change from the law magazines she usually read. She'd bring one out this afternoon, if it wasn't too hot.

She retraced her steps to the path that led back to the house. Upstairs, she dressed in a long, casual floral skirt and a loose thin cotton blouse gathered at the neck. The long sleeves hit just below her elbows and tied with a cotton strap. She stepped into a brown pair of fisherman sandals and plopped a big straw hat on her head. Her set of gold gypsy bracelets clanked as she walked downstairs. She loved this outfit, mostly because it didn't fit her personality, or the persona she should portray.

Well, today she didn't have to worry about those things. She was plain old Charity Dawson, blond gypsy, seeker of adventure. In the entry mirror she checked her silver-dollar-size gold hoop earrings, set the hat at a better angle, and, purse in hand, headed for her car.

The drive into Fredericksburg only took fifteen minutes. She parked the car in front of a small restaurant with patrons sitting outside under a canopy. The block around it and across the street was filled with novelty shops—a veritable paradise. She'd spend all morning touring the shops, enjoy lunch at the bistro, and then head back to the cabin for a nap. Her flight had been more tiring than she'd expected.

Two hours later, with packages, she sat down at one of the tables under the awning. It had grown warmer outside, but the breeze felt pleasant. She put her packages in an empty chair and stacked her hat on top. With her fingers, she fluffed her hair, lifting the damp blond strands away from her scalp. The motion set her bracelets tinkling and several people looked her way. She smiled politely and turned her attention to the menu on the table.

A waiter appeared by her side. She ordered a Reuben and a glass of peach tea. While she waited, she examined the vintage art deco ring she'd bought at one of the shops. Three marquise-cut diamonds banked by emeralds were set in an oblong base of platinum. It had put a dent in her savings account, but she'd not bought anything for herself in a while. Hell, she worked twelve-hour days. There wasn't time to shop for anything other than the business clothes. She needed a bauble to boost her spirits.

Her sandwich was delicious. It was stuffed with sauerkraut. She pulled some free with her fork and popped it in her mouth. The tartness of the cabbage made her cheeks pucker, reminding her of the pinched expression on the jewelry clerk's face when Charity described where she was staying. The older woman mumbled something about "strange doings out there." Before Charity could ask what she meant, a man from the back room muttered, "That'll be enough gossip, Mae."

What doings was she talking about? Drat! Charity wished the guy hadn't stopped Mae's talk. Old folks had interesting tales to share. Oh, well, maybe she could get back to town and visit with her another day—without her guard.

Charity returned to the cabin, packages in tow, shortly after two o'clock that afternoon.

She'd bought a beautiful handmade shawl, in pale blue, for the winter and a pair of soft brown leather boots. The heels were low. They zipped up the side, and came halfway up her calf. Kicking off her sandals, she pulled a thin pair of socks from a drawer, slipped them on, and the boots followed. Actually they didn't look bad with her gypsy skirt and blouse.

She found a quilt on the top shelf of the closet and folded it over her arm. Sunhat on her head, paperback book in her hand, she danced downstairs. As she passed through the parlor, she plucked a decorative pillow off the sofa. In the kitchen, she stopped at the refrigerator to get a bottle of water. On impulse, she grabbed one of the red silk roses from the arrangement on the table, stuck it behind her ear, and left the cabin by the back door. The sun beat down, warming her skin. Hopefully in the shade it would be comfortable.

Her stride was full of purpose as she walked toward the path on the embankment. The boots were better protection for her feet, and she had no difficulty getting down to the creek and the bridge.

As she stepped onto the bridge, a breeze caught her

hat, almost ripping it off her head. She caught it before it became airborne and, laughing, ran the rest of the way across and into the small clearing. The entire area was shaded and felt ten degrees cooler. She spread the blanket on the ground, tossed her hat aside, and stretched out on the quilt with the pillow under her head.

Now she'd read her torrid western historical romance novel. The cover of *Taming the Cowboy* showed two half-dressed people in a serious lip lock. From what she'd read so far, it appeared the heroine was the one being tamed. Set in the Panhandle Plains of Texas, the hero, Rafe, was an alpha male, tall, dark-headed, with black eyes and the shadow of a beard. Julie, the meek little woman, had blond hair, blue eyes, and a streak of determination. She wasn't about to let the ranch manager take over control of *her* ranch.

Charity became engrossed in the story. The lack of respect for a woman's mind in those days and the condescending ways of men amazed her. It was a good thing she wasn't born in that time period. She was halfway through the book and the two'd had sex in the hayloft but argued about every aspect of running the ranch. She yawned and shook her head at the stupidity of people. Dog-earing the page of the book, she set it aside and closed her eyes.

Just a short nap, that's what she needed. It was so peaceful here, no cell phone, no computers, no...what would it be like to live in Texas in the old days? Probably not nearly as romantic as her novel depicted. She chuckled at the idea... Nope, she was a modern woman. On that thought, she drifted to sleep.

****

Prairie, Texas, June 15, 1888

Turner Reardon paced the floor in the small, hot jail cell, anger and frustration eating at his soul. The sound of hammers striking thick nails into boards—boards forming the scaffold for his hanging, pounded against his skull.

Only one person could want Lucinda dead and him to take the blame—Edward Samuelson.

Damn his soul to hell. Edward intended to see him hang for a crime he didn't commit. And for what reason? Lucinda Bowers had spurned Edward's advances for those of Turner. It was a known fact the widow had men in at night, but she never favored more than one man at a time. When she'd told Edward to stop coming by, the man had lost all reason. Her rejection was the final straw. He'd killed Lucinda, or had her killed, and now tried to blame it on Turner.

Edward was the owner of the town's only bank. An upstanding citizen, one above reproach. He was present at church every Sunday, participated in every charitable event the town sponsored, and had a condescending smile that made Turner want to knock his teeth out of his head.

Oh, he was pleasant enough, until Lucinda told him she was seeing someone else and not to come calling again. Then the devil in the man made its appearance. He'd tried to redirect funds from Turner's account, pleading ignorance on the part of a staff member. Then someone had set fire to a section of hay on his land. If the fire hadn't been caught in time, he wouldn't have enough feed for the winter. He would have been forced to sell off some of his cattle. Though he'd suspected Edward was the culprit, his hands were tied until he could prove it.

Turner had been the one to find Lucinda lying on the floor in a pool of blood. The bastard had gutted her with a hunting knife, *his* hunting knife. It had been missing from his saddlebag for over a week. The wound started below the waist and arched across her belly. They'd found his bloody knife behind her house where he'd tied his horse. He'd never hurt Lucinda. He didn't love the woman, but cared for her in his own way. They enjoyed each other's company in and out of bed.

Turner stopped and leaned against the barred window. As often happened, a good wind passed through their town in the panhandle of Texas and dirt twirled around in the street. Women held their bonnets on and struggled to keep their skirts on the ground. Most tried to avoid looking at the scaffold being built on Main Street.

Well, it appeared the little jackass had done it, convinced everyone he was guilty. Tomorrow there'd be a trial. The jury would convict him, and he'd swing from a rope. He flung away from the window and sat on the narrow cot. Elbows on his knees, he dropped his head into his hands and massaged his scalp.

This was one hell of a mess, and he didn't have a clue how to get out of it. Oh, he could have his ranch hands come in, bullets flying, and help him escape, but what would that serve? Nothing. Then he'd be a wanted man and always on the run, as would his men. But it would give him time to prove his innocence.

Maybe that little pissant of a lawyer he'd hired was smarter than he'd given him credit for and would come up with some kind of evidence to free him. He stretched out on the bed, his feet hanging off the end. Jail furniture wasn't built to accommodate his six-foot, four-inch frame.

He went over the scene again in his mind, hoping he'd remember something to help him prove his innocence. Damn if he wasn't in one fine fix. He wasn't ready to die.

****

The sun beat down with a fury. Charity could see it through the cracks in the straw hat she'd put over her face at some point. Her arms stung as if she were sunburned. Yanking the hat from her face, she sat up and stretched. Man, what happened to all that shade and the cool breeze? It felt a hundred degrees. She glanced at her watch. It was seven o'clock. The sun should be setting soon.

She plopped the hat on her head, stood, and reached down to pick up the quilt. As she shook it out, she froze and her mouth fell open. The terrain had changed. The trees were gone, as were the bridge, tank, and cabin. She searched in all four directions, shook her head, blinked her eyes, but she saw the same thing. Miles of wheat waved with the increasing breeze. She stood at the base of a large tree. The ground was covered with a short wild type of grass, small rocks, and dirt.

Her breath hitched in her chest, and she struggled to keep from screaming in fear and confusion. *Okay, be calm, now. There has to be an explanation for this.* Her advice did little to calm her, and the uncertainty was quickly overtaking her reason. She looked around again. There seemed to be nothing for miles around, no buildings or roads—nothing.

In the distance she heard something, a steady

clomp, clomp, clomp, rattling, and the sound of voices—children laughing. She searched the horizon and saw dust stirred up on the other side of the wheat field. There had to be a road over there, and a car traveling at a slow speed.

"Help, help!" she screamed. She drew the quilt over her arm, picked up the book, her water and pillow, and started running across the field. Stalks of wheat caught at her skirt as she jogged through them, but she didn't care, she yanked the material free.

"Wait...please wait!" She gasped for breath and stumbled out to the roadway. It wasn't a car; a wagon pulled by mules had just passed. She dropped to her knees in the dirt, gasping for breath. *Damn.* Only a minute more and she'd have caught them. Sobs caught in her throat and threatened to erupt.

You stop that right now. You're not helpless. You can follow the wagon. It has to be going somewhere.

"Hey, lady, you all right?"

She looked up to see a man and a woman rushing toward her. *Thank you, God!*

They stopped several yards away.

The woman wore an old-fashioned sunbonnet and a long gingham dress. She drew closer and knelt beside Charity. "Miss, are you hurt anywheres?"

Charity shook her head and sucked in air. "No. I'm lost. I don't know where I am, or how I got here."

The man and woman exchanged glances. *They think I'm crazy, and Lord, I probably am.*

He shook his head.

"But Frank, we can't just leave her here on the road." She propped her hands on her hips. "What if it was one of our girls, and someone didn't help them?"

He removed his ragged hat and slapped it against his thigh. Dust flew everywhere. "Oh, hell, Merle, let's get her in the wagon."

They helped her stand. "I won't be a problem, I promise." She stared down at her wrist and took off one of the bracelets. She held it out to the man. "Here, take this. It's twenty-four karat gold. Surely it'll pay for my way to wherever you're going."

The man reached for the bracelet, but he jerked his hand back after seeing the expression on his wife's face.

"Honey, there is no need to pay us. Helping you is the Christian thing to do. This is my husband, Frank Smithers, and my name is Merle."

"I'm Charity Dawson from New York City, but I...."

Merle took Charity's arm and led her toward the wagon. "We're going into town for supplies. We'll camp for the night and should be there by noon tomorrow. Tonight we'll talk and try to help you get things straight in your mind."

Charity climbed in the back of the wagon with the children. "This is Lucy, Amy, and Polly."

"Hello, young ladies. My name is Charity."

The three little girls giggled and studied her with their sky-blue eyes. Finally one got up the nerve to speak. "Pa says there's gonna be a hangin' in a few days."

A hanging? They didn't hang people anymore, did they?

Merle turned around and thumped the girl on the head. "Don't you be talking about such, young lady. The man hasn't even been tried yet."

"Ouch, Ma. That hurt."

"It was supposed to remind you of your manners, Lucy. You don't go around telling tales."

"Yes, ma'am."

Lucy rubbed the sore spot on her head, leaned over, and whispered. "My Pa says they'll probably hang him. They pretty much caught him red-handed, and killin' a woman is worse than killin' a man."

Curious now, Charity couldn't resist. "Mr. Smithers, is it true a man's on trial for his life?"

"Yes, ma'am," he said out of the side of his mouth while keeping his eyes on the mules pulling the wagon. "He's accused of killing a widow lady he'd been seeing. I think he's looking at the end of a hangman's noose."

"Frank Smithers, you know Turner is not the type to kill on the sly, and especially a woman," said Merle. "Now, I can see him killing someone in defense, but not like that woman was killed." Merle shuddered.

Charity wanted to ask for more details but hated to ask in front of the children. She watched the wheat fields pass. Occasionally, another crop grew alongside the dirt road—one that looked like hay. As darkness began to fall, Frank pulled the wagon off the road into a small clearing.

The girls scrambled out of the wagon and ran off to play. Merle yelled, "Don't go far, and watch for snakes."

"Yes, Ma. We will."

Merle pulled a picnic basket to the end of the bed of the wagon while Frank unhitched the mules and led them a short distance away to water and feed them.

"Can I help you, Mrs. Smithers?"

15

"Sure." She tossed a quilt to Charity. "See if you can find a level space without too many rocks, and spread this." She smiled. "And call me Merle."

Charity caught the blanket. "Thank you, I will. And please, call me Charity."

Still smiling, Merle nodded and went about taking things from the basket.

As soon as the quilt was on the ground, Merle laid out the food wrapped in dishcloths. She placed several jars of tea in the center. Straightening, she turned toward the wheat field, stuck two fingers in her mouth and issued an ear-splitting whistle.

"Comin', Ma," echoed across the field.

Merle dropped to the ground. "Sit here by me. If you get stuck in the middle of the girls, they'll talk your ear off."

"They're just excited. I imagine I'm an oddity to them."

"I 'spect you're right," said Merle.

Charity suspected the two adults were curious also, but they were too polite to ask questions.

Frank and the girls dropped to the blanket. He bowed his head and his family followed suit. Charity quickly acted on their example.

"Lord, thank you for the bounty before us. Amen."

Merle uncovered the food. There was a ham, a fresh loaf of bread, and pickles. Two pieces of bread with a thick slice of ham on top of one was placed in Charity's hand. She covered the ham and took a bite. It was heavenly, absolutely the best sandwich she'd ever put in her mouth. Maybe she was hungrier than she thought, or possibly it was the fresh air and excitement. "Merle, this is the best homemade bread I've ever eaten."

"Why I just follow a standard recipe."

"But it's fresh. I'm used to packaged bread. You know, the kind that comes wrapped up in paper and is sold at the grocery store."

Merle glanced at her husband and shook her head. "No, I don't believe I've ever seen packaged bread."

Oh dear, thought Charity. She was really in the boondocks if these people didn't know about store-bought bread. "Do you ever have automobiles drive on this road?"

Frank sat up a little straighter. "Nope, but hopefully someday. We saw a picture of one in the newspaper a while back."

"Why, I read they're noisy and always get stuck in the mud," said Merle. "Seems to be a waste of good money, to me. A mule and wagon get us where we need to go without all that coughing and belching. Why, the machines even run out of gas out in the middle of nowhere."

Charity's stomach churned with anxiety. "What is the name of the town we'll be in tomorrow?"

"Name is Prairie. The reason being it was all grassland back twenty-five years ago when it was settled by four or five families. There are probably thirty families living in town now, and three to four times that many living on outlying farms and ranches." Frank beamed. "We're right proud of how much our little town has grown in just the past ten years."

She had to know, but didn't want to ask. "You know, I can't exactly remember the date. Is it June or July?"

Merle looked concerned. "Did you get hit on the

head?"

Charity touched her head and felt for sore spots. "No."

"It's June 15, 1888."

Her vision blurred, and she gasped a lungful of air. *Oh, God! Is this what Mae meant by "strange doings"?*

Chapter Two

They drove into Prairie at noon. Charity was tired to the bone and on the edge of hysteria. Mr. Smithers stopped the wagon in front of a building with a sign that read Sheriff's Office. He handed the reins to Merle, hopped down, and came around to the back to help Charity out of the wagon. The man had been much nicer this morning. She didn't know if it was because she'd soon be off his hands or if he'd heard her crying half the night and felt sorry for her.

"Here we go, Miss Charity. The sheriff will know how to help you. Now, if things don't work out for you here, ask anyone in town where the Smithers' farm is and they'll point you in the right direction."

"Thank you, Mr. Smithers. You've been very kind."

He cleared his throat. "It's the least a body could do for one of our own lost souls." He walked on into the sheriff's office.

Hell, the man didn't realize how true his statement was. Lost wasn't half the size of it. She walked to the front of the wagon and bid Merle goodbye.

"When you get settled, come out and visit sometime," said Merle.

"I'll do that."

"Here she is, Sheriff. Name's Charity Dawson. Says she's from New York City, but don't have a clue

19

how or why she's here." Frank Smithers stood on the porch with a large bull of a man. Most of his weight was muscle, but his belly had begun to turn to fat and hung over his belt. "Miss Dawson, this is Sheriff Elijah Cannon."

With his brow wrinkled, the sheriff studied her from head to toe. At last he spoke. "Come in, Miss Dawson. Let's see what we can do for you."

She waved to the Smithers before going inside. The room was sparsely furnished with a desk and several chairs. A gun cabinet stood against one wall, and behind the desk a set of large keys hung from a railroad spike hammered into the wood. No doubt they opened the steel door several feet from the keys.

He pulled a chair closer to his desk. "Have a seat," he said. She sat down with the quilt wrapped around her pillow and the paperback book in her lap.

He opened the desk drawer and removed a sheet of paper and a pencil. "All right, little lady, tell me everything you can remember."

She watched his expression as she related just what she'd told the Smithers family—she awoke in a wheat field and couldn't remember how she'd gotten there. His steel gray eyes, that matched his hair and mustache, watched her like a hawk about to close its talons around its prey.

He didn't believe her story. Hell, she wouldn't either if she were him. Under the circumstances, it'd be best if she didn't confide she'd been in the Hill Country when she went to sleep.

"How can you know your name and where you're from without knowing how you got to Prairie?"

"I don't have a clue."

He studied her a minute, then shoved his chair back and stood. With his arm at her elbow, he helped her to her feet. Lord, the man acted like she didn't have the strength to stand on her own.

"Let's get you over to Doc Wilson's and see if you've got a head injury or something."

Running footsteps, coming toward them, pounded on the boardwalk. A voice shouted, "Come on, Sheriff, they're resuming the trial." A breathless young man with a star on his shirt slid to a halt just outside the door.

"John, escort this young woman to Doc Wilson's."

A trial? That's right. Mr. Smithers mentioned a murder trial. "Sheriff, please let me go to the trial. I can see the doctor after it's over."

He shook his head. "I don't know. We need to get you checked out."

"I'm fine," she promised.

"All right, come on. The doc will most likely be at the trial anyhow." He took her bundle and dropped it in the chair, then took her arm and escorted her outside. They walked a block to the square. A brand spanking new courthouse stood majestically in the middle of the large lot. It was made of red bricks, with a tall, wide stairway leading to a porch with white colonial columns.

Inside, they took a seat behind the prosecutor's table. Before she was fully settled on the hard bench, a door opened and a man wearing a marshal's star brought in the prisoner, a tall man wearing a vested suit with a white shirt and tie. His face appeared carved from stone, ready to crack at any minute. He was handsome in a rugged way. Work in the sun had tanned his skin, making his eyes appear robin's egg blue. Dark hair fell in waves to just below his collar, and he tossed his head to get it out of his face.

Good grief, he was a good-looking man. The thought had no more than cleared her mind when he stopped at the prosecutor's table. He glanced at the sheriff, and then turned those blue eyes on her. They immediately turned glacial and fixed her to the bench like a spear of ice. Gooseflesh broke out on her arms, and she shivered. What was wrong with him? She hadn't done anything to him.

Turner couldn't help but stare at the blond-haired woman. He'd never seen a woman with her hair cut so short and wearing such large earrings. Who was she and why was she here? His gaze was drawn to her face— blue eyes, brown eyebrows and lashes, and pink lips. She was lovely. When he peered into the depths of her eyes, he felt an electrical jolt. Did he know her?

He mentally shook himself and continued to the table where his skinny inept lawyer sat. The man tried, but he just didn't have the backbone to go toe to toe with the prosecutor. He might have been better off to defend himself.

The bailiff announced, "All rise for Judge Howell." The judge fluttered in with his black robe flowing and sat down at the desk on the dais. He gave Turner a hard look and then turned to the prosecution.

"Are you ready to finish your charges against the defendant, Mr. Jamison?"

The rotund prosecutor stood and pulled his vest down tightly over his large belly. "Yes, sir, I am. I just have one more thing to add." He turned to his assistant. "Will you please move the chalkboard around to the other side?"

The young man did so. "Now, Doctor Wilson, will you draw a torso and show us how the woman was cut, and how the fatal wound was delivered?"

Doc stood, walked to the chalkboard, and picked up a piece of chalk. It didn't take him long to show the terrible knife wound that started on the victim's left side and continued over and up under her right breast. The thought of Lucinda dying such a horrible death was nauseating. If he ever got out of this fix, he'd find her murderer and make him pay.

Jamison parroted in front of the jury. "Now, Doctor, would you say that was a good rendering? That's exactly how the wound looked?"

Doc Wilson nodded. "Yes."

"How deep did you say the wound was?"

"Jamison, I've said three times already the wound was three inches deep in places." Doc was livid. He turned to the chalkboard, picked up the chalk, and wrote it: three inches deep. "There, do you think that's clear enough for you?"

The room roared with laughter. Judge Howell pounded the gavel. "That'll be enough. Silence, or I'll empty this court." The room settled to a low hum and then became quiet.

Jamison's neck was red as he turned to the jury. "Take a good look at that horrendous wound, folks." Then he pivoted and pointed at Turner. Everyone in the room turned toward him. Some glances were sympathetic, others were filled with hate. He continued to doodle on the pad in front of him and, without luck, tried to ignore their stares. "And that's the man who inflicted it. The state rests, Your Honor."

Turner's attention, along with the audience's, quickly moved to the strange blonde as she struggled with the sheriff. Finally he let her go and she moved to sit behind the defense table. *What could she be up to?*

Judge Howell scowled. "Young woman, you will remain seated in my court."

She stood, nodded, and replied. "Yes, sir, Your Honor." Her voice was warm and scratchy like good rye whiskey. The judge appeared mollified by her dignified answer and nodded back.

Judge Howell turned to Turner's attorney. "Mr. Bailey, are you ready to present your evidence for the defense?"

Bailey stood and, voice quaking, stuttered, "Yes...sir, your...Honor." He started picking through papers. The woman behind them pulled on his coattail, and he bent down while she whispered in his ear. His faced registered shock and he shook his head, but she leaned over, slapped the rail with her palm, and whispered again.

Flustered, he said, "Uh, Your Honor...I have a surprise witness." Sweat was pouring from his face and he pulled at his collar.

"Well, get on with it, Bailey," said the judge.

Bailey appeared to plea to the heavens, but took a deep breath and announced, "Miss Charity Dawson, please take the stand."

The sheriff and Jamison both jumped up at the same time. "I object, Your Honor," said Jamison. The sheriff shouted, "That young woman just arrived here this morning; she can't know anything about the murder."

The judge scowled at the woman. "Is that true,

Miss Dawson?"

"Yes, sir, it is. But I'm a lawyer from New York with some skill in forensic science that I think will greatly help this case. I beg your indulgence, Your Honor. Please let me speak."

Sheriff Cannon threw up his hands. Jamison howled, "I object, Your Honor. Who ever heard of a woman lawyer?"

Judge Howell scratched his head. "I'll allow it, Mr. Bailey, but it better be good."

"Yes, sir, Judge."

Turner watched in fascination as the young woman was sworn in and took the stand. She sat down in the witness box with no fear, as if she did it every day.

"First, miss," said Bailey. "Will you define forensic science for the court?"

She smiled, and her blue eyes lit with excitement. "It is the study of evidence in cases and how to use those facts to prove or disprove someone's innocence or guilt."

A quiet murmur went through the audience.

"Do you have some information that is helpful in this case?"

"Yes, I do."

Jamison jumped up again. "I strongly object, Your Honor."

"Objection so noted, Prosecutor. Now sit down and shut up," ordered the judge. Jamison fell into his chair and closed his mouth. Turner wanted to chuckle but restrained the urge. Doing so would just make the prosecutor more determined to hang him.

"Now, Miss Dawson, please continue," said Judge Howell.

"May I move to the chalkboard, Your Honor? I'd like to point out something about the wound that will be helpful."

Turner didn't know what was going on, but he prayed the woman was for real and knew something they didn't. Pencil clenched in his hand, he watched as the bailiff helped her down from the box.

Turner followed her progress across the front of the court, as did every man in the room. Her hips swayed gracefully under that unusual skirt, and her bracelets jangled with each step she took. The white blouse showed her neck and chest, though her breasts were hidden, and the skin was tanned like she worked in the sun a lot.

She stood before the doctor's diagram and pointed to the wound. "First, let me say a man's strength in his arm is here." She put her hand around her bicep, turned to the jury, and then to the courtroom. "Would you gentlemen in the room agree with that?"

Heads nodded and Turner heard several men say "yes" and "that's true."

"Now, if you've been watching Mr. Reardon during the proceedings, you'll have noted which hand he's been using to write on the pad before him. From your observations, what is your conclusion?"

Head tilted, eyebrow quirked, she opened her left palm and waved it toward the audience.

Some peered around trying to see him, while others sang out, "He's a lefty," and "Used that southpaw ever since I knowed him."

She smiled. "Now, since we've clarified that, look back at the diagram. There is no way the defendant could have caused this wound. It was inflicted by a right-handed man." She pointed to Turner. "As established, the defendant is left-handed. If he'd inflicted the wound, it would've gone in the opposite direction."

The courtroom erupted into a round of loud claps and whistles. The defendant's eyes met hers and a slow, lazy smile softened his features. He nodded, and she returned the courtesy. God, he was a charmer.

Judge Howell started beating on his gavel and shouting, "Order. There will be order in this court." He turned to the bailiff. "The next man to open his mouth is to be removed from the room." The judge turned and fixed his attention on the courtroom.

"Do you want to cross examine this witness, Jamison?"

"I sure as hell do."

"Watch your language, mister. There are women present," ordered the judge.

Charity ducked her head to hide her grin as she made her way back to the witness box.

Jamison rose from behind his table and meandered over to her. "Pardon my rudeness, Miss Dawson." He turned to the court. "Ladies."

Charity merely nodded in acceptance.

"Now, Miss Dawson, you say you're a lawyer. Do you have any identification to prove that?"

"Not with me I don't."

Jamison preened. "Ahem. Well, tell us where you got your law degree?"

"Harvard University in Cambridge." A murmur went through the courtroom. They were impressed.

"Miss Dawson, Harvard does not admit women."

Nose in the air, she spoke through clenched teeth.

"They did this one."

Jamison snorted with disgust and waved his hand. "I have no further questions for this witness, but I do want to call Sheriff Cannon to the stand."

Oh, hell, thought Charity. After the sheriff told his story, everything she'd said would be tossed out, even though it was true. She glanced at Turner. As if he knew the outcome of this trial already, he shrugged and turned back to the paper in front of him.

Sheriff Cannon was sworn in and took a seat in the witness box. He didn't look happy.

"Sheriff, I saw you come in with Miss Dawson. Is she your prisoner?"

"No, she's not." Jamison's disappointment showed in his scowl of displeasure.

Charity released the breath she didn't know she'd been holding.

"Is she in your custody, Sheriff?"

"Sort of," Cannon replied.

"Now just exactly what does that mean?"

"I don't think it's any of your business, Jamison." He turned to the judge. "Or the court's, Your Honor."

Judge Howell's face scrunched as he pondered the sheriff's statement. "I'm sorry, Sheriff, but on this one I have to side with Jamison. Please answer the question."

Jamison was so pleased she feared he'd jump into a jig at any minute. Might be entertaining, thought Charity.

Sheriff Cannon looked at her and then out upon the audience in the courtroom. "Miss Dawson was brought to town by Frank Smithers and his family. She'd stumbled from a wheat field onto the road near Comanche Crossing. Knew her name and where she's from but didn't have any idea how she'd gotten in that wheat field."

Jamison grinned with victory. "Your Honor, I ask that Miss Dawson's testimony be stricken from the record and the jury be ordered to ignore what they heard from her today."

Judge Howell muttered, "So ordered."

"I have no further questions," said Jamison as he returned to his seat.

****

Sheriff Cannon took her arm and hustled her out of the courthouse. "What were you thinking, interrupting court proceedings like that, missy?"

"I was thinking the man's not guilty."

He snorted. "You're lucky the judge didn't throw the book at you."

"For what?" She yanked her arm from his, stopped in the middle of the street, and dug in her heels. "Slow down before I trip over my feet and fall." When she resumed walking, the sheriff shortened his stride to accommodate her shorter legs.

"All I did was prove a point."

"Folks probably think you're crazy, losing your memory and popping up in that wheat field. I'm not so sure they're wrong. Either that or you're trying to pull some scam on us."

He muttered something under his breath.

"What'd you say?"

"I said and then you have the gall to get up in front of the judge and tell him you're a lawyer."

"I am a lawyer. Why is that so hard to believe?"

" 'Cause you're a woman."

Charity couldn't believe the intolerances women

suffered in this day and time. She guessed if the women didn't fight against their restrictions, their men would continue to be intolerant of activities they didn't understand or condone. If she stayed here very long they'd be in for a rude awaking.

His mouth pinched in a firm line, he stopped in front of a building two blocks from the courthouse and helped her step up onto the wooden sidewalk. "Let's get you in to see Doc Wilson and get your head examined."

He opened the door. A bell tinkled overhead and the doctor called from the other room. "Be right there."

A minute later he entered the room. "Sheriff Cannon." Charity relaxed when he smiled at her. "Miss Dawson. What a pleasure to see you again."

She moved to offer her hand and then remembered women in this time period didn't shake hands. Instead, she nodded. "Thank you, Doctor Wilson."

"What can I do for you?" He looked between Charity and the sheriff.

Cannon covered his mouth and coughed. "It's like this, Doc. You heard how Miss Dawson happened to meet the Smithers family on the way into town."

"I did."

"She has no memory of how she got here. She needs to be checked out to make sure her head isn't cracked or something."

The doctor's eyes twinkled and he rubbed his chin. "I see." He took her arm. "Come into the examination room and let's have a look at you."

Charity did as he asked. At the door he stopped. "Sheriff, you have a seat over there. I'll give you my full report as soon as I've finished my assessment." He closed the door.

"Step up here and have a seat on the table." Charity did as he asked and answered his questions as he looked into her eyes, checked her reflexes and felt all over her head. The he pulled a chair up and sat facing her. "Now, young lady, how about you tell me what's going on."

Did she dare tell him what really happened? Would he believe her? What could it hurt?

"Is what I say in private confidential? Will I have to worry about you telling others what I'm about to say?"

He drew himself up, thrusting out his chest. "Of course not. All patient information is confidential."

"Forgive me. I don't mean to offend you, but I had to make sure." She took a deep breath. "What I'm about to tell you will be hard to imagine. It's even hard for me to believe. Yesterday afternoon I was in…"

Dr. Wilson sat and watched her as she talked. He didn't interrupt, get excited, or appear shocked, until she named some of the medical advances in the twenty-first century. When she told him blood groups were identified in 1901, he leaned forward in his chair.

"And you can show me how to type blood into these four different groups?"

"Yes, and how to use that information when giving blood transfusions, so the patient won't have a reaction." Many transfusions during this time were unsuccessful because the patient was given the wrong type blood. It was a hit-or-miss situation. She didn't want to mention the RH factor right now. The man appeared dazed enough.

He stroked his chin and shook his head. "I don't know what to believe." His brow furrowed. "I don't believe in traveling through time, but I do think you're knowledgeable about what you've shared with me today."

A loud snore came from the waiting room. Dr. Wilson's eyebrows shot up an inch, and he grinned. "I think the sheriff got tired of waiting."

With a slap to his thighs, he stood and walked to his glass-front medicine cabinet, where he extracted a small bottle. "These are merely sugar pills. I use these for patients who have imaginary complaints. Seems to help them considerably. I think they'll help reassure the sheriff's mind that you're not demented."

Charity took the bottle and nodded. She offered her hand and, after a slight hesitation, the doctor clasped it in his. "I'll be back some afternoon when you have time for us to work with the microscope you have over there."

Sheriff Cannon shot up from his chair when they exited the examination room. "What's the word, Doc?"

Dr. Wilson cleared his throat, his demeanor serious and professional, and stated, "I can assure you, Elijah, Miss Dawson doesn't have a head injury, nor is she crazy. She merely suffers from a condition similar to amnesia. I've given her medication, and she's to come back in a couple of weeks so I can check her progress."

The sheriff glanced at the bottle Charity had in her hand. "Much obliged, Doc."

"Anytime, Sheriff."

Fifteen minutes later they left the bank with money in Charity's pocket. Her bracelets had brought almost $19.00 an ounce. She now had a tidy amount of money in a savings account, plus enough for a place to stay and a few clothes. What a shame she didn't have her new ring with her, but since diamonds were mine-cut in the 1800s, a jeweler might be suspicious of the new brilliant-cut stones. So it was just as well that the ring remained in the future.

Sheriff Cannon left her in front of the mercantile. His earlier gruff demeanor had softened somewhat. "You finish your shopping and get yourself to Mamie's."

"Yes, sir, Sheriff, and thank you for your help." On impulse she leaned in and kissed his cheek. "You've been very kind."

The man blushed scarlet. "Uh…uh, go on with you now." He turned and stomped off down the boardwalk.

****

The following morning, Turner stood before the judge and jury. The foreman read the verdict.

"We find the defendant, Turner Reardon, guilty as charged." The words hit Turner in the chest like a blow from a two-by-four. For a minute he was unsteady on his feet.

Judge Howell peered down at him, sympathy on his face. "Son, I hate to do this because I don't believe you're guilty, but my job is to administer justice." He hit the gavel. "I hereby sentence you to hang by the neck until you are dead. Execution will be carried out July 19, 1888, two days from now. May God have mercy on your soul."

Charity thought she'd pass out in a dead faint. The man was innocent. She knew it as well as she knew her name.

Mr. Reardon looked back at her before he was taken away. "I appreciate you trying, Miss Dawson."

Throat too choked to speak, she nodded.

She sat there for the longest time, thinking. There had to be a way to save this man's life. She'd go to the courthouse and read every law the city and the state of Texas had, to find a way to clear him. Turner's lawyer, Mr. Bailey, remained in his chair, head down. That man needed help with his courtroom presence and interrogation skills. Maybe they could help each other.

She stood up and, trying not to step on the hem of her new blue-and-yellow cotton twill dress, moved out of the aisle and up to the defendant's table. The dry goods store had taken one of her gold bracelets in payment for several dresses—two for everyday, one for church, and one for town—and some undergarments. She'd passed on the bonnets popular at the time and wore her straw sunhat when outside. After leaving the store, she'd gone to the boarding house Sheriff Cannon had recommended. She was paid up for a week, two meals a day included.

"Mr. Bailey, may I speak with you?"

Startled, he quickly rose from his chair. "Miss Dawson, I didn't realize anyone else was here."

"Mr. Bailey, I need some help. I'm going to find some way to keep Mr. Reardon from hanging, and in payment I'll help you with your courtroom skills."

"Ma'am, I'm sorry, but just like the rest of this town, I can't believe you have a law degree." He blushed at having to admit his mistrust.

She couldn't blame the man. Harvard wouldn't admit women for another eleven years, and then it was to Radcliffe, a part of the university for women. "If you'll give me a few minutes, I'll be able to dispel some of your doubt. Is there somewhere we can go to talk?"

"Well, I suppose we could go to my office."

Mr. Bailey's office was across the street from the courthouse. It sat on the corner, and an outdoor stairway led to his living quarters upstairs. A barbershop, the surveyor's office, and a cafe occupied the remainder of the block, except for the bank at the opposite end. Above his office was a nice sign that read Mr. Jonas Bailey, Attorney at Law. His name was also etched into the glass on the front door.

Inside, the walls were lined with law books, and Charity itched to get her hands on some of the ancient tomes. But the books could wait.

"Have a seat, Miss Dawson." He held a straight-back chair for her while she sat and then rounded his desk and dropped into his leather chair.

"You have a very nice office. Business must be good here."

He coughed. "Actually, my father paid for all of this." His face reddened. "He doesn't know how poor a lawyer I am."

"Don't say that, Jonas. Can I call you Jonas and you call me Charity?"

He nodded. "I'd like that."

She opened the reticule she'd bought with her clothes and withdrew the paperback book. Open to the copyright page, she turned the book around where he could read. "I know this is going to sound crazy, but I'm from the future. I come from the year 2008."

"Now, Miss Dawson, I may not be a good lawyer, but I'm not stupid."

She placed the book in his hand and tapped the copyright page. "Read this."

He glanced down at the print and, as he read, his

eyebrows gradually rose higher. His finger ran along the binding. She knew he felt for stitching.

"In the future, books are bound with glue." He studied her a minute and returned to the paperback.

Before she could stop him, he'd flipped the book to show the cover. One look and he yanked his hand back like it'd been burned. The book landed on the floor.

"Miss Dawson! You could be arrested for having lewd reading material in your possession."

Charity retrieved the book. "No, Jonas, the picture is misleading. The story isn't near as risqué as the cover." Since she hadn't finished it, she hoped she wasn't lying.

"Well, I should hope not. This is some kind of joke you're playing on me, and I don't like it." He pushed his chair back and rose. "I'll thank you to get out of my office."

"Please, Jonas, hear me out. Then if you still don't believe me, I'll leave."

****

It had taken awhile, but Jonas had finally believed her story. Charity and Jonas spent the remainder of the afternoon going through law books, searching for something to help save Turner's life. They'd found nothing. Charity was disappointed and for a few moments considered buying a gun and using it to get the man out of jail.

"I can't believe we've not found one thing."

Jonas had been sitting quietly for several minutes. It appeared he'd given up finding a solution. "There is one more place we can look," he said.

Regaining hope, she asked, "Where?"

"At the courthouse in the County Records Office.

We need to go over every ordinance that's been made since this town started back in 'sixty-eight."

By noon the next day, they'd found what they needed. With permission, Jonas took the paper out on loan for one day. They put it in the small safe in his office and, before she knew it, Charity was the proud owner of one hundred acres of land, with a rundown shack, a mile from town. She was also in debt to Jonas for two thousand dollars, but there was no other alternative.

It was almost five o'clock when they left the law office. Jonas walked her to the boarding house. She was tired to the bone but so stressed she wasn't sure she'd sleep that night.

Jonas asked, "Are you sure you want to do this? It's not something anyone should take lightly."

"I know, but there is no other alternative. We can't let an innocent man hang. I'd never get over it."

He tipped his hat. "All right then. I'll see you in the morning at eight o'clock. The hanging is set for nine."

****

Turner stood when he heard the key in the lock of the metal door. He'd welcome anything to get his mind off his dilemma. To think his life would come to an end the following morning wasn't a pleasant thought. If he were an old man, he might feel differently, but, hell, he was only thirty-four years old. Sheriff Cannon came in with Aunt Ruby. Red-eyed, she carried a pie plate covered by a dishtowel. The smell of cinnamon, nutmeg, and apples filled the air.

"Aunt Ruby, you shouldn't have come. You've got no business in this place."

"You are my business, young man, and don't you

forget it." She passed the pie pan through the slot, turned, and sneered at the sheriff as he stood watch. "Your favorite, apple, and don't you let Sheriff Cannon or any of the deputy boys have one bite."

Turner took it and set it on his cot. "Thank you. I'll enjoy it."

"Ruby, it's not like me and the boys sat on that jury yesterday when they sentenced Turner. We're just following the law," said the sheriff.

"Elijah, you should be ashamed of yourself. You were Turner's daddy's best friend. If you were a true friend, you'd be gettin' this boy out of here until the real killer could be caught."

"Aunt Ruby, leave him alone. He's just doing his job. Come here now, and let me kiss your cheek one last time."

Elijah stepped between them. "Can't let you do that, Turner."

"Why the hell not?"

"You know why. She could pass you something, a weapon."

"Hell, she just passed me a whole pie."

Elijah had the grace to look embarrassed. "We sliced it for you to make sure there wasn't anything planted inside." He cleared his throat. "We didn't want to search Ruby."

Turner hid his smile at the expression of outrage on his aunt's face. She poked Elijah in the chest with one of her bony fingers. It had to hurt. He oughta know, because she'd done it to him enough times.

"It's a good thing, too, young man. I'm not a helpless old woman and can still take a plug outta your hide."

"Yes, ma'am, I know." He put his arms around her shoulders and turned her toward the door. "Now it's getting dark out. Visitation is over. You can see Turner in the morning."

She wailed, "Yeah, hanging by a rope. I can't believe I'll never see my boy alive again."

He waited until Elijah had locked the door, and then went to work on the pie. There was no doubt in his mind that a note would be in there somewhere. He carefully went around the pan, lifting and peering under slice after slice. Ah, there it was under the fourth wedge. A piece of oilcloth hid a small note folded twice. He opened it and held it beneath the last rays of sunlight drifting through the bars so he could read the small words.

Be ready. Will create diversion and come after you before you climb the steps.

Turner smiled at the ray of optimism that rushed through him. He wondered what kind of diversion. Lifting a serving of the spicy pie, he stuffed the wadded piece of paper inside it and started eating. After four slices, he was stuffed and called for the deputy on duty. "Come get the rest of this pie if you want it, else I'll toss it out the window." He chuckled when he heard the key in the lock.

Chapter Three

Charity and Jonas were in front of the sheriff's office by eight thirty, along with a lot of other townspeople. She'd worked with Jonas on how to conduct himself if he had to face down Jamison or anyone else. They'd written up a contract listing what was required for the agreement to be binding.

At a quarter of nine, the door finally opened. Judge Howell came out first, then the sheriff, with a firm grip on Turner, and several deputies brought up the rear. Before they could reach the step down to the street, she shoved Jonas in front of the judge.

"Judge, Miss Dawson is here to buy herself a husband and save Mr. Reardon from hanging." He raised a sheet of paper and waved it in the air, so everyone could see it. "This city ordinance was created in 'sixty-eight. It says if a woman with property needs a husband to help her with said property, she can choose one from criminals about to be hanged."

Jamison shoved his way in and tried to take the paper from Bailey. "Give me that, you fool. I've never heard such nonsense."

Jonas looked ready to retreat and Charity gigged him in the side. He took a deep breath and stood straighter, shoulders squared. "I'll thank you, Mr. Jamison, to keep your hands off my person. This is none of your concern. It's the business of Miss

Dawson, Sheriff Cannon, and Judge Howell."

"It damn sure is my business." Jamison glared at Charity. She returned it with a grin. "This woman doesn't own property. She just got here."

"I beg to differ, Mr. Jamison," said Charity. "I bought one hundred acres and a small house just a mile from town."

He guffawed. "That's not a house, it's a shack."

"That may be, sir, but it's my shack. I need someone to help me repair it and plant crops, so I don't starve this winter."

His eyes narrowed. "And what, pray tell, did you use for money, Miss Dawson?"

"That's not any of your concern." Hands on her hips, she glared. "Do you have anymore questions, sir?"

When he didn't say anything else, she added, "I didn't think so."

"Fire! Fire!" A horse flew down the street, its rider waving his hat as he yelled. He skidded to a halt in front of the jail. "Sheriff, that old shack just outside of town is burning to the ground."

Charity stiffened and turned to Jonas. "I guess that would be my property, wouldn't it, Mr. Bailey?"

"Yes, ma'am, it sounds like the place."

Sheriff Cannon jumped off the boardwalk and ran down the street, to the firehouse she supposed. She peered at Mr. Reardon. His expression of guilt told her just what she needed to know, but she didn't blame him. Within minutes, men on horseback or driving wagons were headed out of town. Shortly after, the fire wagon rolled out, its bell clanging, and followed the riders.

The sheriff returned before the dust settled, having

dispatched the fire brigade, and the men returned to the issue at hand.

"Let me see that, Jonas," said Judge Howell. Jonas handed the ordinance over to him. The judge took a quick glance and turned to the sheriff. "We better go back inside and get this settled."

Turner couldn't believe the talk flying back and forth between Bailey, Jamison, and Miss Dawson. Was it possible she could keep him from hanging by marrying him? If so, he'd agree quick as a lick. Hell, he'd marry old Widow Tate if it would save his neck.

He studied the pretty blonde. She had spunk, all right. She didn't back down from Jamison or the judge, and it appeared she'd added some steel to Bailey's backbone. Her strength didn't scare him. He'd never met a woman he couldn't bend around his little finger. Given the chance, that is.

Sheriff Cannon found chairs for all of them while the judge read the ordinance. When they were all settled, he explained. "Everything Jonas said is true. This ordinance was adopted to help women with property that'd lost their husbands in the war. All they had to do was pay a price. It doesn't give an exact amount, so I don't know how that's figured." He turned to Miss Dawson. "Are you prepared to pay to claim this man?"

"Yes, sir. I have some money." Actually the money was Jonas's, but they didn't need to know the source. "What do you think would be fair?"

The judge scratched his chin. "I don't rightly know. He pondered for a moment while Charity held her breath in expectation. "I reckon fifty dollars would be enough, don't you think, Cannon?"

"Yep, I do, but..." He directed his attention to Charity. "You need to know Doc put Miss Dawson on some medicine. Didn't say she was crazy, but had some illness like amnesia." He shrugged. "What if she's already got a husband?"

"I can assure you I don't have a husband." She raised her chin. "A woman would remember something as important as a husband."

Sheriff Cannon held up his hands. "Just had to say my piece."

"Point taken, Elijah," said Judge Howell. "What about you, Turner? Are you willing to be this young woman's husband?"

Turner looked at Miss Dawson. She didn't bat an eyelash, just studied him casually as if she could care less what his answer would be. Yes, he'd be willing to marry her, but then there was that paper Bailey had spread on Elijah's desk.

"What does that document say that I'd be signing?"

The judge scratched his chin. "It says that you'll help Miss Dawson work the land she owns, you'll be a true and faithful husband, and share your wealth with her. You must agree you'll allow her to practice law if she so wants. If after ten years you don't suit, you'll be free to seek a divorce."

Hope pumped though his veins. The request was more than fair. He asked, "Miss Dawson, why would you do this for me?"

"Why, why wouldn't I? It's wrong for an innocent man to hang, and I don't have any doubt whatsoever that you're guiltless. And given time, I'll prove it."

The woman had more backbone and character than most men he knew. Being her husband wouldn't be a hardship at all. His body wasn't immune to her, and her spunk definitely stirred his interest. Turner watched her carefully and said, "I won't agree to a marriage in name only. I want children."

"So do I, Mr. Reardon."

Sheriff Cannon spoke. "Well, what do you think, Judge?"

"I think we have no choice, and if we don't want this ordinance used again, we better revoke it as soon as possible." He shoved his chair back and stood. "Well, gentlemen, we better gather the ladies, so they can set up the church for a wedding tonight. Turner, you'll remain here until after the ceremony."

"May I speak with my bride-to-be privately for a minute?" asked Turner.

"I expect you can," said Judge Howell, "if she's willing."

Miss Dawson nodded.

The sheriff looked from him to her. "We'll be on the front porch. You've got ten minutes."

Charity leaned back against the desk, both hands braced on the edges. He waited for the door to close before he moved to stand in front of her. She gazed up at him and he looked his fill—the smooth skin, clear blue eyes, and full pink lips. Lips he didn't doubt would be quite enjoyable to taste. He breathed in her scent and felt his groin tighten in response to the clean womanly smell. If she wore perfumed powder, she'd used it sparingly.

He lifted his hand toward her hair, but sought her eyes before he touched the blond tresses. She didn't shrink back in fear. Like corn silk, the strands slid through his fingers.

"Have you seen enough, Mr. Reardon?"

"Well, can't say I wouldn't like to see more."

"You'll have to wait for that until after the ceremony."

He chuckled. "I can wait." His fingers dropped from her hair, his knuckles brushed down her cheek. "Why are you doing this, Miss Dawson?" he asked again.

"You're an innocent man. I'm here in a strange place, a strange time, and I need you to help me. Will that suffice until after the ceremony, when I can explain things further?"

"Yes, if you're sure about this."

"I'm sure."

"It's not often a man gets engaged and marries all in one day. I think a kiss might be in order. And I want to hear you say my name, Charity."

"I agree, Turner, a kiss would definitely seal the deal."

Hands at her waist, Turner lowered his head and softly touched his lips to hers. She didn't back away, so he pulled her closer, crushing her softness to his hard length. She moaned and her arms went around his neck. *Oh, God, she was sweet.*

When the sheriff pounded on the door, they jerked apart just before he opened it. "Ten minutes is up. Come on, Miss Dawson, word's already spread, and the women are waiting for you right now." He slapped Turner on the back and chuckled. "And your Aunt Ruby is leading the pack."

****

From inside the bank, Edward Samuelson peered through the window and wondered what the Sam Hill was happening. It appeared every woman in town was headed for the jail. Surely these gentlewomen weren't going to the hangin', were they?

He grabbed his coat off the rack and slid into it. It was about that time, and he didn't want to miss seeing Turner Reardon swing. Excitement curled in his belly, and damned if his pecker wasn't rising.

He chuckled. The night he'd slit Lucinda open, he'd been afraid he'd spend himself in his clothes. He'd managed to hold it until he reached the outhouse behind the saloon. It hadn't taken but one jerk and he was firing like one of those rockets at the Fourth of July celebration. A delicious shiver went through him at the memory.

The bell above the door rang, and one of his employees came inside. "John, what in tarnation is going on out there? I've never seen a hanging in this town cause such a to-do."

"Ain't going to be a hangin', Mr. Samuelson. That Miss Dawson has bought Turner's sentence, and they're getting married tonight. All the women in town are rushing about to get things ready. You know how they do love a wedding. And I have to say, every female in town over the age of two is crazy about Turner. They want him to have a fine celebration."

Edward sputtered, "I've never heard of such a thing. I better get down there and make sure they're following the law."

"Most likely it wouldn't do any good. It's a done deal. The judge has witnessed Turner and Miss Dawson sign a contract, and she's paid fifty dollars for him. Seems there is an old town ordinance that allows—"

"Never mind, John. Get to work." Damn if Turner

hadn't cheated him again. And if he wasn't mistaken, Turner suspected him of the deed. Yeah, he was a smart fellow, all right, but not as smart as Edward Samuelson. *I'll get you yet, you son-of-a-bitch.*

****

Charity felt like a tornado had hit her. She'd been prodded and poked all afternoon, getting fitted for a wedding gown. This was after they decided between the ten they'd brought which one best suited her. Several women had taken a turn at her hair, but, unable to get it to stay up, they'd agreed she'd have to wear it down.

At last they were finished, and they'd left her alone to rest. It felt wonderful to lie down in her chemise and close her eyes. Remembrance of Turner's kiss earlier kept running through her mind. A streak of desire coiled in her stomach. How could she have the hots for a man she barely knew? When a knock sounded on her door, she shot straight up in bed. In walked Turner's Aunt Ruby. "Your bath is ready. Come along now."

The bathroom was a modern convenience which Miss Mamie, the boarding house owner, was quite pleased to have in her establishment. Sure enough, the tub was full. She washed and rinsed her hair before going to work on her body. When she finished, she cleaned out the tub. Wrapped in a large bath sheet, she padded barefoot back to her room. She'd just stepped into drawers and a chemise—*My God, I can't believe I'm even saying the words, much less wearing them*—when the door opened again.

Thank God that Ruby and Miss Mamie were the only two allowed to help her dress. Charity sat before the window while Ruby brushed her hair dry. When she was dressed in the long white gown and the veil decorated with baby's breath, Ruby burst out in tears. At a loss, Charity patted her on the shoulder. "It's going to be all right, I promise."

Ruby grabbed her in a tight embrace. "I'm sorry, child, but I've been so worried about Turner. Your getting him out of this fix is like a miracle, one I'll thank God for the rest of my life." She pulled back and patted her cheek. "Why are you doing this? I know you don't love each other—you'd never seen each other before two days ago."

"It's a long story, Aunt Ruby. In a sense, Turner is helping me almost as much as I'm helping him. I'll explain everything to you later." Her heart twisted a little, and she smiled. "And maybe in time, we'll learn to love each other."

"All right, you two. Stop that blubbering," said Mamie. "We've got a weddin' to attend." She took Charity by the arm and led her next door. In her own bedroom, she had a large cheval mirror. "Take a look at yourself, young woman. Print this picture in your mind forever."

She couldn't believe what the women had been able to do in one day's time. Long sheer sleeves were caught at the wrist with white ribbons. A low square neck showed off her cleavage but wasn't vulgar. Thank God she'd talked them out of wearing a corset. The top was fitted but low waisted. From there the skirt fell in several layers of a sheer fabric over satin.

Charity could only stare. It was lovely. She sniffed. "Thank all the ladies for me. It is absolutely stunning."

****

Sheriff Cannon slapped him on the back. "Don't act so scared, son. Marriage is a lot better choice than having your neck stretched."

Turner didn't answer because the organist started playing and drowned out every sound but the music. Everyone stood, and his bride appeared in the doorway. The last rays of sun streamed behind her, making her glow like an angel as she walked forward on the arm of the judge. Then the door closed, and he could see her features.

His heart picked up in rhythm, and his palms grew sweaty. She was the most beautiful woman he'd ever seen. And she would be his wife. Or would she? He straightened his shoulders. Hell, yes, she would. He didn't believe in a married man going whoring, and he didn't intend to remain celibate.

Charity couldn't believe she was actually doing this. It wasn't as if she had many options, and being married to Turner would be much nicer than being tied to some of the other men in this town. Not only was he good-looking, he was neat, clean, and from what she'd observed, didn't chew that nasty tobacco.

He appeared as nervous as a cat as she approached. Someone had brought him a dark suit. His hair had been cut, and he'd had a shave. Thank goodness they didn't take too much off those curls of his. She liked his hair long. He was a looker, and a charmer. If she weren't careful, she could lose her heart. As if he could read her thoughts, his half smile turned to a frown of purpose. For a moment, she wasn't so sure she was doing the right thing, but it was too late to dwell on the issue.

When she reached his side, he took her hand and placed it on his arm. His smile of encouragement lessened her uneasiness. She could add kindness to his good traits.

How she kept her voice from shaking when she repeated her vows, she didn't know, but when Turner said his and slipped a plain gold band on her finger, she had to bite her lip to keep from crying. How sweet was that? He'd bought her a ring.

The preacher's voice boomed off the rafters. "I now pronounce you man and wife. Turner, you may kiss your bride."

Charity didn't know what to expect, but Turner carefully lifted her veil and settled it back over the headpiece. He spoke softly. "You are lovely, Mrs. Reardon." His kiss was a soft touching of mouths, sweet and pure, but it held a promise of more to come.

****

As Charity left the church on Turner's arm, about twenty men stood in line.

"These are the men who work for me."

"Why weren't they in the church?"

His face was serious as he looked out at the line. "They're afraid you won't forgive them for burning down your shack. They were trying to create a diversion so I could escape."

Charity shoved her flowers at him and took the two steps down to where the line began. She shook hands with each man as she chatted and placed a kiss on his cheek. Some blushed, some kissed her back, and a few grabbed her in a bear hug. But everyone had a smile on his face. Turner felt something give in his chest and fought the feeling. It was too early to know if this woman was honest in her actions or was putting on a show.

He stepped off the porch and stalked down the line.

"All right, men, you've taken up enough of my wife's time. Looks like you've been forgiven, so we'll see you at the community hall for the reception."

They crowded around him and Charity. "We're mighty happy for you, boss," said Tom, the man who'd been with him the longest.

"Thank you, boys. I've never gotten married before, so I guess maybe we should have a day off tomorrow."

Tom acted thunderstruck. "You mean not work?"

He clapped the older man on the shoulder. "Well, some things have to be done, but others can wait. I'm leaving it up to you to make those decisions."

Yee-haws echoed around the churchyard.

Turner took Charity's arm, and they walked the few blocks to the reception. The town's folk had outdone themselves. A band sat at the far end of the room and when they entered started playing a waltz. He looked down at the woman on his arm. "May I have this dance?"

"Yes, indeed."

Charity was surprised he was such a good dancer, better than she was. She didn't have much time for dancing. As a matter of fact, she'd not had many men to take her out on the town. Turner moved her smoothly around the dance floor. She laughed with pure enjoyment as he smiled down at her, surprised at the heat that coursed through her veins when their bodies touched. When the music stopped, she was breathless.

Aunt Ruby made her way over to them. "Come on, now. It's time to cut the cake." She led them toward the table. Charity was amazed at the beautiful three-tiered cake at one end of the table with a large bowl filled with yellow punch to match the tall gladiolas placed in the center. The opposite end was piled with sandwiches, snacks, and more desserts.

A row of ladies stood against the wall, excitement emanating from their faces. "Ladies, this is so lovely, and you did it so fast. I don't know what to say."

Turner put his arms around her shoulders and said, "We thank you, ladies."

****

Charity hadn't thought about their wedding night, where they'd go, but Turner had reserved a room at the hotel in town. They'd arrived to find their room filled with more food, a bucket of champagne, and on the bed waited a frothy nightgown.

She picked it up and fingered the fine material. "Oh, my, Aunt Ruby has outdone herself. I don't know who she's trying to convince to consummate this marriage, me or you?"

Turner picked up the nightgown, held it up to the light, and chuckled. "Must be you, because she knows I won't need to be persuaded." He came up behind her and started undoing the numerous buttons on her dress. "How about you? Will you need to be won over, wooed?"

"Well, all women enjoy a little wooing, but if you think I'll renege on our bargain, you're wrong." She turned toward him. "Making love with you won't be a chore."

"I'm glad to hear it. I must say I find you very desirable and think we should get comfortable."

He made to smooth the dress down her shoulders, but she stopped him. "I need to tell you some things first. Things you need to know about me."

"All right, but put on something more comfortable, and I'm taking off part of this suit."

Charity rummaged around in the things Ruby had packed for her and pulled out the long cotton gown. It was either that or put on a dress. She moved behind the dressing screen and stepped out of the beautiful wedding gown. She carefully draped it over the panel. With her undergarments still on, she slipped the gown over her head and came out.

Turner sat in one of the chairs, but stood and pulled one over for her. She curled up in it with her feet tucked under her. "What I'm going to say will make you think I'm crazy, but I'm not."

He listened intently, examined the copyright date on the paperback book, looked at the binding, and when he turned it to see the cover, his eyebrows shot up two inches. "It's common for books to have this kind of cover in your time?" he asked.

"Yes, but usually the covers are more risqué than the story."

"I'll be the judge of that." He tossed the book on his stack of clothes.

Feet crossed at the ankles, he said, "I can't say I completely believe your story, but I know strange things do happen. I know women in this era don't dress like you did the day of the trial. Not many would stand up to the judge or Jamison the way you did."

"Are you sure? I bet Aunt Ruby could hold her own with any man."

He chuckled. "You're right, there. She told Elijah Cannon the other night she could still take a plug out of his hide."

Charity covered her mouth. "What'd he say?"

"Can't remember, but he didn't argue."

He studied her for a long while; so long she grew uncomfortable and felt exposed in her long nightgown. Finally he spoke. "Why did you work so hard to save my life?"

"I'm a lawyer. It's my job to save lives. When I saw the drawing of that knife wound, I knew you'd not killed that woman." She sighed deeply. "And I have to be honest, that day in court when you stopped and looked at me, I was immediately drawn to you." His eyes darkened with passion and her stomach flipped. "And I needed a place. I'm here without anyone and doubt I'll be able to return to my time."

He stood. "Are you going to put that wisp of a gown on?"

"Do you want me to?"

He took her hand and pulled her from the chair. His lips touched her neck and traveled up to her ear. She shivered. "No. I'd prefer to undress you right now and have you in bed with nothing on."

She raised her arms and he lifted the cotton gown over her head and tossed it over the side of the dressing screen. He kissed her, his lips igniting a fire in her belly like none she'd ever known. She opened for him and his tongue slipped inside and twirled around hers. Without releasing her mouth, he untied her knickers and they fell in a puddle on the floor. One swift yank and her camisole joined her gown.

He broke the kiss and stepped back. "I want to look at you."

His eyes, dark as the ocean depths, touched her body, warming her. Her skin tingled, and when his hands stroked her breasts she jumped at the sensation they aroused. "Lovely. You are beautiful, Charity."

Her hands sought his body, trying to unbutton his shirt. She wanted to touch his skin, put her lips on his chest, and learn his taste. He brushed her hands aside, turned, and quickly removed his shirt, shoes, and trousers. His back was broad, the muscles rippled as he moved. Her eyes moved down to his trim waist and taut buttocks. Then he turned.

Oh, God, he was magnificent. His chest was covered lightly with dark hair that grew in a line down his belly and thickened as it surrounded his erection. *And oh, my...* Her eyes jerked up to his to see he was watching her. She stepped forward and ran her hands over his shoulders and down his chest. Her lips touched his skin, her tongue flicked out to taste him. He reached for her, pulling her flush with his body.

Their hands roamed, discovered, and learned, drawing sighs and moans of pleasure. He weighed her breasts and thumbed the nipples, making them ache for his mouth. She cupped his buttocks, enjoying the tensing of his muscles as she did so. Capturing her hand, he lifted her and carried her to the bed.

She helped him toss the covers back and scooted over to make room for him. He dropped down beside her and moved to kneel between her thighs. Leaning forward, he took her mouth in a kiss that left her head reeling. She keened low in her throat, and he lowered his head to her shoulder.

Charity couldn't take any more. She raised her legs and wrapped them around his waist, tugging him closer. "Please now, Turner."

"I don't want to hurt you."

"Hurt me? Turner, I'm not a virgin." He stilled and

watched her face. "I've not been with many men, but in my time, very few women remain a virgin past the age of twenty."

He growled. "When was the last time you were with a man?"

"It's been at least a year."

He dropped his forehead to hers.

"Does it matter?"

"No, I guess we're even."

She jerked him forward with her heels. "Well, what are you waiting for, then?"

Later, weight on his elbows, he nibbled at her collarbone and up her neck to her ear. He nipped it gently and growled, "I think I made a damn good bargain."

She laughed and swatted him on the butt. "Maybe we both did."

Chapter Four

Turner lay on his side, head propped on his hand, and watched his wife sleep. After the numerous times they'd made love throughout the night, he grew hard again looking at her bare shoulders. He pulled the sheet down to expose her lovely breasts with their rosy pink nipples and smiled.

Last night, they'd drunk champagne, eaten, and made love twice more before falling into an exhausted sleep. His wife was a passionate woman, one who welcomed his advances. God, how had he been so lucky? True, he was disappointed there had been other men, but...at least she wasn't cold and afraid of his touch.

He leaned down and kissed her. "Wake up, sleepy head. We've got a long day."

Startled, she sat up and looked around in alarm. Awake and remembering all at the same time, she smiled and lay back down, taking him with her.

"Good morning," she said between kisses.

"Yes, it is, and time to get up. I'm ready for my bacon and eggs." His stomach rumbled to prove his point. He was tempted to stay in bed half the day, but he wanted Charity at the ranch before nightfall.

He watched, mesmerized, as she stretched, rose from the bed in all her naked splendor, and walked behind the dressing screen. He started pulling on his drawers and pants. If he didn't, he'd be tossing her in the bed for another romp.

"After breakfast, we'll stop by the mercantile and pick up some clothes for you—a riding skirt, some unmentionables, and decent boots."

"What's wrong with my boots? I'll have you know they are expensive leather and cost almost $300.00."

"Thunderation, woman. You paid that much for those flimsy things you've been wearing? Hell, that much money would buy three horses and saddles."

"I know. Things are more expensive in the future, but people make more money. Some women pay a thousand dollars or more for a pair of shoes."

He couldn't imagine such, and a niggling of doubt poked at his brain. Would she expect fancy things? Nah, she didn't act like a money-grubbing woman.

"A man would have to be rich to buy such expensive doodads for his wife."

"The women I knew worked and paid for the items themselves."

She lifted her gown from the screen panel and tossed it toward the chair where her small reticule sat. He rolled the garment into a ball and stuffed it into the bag. Just to be safe, they'd have a serious talk about money at home.

"After shopping, we'll borrow you a horse from the stable and ride out to the ranch."

Her head peeked over the screen. "I can't ride a horse. I'm used to driving a car."

"You mean one of those ugly contraptions some man over in Germany made?"

She laughed, the sound giving him immense pleasure. "No, much more modern. You turn a key and

58

they start, cool or warm the air inside, and they'll go over a hundred miles per hour."

He couldn't imagine it and wasn't sure he wanted to. Was she really from the future? Maybe, but it didn't change the here and now. "Guess you can ride double with me, and I'll teach you when we get home."

"I'd really like a bath, but that would take too long."

"By the time we get to the ranch, we'll be caked with dirt anyway. We'll have a bath at home."

They left the room and went downstairs to find a table in the dining room. It was full this morning, and Turner didn't doubt folks were all here to see them. The owner had saved them a table in a little hidden alcove. At least someone around here believed in giving them privacy.

By eight o'clock they were ready to leave town. Turner pulled Charity up behind him on Chester, his bay cutting horse. The animal didn't seem to mind the extra weight.

Charity bounced and giggled all the way out of town. Lord, the woman was just like a child about some things. She took a great deal of pleasure in her surroundings. Her situation before must have been confining, as she looked at each new experience as an adventure.

Her arms were tight around his waist, her breasts pressed to his back. Damn, if the pressure of the lush globes didn't make him burn with want. Hellfire, he'd better get his mind on something else.

Charity's carpetbag had proved too small to hold their purchases, so, wrapped in brown paper and tied with string, the packages were strapped down at the front of Chester's saddle. The paper rattled as they rode. Poor horse deserved extra rations tonight, and a long rub down.

"You doing all right back there?" he asked.

"Fine. Hey! Is that my shack over there?"

Turner considered the pile of burned rubble and scorched grass. "You mean you bought this place and haven't ever seen it?"

"We didn't have the time. Jonas had seen it and said it was good land. And yes, he told me the shack was worthless." She squeezed his waist. "Let's stop a minute."

The house was about a quarter of a mile off the road. As they approached the charred remains, he noted the soil was rich. It'd be a good place to plant hay for the cattle. He drew Chester to a halt, and taking Charity's arm, he swung her to the ground before dismounting. The horse started chewing on the grass, and Turner let the reins drag the ground.

Turner couldn't resist. His body shook with restrained laughter.

"What's so funny?"

"At least the outhouse didn't burn."

She punched him in the arm. "Very funny."

"Hey, woman."

"This isn't a laughing matter, mister." She directed her attention to the burned wreckage. "I think when we rebuild the house, it should be a little closer to the road. We can clear this area off here and put a lean-to for the horses." She whirled to face him. "What do you think?"

Well, hell, at least she asked. "I don't see the need to rebuild here. You don't need it; you'll be living with me."

"I do need it, and you agreed." She peered up at him from under her sunhat. "I need to be in town a couple of days a week to help Jonas. It was our deal. I'm now his partner. A place to stay here would be more convenient than riding six miles all the way to your ranch."

"You mean with all that's been going on, you think I'd let you stay out here by yourself?" The idea was ridiculous.

"I know there's a killer out there, but he'll be caught one day, and then it will be safe."

"Safe or not, I couldn't let you do it. If you need to stay here, I'll stay with you. Besides, I've found I like having you sleep beside me."

"Now how do you plan to do that and run your ranch, farm, whatever it is you have?" she asked.

"My dear, I have a spread. We raise cattle but do plant and harvest hay for our beefs."

"Okay, still, how will you manage it?"

"I don't know, but I will."

"How long do you think it would take to build a little two-room house? Just a kitchen, eating, and living area with one bedroom."

Hell, she just wasn't going to give up on the subject. Having a place closer to town might be convenient on occasion. But that was a lot of money to spend for a convenience. "With some help, we could have it up in a couple of days."

She clapped her hands. "Good. I want to get started as soon as you get caught up and can spare the time."

"That may be a month or so."

"That's too long. I've got an idea how to snare our killer." She put her arm around his waist and leaned

61

into his side. "We'll use me as bait and lure him out here."

Terror twisted his gut. She could be killed. "It's not going to happen, madam."

****

As they left the main road for the one that led to Charity's new home, all she could see was the roof and part of the second floor. From this distance, it didn't look very big, but she had no idea how far it was to the house.

"How far is it from the road to your house?"

"Two miles." She breathed a sigh of relief. Her brain had to be scrambled from all the bouncing up and down, and her butt wasn't in the greatest shape either. No doubt she'd have bruises for weeks. Turner had been right about the dirt. It had to be at least a half-inch thick on her face.

A dog met them about half way there. He barked and pranced along beside the horse but kept well out of the way of the animal's hooves.

"Hush, Snowball."

Charity laughed. "How on earth did he get his name? He only has a few white spots."

"The man who gave him to us had a sense of humor."

When they drove into the yard, Charity squeezed Turner's arm. "It's a lovely place."

"My grandfather built it when he moved his family here some years before Prairie became a town."

"I love the wraparound porch." Rose bushes grew around the perimeter. "All it lacks is a white picket fence."

"Anything my sweet wife desires, she shall have—

within reason, that is."

The front door flew open. Aunt Ruby ran out, wiping her hands on her apron. "Children, I'm so glad you're home." She flew down the steps and grabbed them each in a bone-bruising hug.

"Whoa, Aunt Ruby. Ease up a little."

"I'm just so happy you're alive, my boy. And now you have a wife—a lovely one, I might say. About time, too, if you ask me." She brushed tears away with the hem of her apron. "I'd about given up hope of havin' any babies in this big old house."

"Now, Aunt Ruby, no need to be dramatic. You act like I'm nearing sixty. Could be I was waitin' for the right woman."

She snorted. "An old woman's got a right to be a little melodramatic on occasion."

Ruby took Charity's arm and led her toward the house. "Soon as you get back from the barn, lunch will be on the table."

Charity turned back. "Wait. I need to get those packages in the house."

"No need. I'll set them on the front porch. You and Aunt Ruby can collect them later." He leaned down and dropped a quick kiss on her lips. "See you shortly."

Aunt Ruby beamed and wiped another tear away before taking Charity's arm again.

A long wide hallway divided two sides of the house. On the right must be the living area and on the left the dining room and kitchen. "Your home is lovely."

"It's your home now, young woman." She led her out to a big porch behind the kitchen. A washstand held a big bowl and pitcher. "The water is still warm. Take your time and wash up. Look around while I get the food on the table."

Charity washed her face, neck, and arms. The water was almost brown when she finished, but she felt considerably better. She tossed the dirty water out the back door. Before exploring, she stuck her head in the kitchen door. "You sure you don't need help?"

"Honey, I've been doing this for years by myself. One more day won't make a difference."

Charity retraced her steps and stepped into the parlor. There was nothing fancy about the furnishings, but the wide plank floors wore a soft patina, as did the wood furniture in the dining room and parlor. A horsehair sofa sat in the center of the room facing the large fireplace. Several chairs rounded out the arrangement.

Other chairs and tables occupied corners of the room. Evidently either Turner or Ruby enjoyed reading, as bookshelves lined two walls. Charity gazed around the room at the chintz curtains at the windows and the handmade pillows tossed about on the furniture. Yes, if she had to stay in 1888, this would be a good place.

She didn't love Turner, but she enjoyed his company, so love might be in their future. And she could serve a purpose here in this time. Jonas needed her help in his practice. First she needed to discover who tried to frame Turner for murder.

****

"Git those kids outta the way of these wagons, Merle, 'fore one gets run over."

Merle ran before her husband's wagon with a long, thin twig. "Get outta here, you kids, less you want a feel of this switch." Kids scattered, only three of them

Merle's.

It had been two weeks since Charity and Turner stood before the pile of burned wood that had been her shack. Today men and women from Prairie and surrounding areas, along with some of Turner's men, gathered to build a cabin. Wagons drove up to unload lumber, while others parked along the road to the site. The women set up makeshift tables using sawhorses, barrels, and lumber that wouldn't be needed until after the meal.

The tables groaned under the weight of the food the women had prepared. The men ate in shifts, relaxed awhile, and then went back to work. The women and children ate last. At first Charity was miffed, but this way they didn't have to rush to finish. They sat around and visited.

Charity sat on a quilt with Merle, Aunt Ruby, and Mamie from the boarding house. Merle's girls sat with a group of children not far away. Their laughter mingled with the pounding of hammers and the laughs and shouts of the men as they worked.

At dusk, some of their neighbors drove or rode away, while others stayed. They'd make beds on quilts or bedrolls under the stars.

"What do you think, Wife?" Hands linked, Charity and Turner stood outside and admired their new dwelling.

"It's beautiful."

"Is it worth turning loose of some of the money you got for those gold bracelets of yours?"

"Absolutely."

"All right, then. Let's turn in. I'm worn out."

They'd found a bed and chest for the bedroom, a

Linda LaRoque

table and four chairs, and an old sofa Aunt Ruby had stored in the attic, but they wouldn't arrive until tomorrow. Tonight they'd sleep on the new pine floor. Frank, Merle, and their children were camped out in the living area. Charity grinned. It was like one big slumber party.

The floor was darned hard, but Charity finally found a comfortable spot. She kissed Turner's shoulder and received a snore in response.

From the other room, one of Merle's girls called out, "Night, Mama, night, Daddy."

Charity heard a soft response and couldn't resist calling out, "Night, John Boy."

"Mama, who's John Boy?"

"Shhh." Charity chuckled at Merle's muffled hiss.

****

Charity closed her small carpetbag and looked around the room to make sure they'd not forgotten anything. She'd brought a few clothes, but not enough to be leaving any. Turner waited on the porch, their horses saddled. She wasn't comfortable on the animal yet, but she'd not been thrown. As soon as they got home, riding lessons would resume. He was determined she become a good horsewoman.

Turner strode through the door. "Rider coming."

He took the bag and held the front door for her to step out onto the front porch. She shaded her eyes from the sun and watched for their visitor to arrive. It was Sheriff Cannon. He slowed his horse, stopped several yards from the porch, and dismounted. Hat in his hand, he approached. His face was grim. "Turner, ma'am."

They stepped off the porch to join him. Turner said, "From the expression on your face, I suspect this isn't a social call."

"Afraid not. Doc sent me." He nodded to Charity. "He thinks Mrs. Reardon can help him with something."

"What's happened?" she asked.

"There's been another murder—a victim with a wound similar to Lucinda's."

"God," swore Turner. Face pale, he bit out, "I don't want Charity to witness a scene like that."

She touched his arm. "It's all right, Turner. If I can help, that's what I need to do."

He nodded. "We'll follow you into town, Sheriff."

Charity knew he needed to get back to work at the ranch. His workers couldn't keep taking up the slack for his absence. It wasn't fair.

She turned and placed her hands at his waist. "Turner, if you need to get back to the ranch, I'm sure I can ride with the Sheriff and stay at Mamie's until this is cleared up."

"No," he said. "I'll not leave you in town or anywhere else by yourself. The boys will just have to manage."

He tied her bag to the saddle horn and tossed her into the saddle, then mounted his own horse.

As they rode, Sheriff Cannon explained the situation.

The victim was a woman who lived alone on the edge of town. Her neighbor had stopped by on her way to town to see how her evening had gone. Mrs. Hall had been expecting a gentleman caller last night but didn't give his name. Her body had been taken to Doc's for examination before going to the undertaker's.

Twenty minutes later they pulled up in front of Dr.

Wilson's office, where a small crowd was gathered. Sheriff Cannon tried to calm them, with little success. Folks were scared. This was the second knifing of one of the town's women, and it was evident now Turner Reardon had almost hanged when he was innocent.

Charity saw Turner's shoulders relax at the comments passed between the people. She hoped he felt vindicated at last. She noticed his lips quiver and his difficulty hiding his grin when someone said Mrs. Reardon was smarter than the sheriff or Jamison. She was sure neither man liked having his expertise slandered.

Dr. Wilson met them inside. He said, "Turner, you better sit here. I'd like Mrs. Reardon to go in alone with me. For the dignity of the woman, you understand."

Turner nodded and sat in one of the chairs.

Cannon walked to the door. "I'll be in my office if you need me."

Charity wasn't sure what to expect, but Doctor Williams had the woman covered with a sheet. She carefully folded it down. The woman was already in rigor mortis, her lips blue. The knife wound was similar to the one she'd seen in the courtroom, but that had been a drawing and this one wasn't nearly as neat. "Is the wound like the other victim's?"

"In some ways, but this one is a lot messier, the angle different, as if she were struggling."

She noted the purple bruises around the woman's neck. They didn't appear to be caused by hands but something with padding, maybe an arm. She uncovered the victim's hands and saw blood and skin under her nails.

"Was she clothed when she was found?"

"Yes, we removed her dress and undergarments here."

She carefully pulled the sheet up to cover the body. "Where are her clothes? Can I see them?"

He scratched his chin. "Well, I had my assistant drop them out back in the trash barrel."

"Do you have a back door?"

"Yes." He pointed toward a hallway.

"We need those clothes, Doctor. There may be evidence on them." She started for the exit then turned back. "Will you get Turner for me?"

Charity had just found the trash barrel when Turner and Doc Wilson joined her. The garment lay at the very bottom, rolled into a wad. "I can't reach down that far. We need a stick."

Turner looked around and found a rake. With the forked end, he tried several times to raise the bundle—using the side of the can for leverage.

"Be careful. Keep it away from the sides if possible. We don't want to contaminate the material." Not anymore than it already had been, at the bottom of the dirty drum.

Inside they laid the dress on a long table and moved it in front of a closed window so she'd have plenty of light. "I need a magnifying glass." Doc produced one and she went to work. "Do you have a pair of tweezers?"

Doc handed her the tweezers, and with the large magnifying glass, she bent over the fabric and studied every inch.

The dress was dark navy serge, the weave tight, something terribly heavy and confining to be wearing in this hot weather. With the tweezers, she picked up a different color thread off the fabric.

"Now I need some gauze." Doc supplied her with whatever she asked. She lined different color threads on the piece of gauze. She also found pieces of rust and other debris. At least the can was empty when the dress was tossed inside. "We need to put these samples where they won't blow away."

He unlocked a medicine cabinet, and she carefully placed their evidence inside and closed the door. Turner stood close and watched but stayed out of their way. She and Doc returned to the dress.

"Now, let's carefully turn it over." On the back, across the shoulders, she found several hairs. Some were gray and others auburn. Those were laid out on a piece of gauze.

She and Doctor Wilson examined a large, light stain on the back of the skirt in which several fibers were stuck. It looked like a concentrated semen stain. She touched it lightly.

"Good, it's still a little wet, so the cells won't be dried out." Charity quickly removed the fiber samples and placed them on a fresh piece of gauze. Then, with a pair of scissors, she cut a small piece of the area out of the dress. "Dr. Wilson, will you bring your microscope over?"

He moved to a table and uncovered a model Charity had never seen before. It was old, had a patent date of 1852, but if it worked, that was all that mattered.

"Good. Now, I need slides, diluted saltwater solution, and a spoon. This will be crude, but it just may work. We've got to work fast."

Using the spoon Doctor Wilson placed in her hand, she carefully scraped some of the white thick secretion onto one of the slides. She dropped several droppers of saline solution onto the slide—placed another piece of glass over it, and then put both under the lens. She focused and studied what she'd found. She nodded to Doctor Wilson. "It's semen, all right."

She stepped aside so he could look.

He studied the sample and turned to her in astonishment. "Where did you learn to do that?"

"Biology 101 lab in college."

He turned back to the microscope and adjusted the lens to get a closer look. Charity could understand his awe. This was something he'd never seen before. Though sperm had first been isolated and identified earlier, probably not many country doctors had had the opportunity to actually view them through a lens.

"Doctor, you know what this means. There is a sexual predator out there. He's killed twice now and in less than a month. Based on this pattern, he'll most likely strike again in a couple of weeks."

Turner's face had turned to stone. He said, "I'll go after Sheriff Cannon. He'll need to decide how to warn the citizens of this town."

The sheriff arrived, moments later, with the judge in tow. Turner had obviously told them of the situation.

The doctor led them to the medicine cabinet to observe their evidence. "Not a doubt in my mind after Mrs. Reardon confirmed my suspicions. Now as far as the thread samples, those will be almost impossible to identify. The hair samples may be useful."

Judge Howell shook his head and said, "Lord, what a sorry mess. How are we going to explain this to the citizens of this town?"

"Simple, Judge," said Charity. "You just call them

together and announce that though the killer doesn't rape his victims, he gets sexual pleasure from killing them. It's a delicate subject, but not near as bad as seeing more women murdered."

"You're right, of course." He turned to Sheriff Cannon. "Elijah, we better get some flyers printed up. We'll have two meetings, one in the church and one in the saloon. That way maybe we'll get the word out to 'most everyone."

Charity interrupted. "Gentlemen, if you could, I'd put the announcement off until after this woman's funeral. The killer may show up and give himself away."

Sheriff Cannon headed for the door. "I'll talk to the pastor and have him conduct a graveside service at four o'clock. At that time we can announce about the two meetings."

Charity glanced up to see Turner watching her. He looked physically ill. She went to him. "Are you all right?"

He spoke through clenched teeth. "I'm fine." He took her arm. "Come on, let's get some fresh air." Arm around her shoulders, he guided her out the door. He walked at a fast clip down the street, like a man on a mission.

"Slow down, Turner. My legs aren't as long as yours."

He stopped, took a deep breath of air, and released it. "I'm sorry. I just can't believe this is happening. I want to get you to the ranch tonight, before the meetings, so you'll be safe."

Chapter Five

Charity absolutely refused to leave. He could tie her to her horse, but she'd have found a way back. He'd just have to stick to her every minute. The thought of her getting hurt, especially by the sick bastard they were hunting, felt like a dead weight in his stomach.

"Turner, I appreciate your concern, but I'm needed here. I want to go to the funeral and watch those who come. If I can help, that's what I'd like to do. Thank you for agreeing to stay here tonight." She walked into the hotel room as he held the door for her.

"I can't pretend I'm happy about it, but we'll do what you want. We'll use the time in between to visit the mercantile. I need to order supplies, and you might want to buy a few items for the cabin. I know Aunt Ruby gave us a lot from the attic, but something new might be nice."

"Yes, it would." She stood at the window in the room looking out on the street. He'd kicked off his boots and was stretched out on the bed.

"Turner, you know your innocence is proven now. If you want to file for divorce, I'll not fight."

His breath caught in his chest. "What, Charity? Do you want a divorce?"

She turned toward him. Her smile hesitant, she said, "I find I rather like being married to you, but I'll abide by your decision."

He could breathe again. He held out a hand to her. "Come here, Charity." When her fingers curled around his, he pulled her down on top of him. Arms around her shoulders and waist, he rolled them to their sides and threw a leg over hers. "You're mine now, Mrs. Reardon, and the idea of giving you up doesn't sit well with me."

She nestled her face in his neck. A strange sense of completeness washed over him. Hell, he'd fight tooth and nail to keep her right here beside him. Is that what love felt like? The thought scared him to death. All the people he'd ever loved, he'd lost. Except for Aunt Ruby, that is. His brother died of whooping cough the winter of 'seventy-five. The kid had only been eight at the time. Nine years later, just four years ago, both his folks had died in a flash flood.

They'd been to town for supplies when a storm broke. They'd stopped to unhitch the horses and wait out the rain under a tarp. Before his father could get the animals loose, lightning spooked them and they ran. Even with the brake on, they were able to drag the wagon down into a wash. Before his ma and pa could get to safety, water rushed through and whisked them away to their deaths.

The next day, a rancher in the neighboring county found their bodies caught in debris.

Charity's hand covered his heart. "Turner."

"Hmmm?"

"What are you thinking?"

He raised her hand and kissed her palm. "I'm thinking my folks would have liked you."

"Oh, God!" she cried.

He pushed up and looked down at her. "What?

What's wrong?"

"My father is probably worried sick. I just disappeared off the face of the earth. He'll think I'm dead." She covered her face with her hands. "I've been so selfish, thinking of only myself, never giving any thought to what he might be going through."

"Honey, it's not like you could do anything about it. You've been busy surviving and doing what you know how to do to help me and now other folks in this town."

"Yeah, but I could've at least worried about him wondering where I was." She clasped his arm, her blue eyes about to overflow with tears. "I love my daddy. I really do."

"Of course you do. You had a big shock, being plunked down in the wheat field. I'd say a body would need some time to come to grips with it all."

"I...guess."

He gathered her close, and she sobbed against his chest. Words couldn't ease her heart. The man must be beside himself with fear, but there was absolutely nothing he could do to help her. Her body stopped shuddering and he heard the steady breathing of sleep. He closed his eyes. She was worn to a frazzle. He didn't know, but didn't doubt time travel was tiring on a person.

****

Edward stood with the some thirty mourners at Mrs. Hall's gravesite. *Ah, madam, I did give you a mighty fine send-off. Or I should say you gave me one.* He wanted to chuckle at his little joke.

She'd struggled so hard he'd had to hold her from behind in a headlock. The bitch had scratched his face with her nails. Thank goodness his beard hid the marks. When the knife hit her belly, she'd struggled for a minute to still his hand. Then she went limp, her arms at her sides. He was already near the point of exploding. Too late to get outside.

Dropping her face down over the back of the sofa, he'd opened his pants, grabbed her hips, and ground against her plump warm buttocks. *Oh, God, the joy of it, the pure ecstasy.*

He held his hat in both hands to cover his erection. That bitch Miss Dawson eyed people from under that sunhat of hers. No, her name wasn't Miss Dawson anymore. It was Mrs. Turner Reardon. She'd ruined everything for him. She wouldn't go unpunished for long. He'd see she paid.

****

"I would almost swear that's our man, Sheriff Cannon, but I can't prove it, and if you approach him, he'll run," said Charity. The sheriff sat behind his desk, while Turner and the judge paced the floor.

"Who would've thought it of our distinguished banker?" said Elijah.

Turner stopped. "I've suspected him all along. He didn't like it one bit Lucinda quit seeing him when I started calling on her." His eyes flicked to Charity's as if he'd been caught cheating. Charity hid her expression from him. He didn't need to see she was jealous of the woman.

"He tried to misdirect funds from my account at his bank and blamed it on an employee—fired the poor young man over it. Then, as if that wasn't enough, I believe he or someone he hired set fire to a field of my hay."

"How come you didn't tell me about this before, Turner?" asked Elijah.

"There wasn't anything you could do without proof, and I didn't have any."

Elijah sadly shook his head. "I don't think I could've forgiven myself if you'd died and the murders had continued." He looked at Charity. "Ma'am, we owe you a debt of gratitude. I was wrong to doubt you."

Before she could answer, Jamison flew through the door, panting from exertion like he'd run a marathon. "What's…going on, Judge?"

He turned to Turner and offered his hand. Turner took it. "I'm mighty sorry, young man, that we almost hanged you over a crime someone else committed."

"You were just doing your job, Mr. Jamison. No hard feelings."

He turned to Charity. "You too, Mrs. Reardon. My apologies."

"They're accepted, Mr. Jamison," she said.

Sheriff Cannon told Jamison all that had happened and how they believed the town's banker was the killer. Aghast, he muttered, "I just can't believe such an upstanding man could do such a thing."

"Son," said Judge Howell, "you'd be shocked at what I've seen supposedly good people do over the years."

"Are you going to arrest him?" Jamison asked.

"We can't without proof. No one can let on we suspect him. Let's see what happens after tonight's meetings. The word being out about how perverted he is may make him more cautious—or reckless."

****

The sheriff and Mr. Jamison had volunteered to

conduct the meeting at the saloon. The judge, with the help of the pastor, would handle the one at the church. The room was filled to overflowing. People had to stand around the walls and were squeezed into the pews like sardines.

Judge Howell rose to speak. "Folks, you've heard the rumors. We've got a killer amongst our town folk, a man who enjoys the terror he inflicts on the women." He cleared his throat. "He doesn't rape them, but he derives sexual pleasure from the violence."

The room echoed with angry mutters.

"Sheriff, I've got a wife and three young daughters to protect. Don't you have some idea who this monster could be?" Charity recognized the voice of Mr. Smithers. Voices rose to a deafening roar. Questions flew around the room.

"Quiet, folks," shouted the judge. "Quiet!" The noise slowly abated. "No, we have no idea who he is, but I assure you, myself, Sheriff Cannon, and with some help from Mrs. Reardon, we have some evidence and are closing in on the depraved man."

He raised his hand to stave off questions. "Mr. Smithers, I can't reveal anything I know. We don't want this person to run." He scratched his chin. "Actually, if he did, that would make him even more suspect. Now, this is what you need to do. Men, stay with your women if at all possible. Those of you women who live alone, you might want to find someone to stay with until this is all over."

The meeting broke up with a very subdued crowd. Nothing had happened like this in their town before, and they were afraid. Charity wondered what they'd think about the crazy world of 2008.

Chapter Six

Edward sat at his desk, beside himself with frustration. His anger and hate for Turner and Charity Reardon was growing like a festering sore. Yeah, like a boil on his butt. He needed to get rid of them, but the bitch first. Then he'd go after Turner.

The town stayed on alert. He'd not seen one woman out alone, and he'd not dared to court another widow. The demon in his body cried out for release. Sure, he could pleasure himself, but it just wasn't the same as smelling fear combined with a woman's scent and the feel of her body struggling against his swollen sex. He shuddered in response to the desire coursing through his veins.

It had started in Galveston when his fiancée, Sara Bell, broke off with him. He'd wanted to die. When she married someone else a week later, he'd wanted *her* to die. And she did. Her family never suspected him of the deed. Two years and four women later, he decided to leave South Texas before he got caught. When he arrived in Prairie, he'd been able to control himself, until Lucinda had spurned him for Reardon. The devil within him had roared in fury. *Make him pay. Kill his lover.* Gutting Lucinda had given him so much pleasure, he'd needed to kill again, feel that glorious release once more. His blood lust grew stronger with each victim.

Activity at the bank entrance drew his attention. He watched Mamie from the boardinghouse enter and stop at one of the teller windows. For an older woman, she wasn't bad looking. He imagined her warm flesh against his crotch and reached under his desk to rub his growing erection. Shocked at his behavior, he scratched his knee and brought his hand to the paperwork on his desk. *Not here, you fool.*

A wagon pulled up out front, and through the big glass window in his office he could see it was Tom, Reardon's top hand. He had some woman with him. She turned and smiled at someone on the street. Why, it was the beautiful Mrs. Reardon herself. What was she doing in town with Tom? She remained in the wagon while Tom entered the bank and went to stand behind Mamie. From where he sat, Edward could hear their conversation.

"Tom, what are you doing in town?" Mamie asked.

"We needed some supplies, and on the way out of town, I'm to deliver the missus to the 'little house' outside of town."

She peered around him to stare at the woman in the wagon. "Ah, so Turner will be meeting her there."

"Nope, not this time. He couldn't make it, and Mrs. Reardon wants to come back to the law office again tomorrow. That's why we've got her horse tied to the back of the wagon." He grinned. "She rode in with me 'cause she hasn't taken to riding that horse too well."

Mamie drew herself up to her full height. "You mean she's going to spend the night there alone?"

Tom held up a hand. "I know, I know, but not one thing I can do about it. Turner would have to lock her up to keep her from doing what she sets her mind to. At least she's packing a pistol."

"Well, I'll be having a talk with that young lady. Packing a pistol, indeed."

Edward watched through the window as Mamie stopped to talk to Charity. The older woman didn't act happy when she left to cross the street. Tom exited without glancing his way. They drove toward the mercantile.

Edward grinned. Tonight the bitch would pay. He'd enjoy this killing more than the other two put together.

****

Edward didn't leave town until it was completely dark. The knife he'd stolen off a customer's horse tethered outside the bank days ago was tucked in his boot. As backup, he had a .32 caliber pocket pistol in his trousers. Not that he expected to need it.

Hidden in the tall grasses growing around the home, he watched the pretty woman move through the house. She sang, but he couldn't make out the words. Once she stopped and swung a towel or something around her head in the air. Didn't look like ladylike behavior to him, but she was alone, so he guessed she didn't have to worry about what her dear husband would think.

The thought of Turner finding her dead the next morning made him smile. Oh, how he would like to be a spider on the wall to witness his sorrow. Sorrow, hell. Turner would be mad enough to kill. It was obvious to anyone with eyes he cared about the woman. Damn! He should've thought to bring something of Turner's that would tie him to the scene. Too late for that now.

Finally, she carried the kerosene lamp into the

bedroom. His body hardened at the thought of her undressing. She disappeared from sight, then returned a few minutes later in a white nightgown. He could see her silhouette through the gown and groaned at the rising desire he felt. *Hurry up, woman, and turn out that light.* As if hearing his request, she blew out the lamp. He'd give her a good hour to fall asleep; then he'd make his move.

****

Charity lay as still as she could and tried to look as if she were asleep. She'd left all the windows open so she'd get a cross breeze. Of course, she also got a lot of flies and mosquitoes. Turner had promised to put screens on next week.

She sighed. It had already been a trying day. They had refused to consider her for the bar exam. As if that wasn't enough, now she was laid up here in bed waiting for a murderer to carve up her body.

Butterflies danced in her stomach, and she broke out in a cold sweat. She didn't doubt for a minute if Edward knew she was alone he'd take a chance and try to kill her.

Moonlight cast shadows across the floor, and for just a second she saw something move, breaking the light pattern. She stiffened and listened for some kind of sound. A board creaked on the small porch, and then nothing. Several minutes later, a footstep sounded in the room outside her door. She trembled, unable to control her movements.

Thru the slits of her eyes, she saw him come into the bedroom. He stood at the door for a moment as if making sure she was asleep. He bent and pulled a large-bladed knife from his boot. It gleamed in the moonlight.

She squeezed her eyes shut, cutting out all light. His breathing was loud in the small room. She couldn't take much more. Just when she thought she'd scream, she heard the cocking of a pistol.

"Don't move a muscle, Edward. I'd love to have an excuse to shoot you, but the judge and Sheriff Cannon have different plans. I think it has to do with you swinging by your neck."

Edward swung around, knife poised to strike. Charity didn't think. She lifted the .38 revolver she had tucked at her side and fired, hitting him square in the back. As he howled in rage and pain, Turner knocked the knife from his hand.

Charity jumped out of bed and lit the kerosene lamp. Turner bent over Edward, probing at the wound to the sound of Edward's wails. "Looks like you'll live long enough to go to trial, Edward. More's the pity."

He stood and came to her side, wrapping both arms around her. "Are you all right?"

"A little shaky. Otherwise, fine."

"You did real good." He bent down and kissed her forehead. "I'm proud of you."

Her heart swelled. Shoot, she was pretty darn pleased with herself too.

Edward moaned. "You going to let me bleed to death while cozying up to your woman?"

Turner nudged him with his boot. "Just might."

Within minutes, they heard the judge and the sheriff stomping through the back door at a run. Both appeared delighted their prisoner was alive. Turner helped carry Edward outside and tie him across the saddle of the extra horse the sheriff had brought. Edward carried on so, Elijah popped him on the head with his gun butt to quiet him.

As they mounted their horses, Sheriff Cannon said, "See you two in town tomorrow so I can write up a report. Don't believe we'd have caught him without your help, Mrs. Reardon."

"Please, call me Charity. I imagine you'll be seeing a lot of me around town."

"I'm right sorry about you not being able to get your license to practice law," said the judge. "I believe you have skills we could all learn from."

"It's not such a big deal. I'm going to be Jonas's partner and help with all the research and investigation. For the past two days we've been brushing up on his courtroom skills."

"Good, good. The boy needs some serious help." He tipped his hat. "Goodnight to you folks. See you in the morning."

****

Charity and Turner lay in bed with the covers kicked back and a light breeze flowing over their damp bodies sated from lovemaking. With both arms and legs wrapped around her, pinning her to his body, Turner squeezed her. "Woman, you will never do something like this again. Sitting behind that dressing screen, I feared I'd die of a heart attack before Edward ever got here."

"The thought of doing undercover work again doesn't excite me. I was trembling so hard I was afraid the bed shook."

He growled into her hair. "Hon, I don't care if you have covers or not, no more of this catching killers."

Have covers? Charity started giggling. Unable to stop she howled with laughter.

"What the hell is so funny?" he demanded.

"Oh...Turner. I'm just so happy." She pulled his face down for her kiss. When she broke contact, she whispered against his neck. "I love you, Turner Reardon."

She yelped as he about squeezed the life out of her. He relaxed his hold and pulled her head back to stare in her eyes. "I love you too, Charity."

Later, she lay still as Turner ran his fingers up and down her back so softly it almost tickled.

She shivered as he whispered against her ear. "What about your father, sweetheart? Are you sure you can be content without him in your life?"

Did she have a choice? No. After loving Turner, no way could she go back to her own time and live without him. She'd miss her father, but if she could get a message to him... "If I could let him know my whereabouts, it would be a big load off my mind. I want him to know I'm safe and happy."

"Is your father's law firm a family business? When was it established?"

"Daddy's grandfather bought the firm in 1908 from Walter Haygood. He'd been in business for over seventy-five years." She shoved Turner to his back and, laughing, straddled his waist. "That's it, that's it!" Arms twined around his neck, she planted a loud wet kiss on his mouth. "I know how to let him know where I am."

She explained her plan.

He fanned his fingers through her hair, brushing it back from her face. "I've got one smart wife." This man's every touch made her feel so special.

She scooted down his body and dropped her head

to his chest. "I just hope it works."

"No reason why it wouldn't. If anyone can make it happen, it's you. Are you sure you're not too disappointed about not getting your license?"

"No, I'll do what I want, and if I get in trouble I'll plead ignorance. Or Jonas will plead for me." She tilted her head up to kiss him. "Heck, I may even make a few laws of my own." She listened to the steady thump of his heart. "And in time, women will be allowed into the profession. I'll be ready and be one of the first."

"I wouldn't put it past you. You're a hard woman to keep on a leash."

"Yes, and don't you forget it." She chuckled. "Anyway, I need to spend some of my time being a wife, learning what life is like on a Texas spread."

"Yes, you do, darlin', in particular, learning to ride your horse without bouncing in the saddle. As for me, I think I need to read *Taming the Cowboy* so I can learn how you women from the future expect me to act."

****

Charity stomped her feet outside the post office to remove as much snow as possible. No need to track up the floor and cause someone to fall. A bell tinkled over her head as she entered. Behind the counter, Mr. Doud looked up from sorting mail.

"Howdy, Mrs. Reardon. Bet you're here for your package."

"It came?" She'd waited so long she'd about given up hope.

"Sure did—all the way from New York City. I'll get it for you."

He returned from the back room carrying a cardboard box approximately fourteen inches long and nine inches wide.

"Here you go, ma'am." She looked down at the box in her hand. There on the label she read: Mrs. Charity Reardon, Prairie, Texas.

She couldn't contain her excitement and stifled a laugh. The man would think her nuts. "Thank you, Mr. Doud."

"You're just mighty welcome." He hustled around the counter. "Let me get the door for you."

Charity strolled outside and to the law office a block away.

Jonas opened the door for her. "I see it came."

"Yes. I can't wait to see them." She pulled open a drawer of the desk he'd brought in for her and pushed items around. "Do you have a pair of scissors?"

He rummaged around in his desk and produced a large pair. Charity took them and snipped the twine and some type of tape. Heck, she didn't know tape had been invented yet, or, for that matter, cardboard boxes.

The carton had been wrapped several times. She appreciated the care with which they'd readied the books for mail.

Carefully, so as not to damage the books inside, she used the scissors to slit the tape across the top of the box and lifted out a thick tome. She ran her hand across the fine bound leather and inhaled its wonderful scent.

Charity opened the book to the copyright page. "Look, Jonas, 1880." She handed it to him. "This is for you."

His mouth fell open. "For me? Why?"

"For being my friend, believing my story about how I got here, and letting me work with you."

He stuttered, "I…I…don't know what to say."

"How about 'thank you'?"

His eyes glistened, and he hugged the book to his chest. "Thank you. Not for just the book, but for making me into a better lawyer."

She patted his arm. "I've enjoyed every minute of working with you."

Charity lifted the other book from the box. It was identical to the one she'd given Jonas.

"This one is for Daddy."

****

New York, July 15, 2008

Buford "Bull" Dawson stared at the heavy aged brown-paper-wrapped package he'd removed from the vault. Years ago, he'd wished it would disappear. Now, it was as dear to him as his life.

After joining his father's law firm, he'd been going through business items they'd inherited from the former owner and was stunned to see his name written across the old paper wrapping. A note had been attached, indicating it should be delivered on July 15, 2008, but he'd been unable to resist temptation.

Charity had been five years old at the time, and the contents had filled him with dread. He'd done everything in his power to keep his girl close, to avoid what he feared most in life.

Years ago he'd replaced the string that had broken on one side. His name was written with liquid ink, the kind he'd used in school as a boy until ballpoint pens had been invented. The handwriting he'd know anywhere.

His throat closed in panic as he studied the return address and date—the one that had haunted his days and nights for the past twenty-three years—Charity

Dawson Reardon, Prairie, Texas, 1888. This time he knew what was happening. This wasn't a joke or a bad dream.

Hands shaking, he took scissors from his desk drawer and carefully cut the string, then folded back the edges of the paper, making sure he didn't damage it, to reveal an antique law book. A beautiful tome. He couldn't resist running his hand over the fine cover and breathing in the scent of old leather. The print date was 1880.

The pages fell open to reveal a folded sheet of paper. He lifted it from the book, opened it, and read the words, knowing this time they were indeed true.

Dear Daddy, I know this will be a big shock, but…

A Marshal

of

Her Own

by

Linda LaRoque

Dedication

Many thanks to my critique partners
Golden, Lynn, and Lynette
for their invaluable help, advice, and support.

Chapter One

November 15, 2010, Fredericksburg, Texas

"Strange doings."

Strange doings, indeed. Investigative reporter Dessa Wade wasn't buying the outlandish explanation for the disappearance of several women. The older woman she interviewed today at the jewelry store had clutched Dessa's hand and said, "You be careful at that cabin, young woman." She pulled Dessa closer. "Strange doings out there." Dessa believed in facts.

She'd driven to the small Hill Country town to gather information on the 2008 disappearance of Charity Dawson. The young corporate lawyer had disappeared without a trace. Known for digging out the whole story, Dessa was anxious to get started. Plus, the storekeeper's comments about strange events had piqued her interest.

She parked in front of the quaint log structure located several miles outside of Fredericksburg, a picturesque German town loaded with antique shops and other tourist attractions. Dessa gazed at the building with a keen journalist's eye. Made of roughhewn logs, its tin roof extended over the deep porch stretching across the front of the dwelling. How could something out of the ordinary take place here? The cabin resembled one her sweet great-grandmother might have lived in back in the early nineteen hundreds. Dessa almost expected, when she got out of the car, to encounter the fragrance of freshly baked gingerbread wafting on the fall breeze.

Oh well, looks could be deceiving, so nothing to do but check out the rumor. The cottage was hers for the next week. If there was anything strange about the place, she'd find answers. The rollers on her suitcase caught on the pea-sized gravel covering the path, and she carried the bag past the claw foot bathtub filled with purple and yellow pansies. The cactus garden on the opposite side of the walkway looked drab this time of year, but purple asters lined the path to the porch, where two rocking chairs creaked in the breeze. She snickered. Maybe ghosts were observing her arrival.

She plunked her luggage down next to the first rocker and went back down the steps to lift the green frog in the flowerbed. The owner had said she'd find the key there, and she did. With it clutched in her hand, she returned to the entrance, unlocked the door, and lugged her suitcase inside. The cozy living area held a stuffed sofa and chair, a bookshelf, end tables and lamps. A fireplace covered almost the entire wall opposite the couch. Logs stacked on the hearth promised a fire-lit evening if the cool weather held out. Dessa dropped her suitcase and closed the door on the world outside.

In the kitchen, she found the small vintage fridge stocked with enough food to stave off her hunger for several days. A bottle of Bordeaux wine sat on the counter, but the dark red was a little dry for her taste. She'd bought her own while touring the winery in town, where she'd found a couple of yummy semi-sweet varieties at the wine-tasting. If she brought them in and put them in the refrigerator, they could chill while she got her bath.

Beyond the window above the kitchen sink she could see another covered porch protected the cabin from the sun's rays on that side. A picturesque pond spread beyond the back steps. Curious, she stepped outside and walked around the berm that surrounded the water on three sides. On the far side, the earth dropped several feet to an area covered with prairie grass, live oak trees, and other indigenous plants.

Oak leaves fell, fluttering around her as the wind blew. The breeze ruffled the short sprigs of her dark, spiky hair. She took a deep breath, enjoying the scents of nature. A gurgling stream drew her gaze to the back of the property, and she slid down the slope to investigate what she saw there. An arched bridge spanned the creek to the clearing beyond, but she resisted the urge to go across. Her stomach grumbled its hunger, and dusk was fast approaching. Tomorrow would be soon enough to explore.

An hour later, bathed and in long, pink fleece pajamas sporting red hearts and her fluffy house shoes, she sat cross-legged on the comfortable couch eating cheese, slices of Canadian bacon, crackers, and juicy red grapes. A fire blazed and crackled in the fireplace, emitting the slight scent of apples. A book stacked with others on the hearth, *Outlaws of Texas*, drew her eye, and she spent an hour flipping the pages, reading accounts of notorious gangs. One caught her interest—the Faradays—because they'd been apprehended in 1890 with the help of a woman. How cool was that? As an investigative reporter, Dessa felt an instant kinship with this woman from the nineteenth century. She must have had some of the same instincts Dessa did.

Setting the volume aside, she placed her glass of wine on the end table and pulled her laptop onto her lap to review her notes on Charity Dawson. The young woman, a corporate New York lawyer, spent one night in this cabin and then disappeared, never to be seen or heard from again. Her car, clothes, luggage, purse—all of her personal items were abandoned at the cottage.

When Charity's disappearance hit the headlines in San Antonio, it captured Dessa's attention. Dessa unraveled leads from the missing person report that came through the news feed, but every thread of the story left her hanging. She'd gathered as much data as she could before committing to the story. Strangest of all was the fact Charity's father, Buford "Bull" Dawson, refused to search for his daughter.

Dessa flew to New York to talk with him. His words, "I know my daughter's whereabouts. She sent me a message from the past. She's happy and doesn't want to be located, so leave it alone. Please, Miss Wade...don't dredge up her disappearance again."

He'd gone through police and FBI scrutiny for over a year. Charity's body was never found. Mr. Dawson had shared a little information with the authorities—an outlandish story about time travel. Evidently the police ran out of leads and quit hounding him, but Dessa didn't doubt the FBI kept him under close surveillance.

"Time travel, my ass." The woman was either well hidden or buried somewhere. Whatever the answer, Bull Dawson was a broken man struggling to return his life to normal. He mourned his daughter's absence. All the more reason for Dessa to locate Charity's body and give the grieving father closure.

Dessa picked up her wineglass and swirled the light red liquid around in the crystal bowl. The beverage formed a vortex, a movement of mystery much like her mission. She smiled and took a sip, enjoying the sweetness with a hint of tart aftertaste. Lifting her glass, she toasted her assignment. "May my success be as sweet as this wine." She hoped any tartness didn't make a showing.

****

Dessa woke before the sun cleared the trees behind the cabin. She ran downstairs to start coffee and then quickly dressed in jeans, a bright yellow turtleneck sweater, and tennis shoes. The java was rich, and the aroma filled the small cottage and smelled heavenly. She poured a large mug full and stepped out onto the back porch to watch the sun's rays creep toward the pond. The chilly air wafted around her, rustling her hair. She sipped the hot liquid, its warmth heating her insides for a moment.

A mist hung over the water and extended beyond to the clearing. Soon the sun would burn the moisture off, but for now the haze was beautiful—a scene she'd like to capture and savor again later. Where the heck was her camera when she wanted to snap a picture? Upstairs, probably.

She turned and went inside. In the kitchen she refilled her cup and then stepped into the living room to grab the patchwork quilt off the back of the sofa. She wrapped the throw over her shoulders and arms like a shawl. It'd be just what she needed to ward off the chill in the air. With coffee in hand, she stepped out onto the porch and struck off toward the barrier around the pond.

Sunlight made the mist sparkle like a lake of crushed diamonds—only this body of water extended beyond its borders as it drifted into the trees. Fascinated, she watched her feet and half her calves gradually disappear the farther she walked. Near where she thought the small bridge across the creek was located, she eased sideways down the incline and inched toward the bridge railings peeking through the mist.

When Dessa stepped off the bridge, she was completely covered by the fog. Fre...eaky. She stood, gaze darting left and right as she struggled to get her bearings. Both hands wrapped around her coffee mug, she tilted the cup to her lips and took a healthy swallow. What was she doing walking about in vapor so thick she couldn't see? It'd be her luck to fall and break a leg. Who knew how many days it would be before someone found her. *If you have a lick of sense, Dessa, you'll march your butt back the way you came and park it on the sofa until the sun burns away the moisture.*

Yeah, yeah, Mother always said her curiosity would get her in trouble one day, but disaster hadn't happened. Yet. She searched the ground as she eased forward. With every step, the mist lessened. A light glowed in the distance as she trudged on.

She slowed at the sound of voices—and a thud and a yelp.

"What the hell was that for?"

"I said get up. We need to hightail it out of here. If that posse catches us, I'll be hitting you with a bullet instead of a rock."

More grumbling followed, accompanied by laughter from two more men. What on earth had she stepped into? Posse? Maybe Mama was right. She started inching backward and then stopped. Her head told her to keep retreating, but curiosity said, "Go forth and investigate." The wind took the decision out of her hands as it picked up speed, and leaves and debris swirled around her. The air churned faster. It lifted and propelled her forward into the midst of the men.

She swayed, caught her balance, and stood stock still with the fire at her back. A crusty-looking bunch, clothes filthy, mouths agape, their gazes flew from her to each other and to her again. The cup fell from her grasp and shattered on the ground as a shriek burst from her mouth. The men yelled and scrambled for their horses.

A shot rang out. "Freeze or we'll shoot! Federal Marshal. You're all under arrest."

Dessa froze. The men stilled for a minute and then dove into the trees. Shots sounded all around them. She screamed and hit the ground.

****

Marshal Cole Jeffers, concealed in the trees with two deputies, couldn't believe his eyes. A person, wrapped in a quilt, appeared out of nowhere—like magic. Nah, he'd been hidden behind something and stood when Cole glanced away. But something spooked the man, because he screamed. Damn, it was a woman. Faraday's men ran into each other in confusion. No matter. The outlaws were in his sights, and he intended to bring them in for trial. They'd robbed one bank too many. Yesterday in Prairie they'd wounded one of the tellers.

Jeffers fired a warning shot. "Freeze or we'll shoot! Federal Marshal. You're all under arrest."

The woman and the men stilled for a minute, but then the men made for the trees.

He yelled, "Open fire." His men obeyed. He and his men fired, hitting two of the robbers. The female screamed and dropped to the ground. Rear end in the air, she crawled toward the brush. His deputies took off after the two escapees. Naturally, one was Faraday. He checked the two fallen robbers—one dead—and removed the wounded kid's weapons and cuffed him. A minor wound, but the way the kid howled you'd think he'd die at any minute. He exhaled a sigh of relief, glad the boy would live. Maybe after a stint in prison he'd straighten up.

****

Dessa resisted the urge to scream again. She bit her bottom lip as a reminder to stay silent and not draw attention to herself. Her heart thundered in her chest, threatening to jump from her body. This couldn't be happening. *God, please tell me I'm dreaming. Wake me up. Please...please...* Just in case God wasn't listening, she was getting out of Dodge.

On her hands and knees she crawled toward the safety of the trees and the shadows. Afraid to look up, she continued forward as fast as her limbs would take her. Rocks and debris scratched her hands and gouged into her kneecaps, but she didn't care.

She bumped into something and shifted to the left, but whatever was in her way moved with her. Uh-oh. Dread inched up her spine. She stiffened. She might be caught, but she darn well wouldn't go peacefully. After all, she was a victim here. Tilting her head up slightly, she eyed a pair of well-worn boots. As her eyes moved upward she noted faded denims, sculpted muscled thighs, and...oh my...just below his gun belt. She blushed and pushed herself up to sit on her haunches, putting a little distance between them.

From that angle, she got a full view of the man. His wool coat bore a silver star. She gave a sigh of relief, then a gasp. He was a lawman, a darn good-looking one, at that. *Focus Dessa.* She'd been saved. "Thank goodness. I'm so glad you're here."

Her smile vanished at the expression on his face. Steel blue eyes assessed her beneath the black felt hat. Rugged planes displayed a scowl that didn't bode well for her, nor did the shotgun held loosely in his right hand.

Well, she'd done nothing wrong. She pulled the quilt—how she'd managed to keep it on in her race for freedom she didn't have a clue—closer around her shoulders and then extended her hand. He didn't take it and help her up.

"Do you have no manners? I need help."

He took her hand and pulled her to her feet. "I'm not in the habit of being courteous to outlaws."

She rocked for a minute, catching her balance, as his comment registered on her brain. "Outlaw? What are you talking about? I'm not an outlaw."

He snorted. "Tell that to the judge. Being in the company of the Faraday gang makes you one of them— a bank robber or an accomplice."

She sputtered and waved her arm in the direction of the cabin. "I'm not with them. I live right over yonder, just across that little bridge."

"What little bridge?" He glanced in the direction she indicated. "There's no water for several miles around here."

"I beg to differ." She backhanded him on the arm. "Come on, I'll show you." She started walking, but he halted her.

"You're not going anywhere." His men came riding in. He squeezed her shoulder. "Either stand here and don't try to run, or I'll tie you to a tree."

She crossed her arms, a mutinous expression on her face, but nodded.

The deputy closest to them jumped from his horse. "Sorry, Marshal. They got away. You want us to go back and try to pick up their trail?"

Dessa stood still and watched as they conversed. Something stank to high heaven about this entire situation. Why were the cops chasing robbers on horseback? It's not like Fredericksburg was that isolated. She glanced at the captured men. The boy moaned, and she made a step to go over and help him. The marshal spun, and the expression in his eyes froze her in place.

"He needs first aid."

"He's fine. Doc will tend to him when we get to the jail."

"You could at least call 911 and let them patch him up for you." She nodded to the man lying so still with his eyes closed. "Your other prisoner doesn't look so good. He's going to die on you if you don't start CPR or get him some help."

"Lady, no one is going to hear a yell from out here. Never heard of any 911 or CPR." He propped on his hip the hand not holding the shotgun and threw her a disgusted look. "Are you blind? That man is dead, shot through the heart."

Her head swam for a moment, and she struggled

not to give in to the sensation and faint. She drew in deep gulps of air. "Well...well...what about the coroner and the meat wagon, not to mention the CSI folks? If you don't get them to record the scene, how are you going to cover your butt? The authorities might say you shot him in cold blood."

He looked at her like she'd sprouted an extra head. "I don't know what the hell you are talking about, woman. No one will question my authority. I'm the law in this county. Now, be quiet, or I'm going to gag you."

His deputies put the wounded boy, with his hands tied, on his horse and controlled his mount with a lead rope. The dead man received the same treatment, but he was placed face down. Before she could object, the marshal lifted her, quilt and all, set her astride his horse, and mounted behind her.

She grabbed a handful of the horse's mane and hung on as he kicked the animal into a trot. The other two on a lead rope followed. His arm locked around her waist, slamming her back against his broad chest.

The air left her lungs with a whoosh. "You're squeezing the life out of me."

"Relax, and I'll ease up." She took a deep breath and tried to concentrate on the scenery. The trees thinned and—

A howl of pain came from the kid. With her elbow, she gigged the marshal in the side. "Aren't you going to do something? He's hurting."

"Nope. Nothing I can do but tie him across the saddle like his dead buddy. Either way he's going to hurt. It's best to ignore him."

Dessa didn't agree, but decided arguing with him wouldn't change his mind.

They'd left the trees and were riding through prairie. Odd. She didn't remember seeing this much grassland around the Fredericksburg area.

"Where are we going?"

"I'm taking you and your cohorts to jail in town."

"Good. The lady I rented the cabin from is in Fredericksburg. She'll tell you I couldn't have known these men. I just got into the area yesterday."

"Fredericksburg?" He laughed, the sound a deep rumbling in his chest that vibrated to her back. "Are you nuts, lady? Fredericksburg is over four hundred miles away."

Chapter Two

His prisoner stiffened in his arms and tried to turn. "You're lying. There's no way I walked four hundred miles on my ten-minute walk this morning."

His grip on her waist tightened. "Quit squirming." Hell, if she moved around much more she'd know what her soft bottom was doing to his body. "I'm not lying. In another hour we'll be in Prairie."

"Prairie what?"

"Hell, woman. Prairie, Texas. What did you think I meant?"

"I've never heard of Prairie, Texas."

Yeah, right. She was a good actress, he'd give her that. Her head dropped forward, and she shuddered.

"Are you cold?" He tucked the quilt more securely around her. She didn't answer but shook her head and sniffled. Ah, hell, not tears.

"Stop that bawling, now. Tears won't help you one bit." Damned if they'd soften him up. He had a job to do—take her to jail—and he never failed to do his duty.

"I must be...crazy. I have to be. Why...why, not two hours ago...I got out of bed, made a pot of coffee, and left the cabin for a walk. Mist was everywhere." She swiped at her tears and sobbed, "I didn't even get to eat breakfast." She threw her hands in the air and wailed, "And here I am in...in... Where the hell am I?"

The woman's raving had stopped the kid's

moaning. He now gaped at the woman in wonder. Hell, maybe she was nuts. She continued to snivel but no longer talked.

Cole had to admit she was an odd little thing. Her short hair appeared to have been cut with a knife. It stuck up at weird angles, leaving her neck and ears bare. The lobes had little holes in them. For earbobs, he supposed. Though her hair was dark and glossy, leaves and dirt were caught in its strands. He reached up to brush them away, then lowered his hand. Why would any woman cut her hair that short? He peered closely at the hair so near to his chin and breathed a sigh of relief. No head lice.

Her eyes were dark, her pale skin a striking contrast to her sweater, the color of sunshine. Never before had he seen a woman in pants. The ones she wore were tight and hugged her legs and rear end. He shifted in the saddle. He couldn't deny his attraction to her.

To aggravate him further, a sweet scent, like flowers, reached his nostrils. He sniffed to make sure his nose wasn't lying to him. Nope, it wasn't a flower, but vanilla. Odd. As close as she'd been to the fire, she should smell like wood smoke and be filthy. Though she'd dirtied her denims and hands in her crawl to get away, she was clean elsewhere.

The woman made him think about things he didn't have. He loved his job, but he often wished he had a wife and children to come home to. At thirty-five, he was past the age when most men settled down. His younger brother already had three kids. He'd had a few sweethearts but none willing to have him gone for several weeks, sometimes months at a time. Not that he blamed them. He wasn't good husband material, but the fact didn't wholly dispel the idea from his mind. Yep, she was a beautiful woman. What a shame she'd strayed outside the law.

****

Atop the horse, Dessa jostled along in front of the marshal. Her head bounced against his shoulder. If only she could relax, go to sleep, and wake up to realize this was all a dream—a bad one, at that. Nothing made sense. Why, she'd just been enjoying her morning cup of coffee, taking a walk, when zap! and she'd landed in la-la land, bullets flying. And then the handsome marshal arrived. She had to admit, as bad dreams went, he was an interesting twist.

Her chuckle died in her throat as they topped the hill. A western movie picture set appeared on the horizon. She whooped with joy. That was it. She'd gotten caught up in the production of a movie.

She whirled on the marshal. "Why didn't you tell me you were an actor making a movie?"

He frowned, expression indignant. "I'm no actor. And I've never heard of a movie."

"Yeah, right. This is all a joke, isn't it? Someone is playing a trick on me."

"Lady, think whatever makes you happy. Won't change facts." He nodded to the man face down on his horse. "Sure as heck won't make him any less dead."

Dessa's heart sank. She'd not seen a dead person before, but the outlaw, if alive, would find his position on the horse most uncomfortable. No way could he have pretended to be dead and remained still all this time. Hell's bells, a dead man. She'd seen a man killed, shot deader than a doornail. Every cliché she'd heard describing death popped into her head. She shuddered and pushed the pictures aside.

Her shudder didn't end but turned into a quake that racked her body. She moaned and bit back a sob.

The marshal held her tighter. "Are you all right?"

"No. I'll never be okay again."

As they drew closer to the town—Prairie, she supposed—Dessa saw people going about their daily business. A stagecoach drove out of town. The driver shouted, "Howdy, Marshal."

"Hey, Samuel."

The stagecoach passed in a flurry of dust. Dessa covered her mouth and nose with part of the quilt and continued to study the scene before her. People stopped their activities to stare as the lawman and his prisoners passed. Did a bug under the microscope want to hide? She sure did, but hiding wasn't an option. Folks flocked to the jail and waited for the marshal to turn over his prisoners.

Dessa couldn't believe her eyes. A few structures had false fronts, but the majority were actual buildings, all in good repair. The dirt street bore ruts formed by repeated activity during rainy weather. A suspicion of doom inched up her spine, leaving goose bumps in its wake.

The door to the sheriff's office opened, drawing her attention back to her predicament. A big man stepped from the jail. He looked from the dead prisoner to the wounded kid to Dessa. "What you got here, Jeffers?"

The marshal dismounted and helped Dessa off the horse. "Looks like the Faradays recruited a woman. Found her in their camp."

The sheriff scratched his chin. "Is that so?"

Her sense of panic evaporated, to be replaced by anger. "No, it's not. I told you I'd never seen those men before." She backhanded the marshal on the chest. A gasp echoed through the crowd. "Until the marshal rode in with guns roaring, that is."

"Harrumph. Well, bring 'em in the jail and let's hash this out." He waved at a deputy. "Get the boy down, Hank, and then go get the doc."

Inside, the sheriff tossed the marshal a large set of keys. "Lock her up. Good thing we've got just two prisoners. Not much privacy in there."

The marshal walked her past a large metal door to a cell and locked her inside. She clutched the bars. "Wait. I don't even know your name."

He tipped his hat. "Marshal Cole Jeffers, ma'am."

"Uh, I need to go to the bathroom."

He pointed to a porcelain container under the bed.

She eyed it with disgust. "Not going to happen. Surely there is another...er...a...facility?"

He yelled at the sheriff. "Get a sheet up in here, Elijah. I'm escorting the prisoner out back."

If he thought she was squatting in the bushes, he'd better think again. They stopped in front of a ramshackle building about four feet by four feet and probably eight feet tall. An outhouse. She stared. Well, it was better than the pot under the cot. She squared her shoulders and went inside.

Dessa kicked at the dust on their way back. If she could delay going back inside, she would. To the west, the sun crept toward the horizon, yet it would hours before dark. Sounds of activity rose faintly from the streets beyond the alley. In the distance, a dog barked,

17

but nothing else stirred. She sighed and plodded forward.

She entered her cell to find water for washing.

"One of us will be back for you in a few minutes." The marshal turned on his heel and left the lockup area.

She washed as best she could without completely disrobing. She'd just finished when Sheriff Cannon barreled through the secure doorway and unlocked her cage to escort her into his office.

"Have a seat, ma'am." She sat in the chair before his desk, hands folded in her lap.

Marshal Jeffers stood by the window. Hatless, his dark hair still bore the imprint and shone with good health. Would the strands be soft to the touch, or coarse? She mentally shook herself. *Stop mooning over the man. He's trying to arrest you for robbing a bank.*

The sheriff licked the lead in his pencil. "Name?"

"Dessa Wade."

"Where you from, Miss Wade?"

"San Antonio."

He looked up from the paper, pencil stilled in mid writing. "You're a long way from home. What're you doing in these parts?"

She glanced at Jeffers, but he turned his back and looked out the window, blocking much of the sunlight. His tall frame exuded strength. The blue chambray shirt he wore stretched taut across his wide shoulders to be tucked into his denim pants. Though not tight, they emphasized his muscular legs and butt. Yes, indeed, he was one hunky man.

The clearing of a throat startled her. "Miss Wade?" Sheriff Cannon watched her with a smirk on his face.

She ducked her head to cover her rosy cheeks and

sighed. "You see, I'm an investigative reporter working on a story. I drove to Fredericksburg to research the disappearance of Charity Dawson back in 2008."

Jeffers turned and moved closer. He propped one hip on the desk and fixed her with his gaze. "Don't you mean 1888?"

She fidgeted under his perusal. "No, July 15, 2008."

The two men exchanged a glance. The fact they didn't believe her was evident, but Cannon said, "Go on."

She described the morning's events. They listened without interrupting.

"Jeffers, did you see the bridge Miss Wade mentioned?"

"Nope. Elijah, you know there's no water within two miles of the spot the Faradays were hid out."

The sheriff continued. "Then a wind picks you up and sets you down just ten miles from Prairie." He shook his head. "You expect us to believe such a wild story?"

"But it's the truth. I swear it. Give me a lie detector test."

"A what?" Marshal Jeffers slapped both hands down on the desk. "Elijah, I told you she talked all sorts of nonsense. Wanted me to call somebody and do something called CRP."

She leaned forward and backhanded him across the arm. "CPR and 911, you oaf."

He grabbed her hand and bit out, "Do not hit me again."

"Well, okay." She yanked from his grasp.

The sheriff folded his hands across his hefty belly

and twirled his thumbs. "Miss, you say you were in Fredericksburg and you were investigating a disappearance that occurred in 2008."

She nodded. "That's correct."

His thumbs increased in speed, and Dessa resisted the urge to giggle.

"And what exactly is today's date?"

"What the heck does that have to do with anything?"

Neither man answered, just waited.

"Oh, all right. It's November 15, 2010."

The sheriff rapped his knuckles on the desk top. "Miss Wade, you're either lying or crazy. Today is November 15, 1890."

Dessa laughed, but at the expression of pity on their faces, her humor fled and quickly turned into a sob. She shook her head. "No, you're lying."

The marshal reached for the calendar she'd not noticed before, lifted it from the nail on the wall, and handed it to her. She flipped through the pages, then fell back into her chair, dropping her head into her hands and wailing, "Oh, God. Please tell me this is a bad dream. I mean, there is no such thing as time travel, right?"

****

Cole resisted the urge to go inside the cell and put his arm around Miss Wade's shoulders in reassurance. Since their discussion before supper, she had remained quiet—a state he didn't think was natural for her. She'd certainly gabbed enough on the ride in to Prairie. He knew she'd been hungry, but she ate little of the food brought from the café. She was too demure for his liking, but, hell, maybe she'd decided the ruse was up and she'd better face the consequences. Still, he wanted to see her spunky attitude return.

Now she sat on her cot, head down, talking quietly to Jonas Bailey. The lawyer, listening intently, occupied a chair Cole had dragged in for him. The odd little man had grown a backbone since he'd taken Turner Reardon's wife on as a partner of sorts. Interesting story, that. Turner Reardon on trial for murder and a woman shows up out of nowhere to prove he couldn't have done the deed. Jurors convicted him anyway, but the woman married him to keep him from hanging and then proved the banker did the killing.

The sheet covering the bars had been pulled back. The kid in the cell next door was snoring softly, but the wall between the units was relatively thick, allowing a scrap of privacy. Earlier, Cole had questioned the boy about the gang's next destination. Either he played dumb or he really didn't know. As to the lady, they'd never seen her before. In his words, "Scared the dickens out of us when she just popped up out of nowhere." Cole didn't know what to believe, but he'd convinced Elijah to keep the information quiet for a few days. The longer they could keep Miss Wade close, the better. She knew something about the Faradays. He felt it in his bones.

Jonas patted Miss Wade's leg. Cole stiffened, ready to intervene if the man got fresh, but, smiling, the lawyer stood. They'd been talking in whispers, but now he spoke up so Cole could hear. "Don't you worry, ma'am. Everything will be just fine." He exited the cubicle and nodded to Cole. "Thank you, Marshal."

"Anytime, Jonah."

Cole moved to the cell door. "Do you need

anything, Miss Wade?"

A half smile tilted her lips. "No, Marshal, but thank you." She lay down on the cot, pulled the quilt over her shoulders, and closed her eyes.

Not thirty minutes later the jail door opened and Mrs. Reardon, with her husband on her heels, rushed through.

"Charity, slow down or I'm going to get Sheriff Cannon to lock you behind bars until the baby comes."

"I am fine, Turner."

"Harrumph. Well, at least sit down." He shoved a chair under her. She eased into it and placed a protective hand on her massive belly.

Truth be told, Cole had never seen a woman so large with pregnancy out in public. Most women stayed at home, but Mrs. Reardon didn't act like other females. She'd set the town on its ear with her sometimes outlandish ways of doing things. The local ladies accepted her and her oddities, although some of the men weren't pleased at their wives' new behavior.

Cole restrained a chuckle at the look of shock on Sheriff Cannon's face. His mouth opened and closed as he tried to speak. "Ma...ma'am...what in thunderation are you doing, rushing about in your condition?"

She rolled her eyes. "I'm pregnant, Sheriff, not dying. Now, I need to see your female prisoner."

****

The metal door clanked open, and Dessa watched Sheriff Cannon stride toward her. "You have a visitor, Miss Wade." He unlocked her cell, and, taking her arm, walked her out to the front office.

A tall, dark-headed man stood, his hands on the shoulders of a pretty blonde woman sitting in front of the desk. Dessa's eyes dropped to note her large abdomen and then shifted to her face. Blue eyes, bright with curiosity, considered Dessa. The woman's gaze moved from the top of Dessa's head to the tennis shoes on her feet.

Dessa studied her in return. There was something familiar about her. The hair was different, but those eyes... *My, God, it's Charity Dawson. No...no, she couldn't be here, could she? Time travel...Mr. Dawson said time travel. Oh, my stars, could it be true?*

"Miss Wade, this is Mr. and Mrs. Reardon."

As if making up her mind, Mrs. Reardon stood and, with arms open, approached. "Dessa, honey, I'm so glad to see you. We've been worried sick about you."

Dessa was wrapped in a warm embrace. A whisper rustled the hair by her ear. "Follow my lead. I'm a time traveler too."

Chapter Three

Dessa whispered, "Charity? Charity Dawson?"

"Yes." She squeezed her tightly and spoke softly. "We'll talk later."

Dessa gave a slight nod.

With one arm around Dessa, the woman turned them both to face the men. "Sheriff, Dessa is my cousin from...from..."

"San Antonio," Dessa blurted.

"Yes, that's right." Charity batted her eyes at the sheriff. "You know, Elijah, even after all this time there are still gaps in my memory."

He coughed. "Yes, ma'am. I expect so."

"Anyway, I'd like to take Dessa with us to stay at Miss Mamie's until we return to the ranch." She laid her free hand over her huge belly. "You know, 'til the baby comes."

Sheriff Cannon blushed scarlet, but blustered, "Well, now. I'm right sorry, Mrs. Reardon, but Miss Wade has to stay here until we determine her ties with the Faraday gang."

"Surely you don't believe she had anything to do with those bank robberies. She's just a victim. They probably kidnapped her, kept her hostage. Why, the dear girl's been missing for a month, ever since that week-long Bible retreat she attended while visiting our aunt in Lubbock, back in early October."

Boy, Charity knew how to weave a tale. It sounded plausible to Dessa, but would the sheriff buy the story? He might, but the stubborn expression on Marshal Jeffers' face said *he* didn't.

****

Cole smothered his snort with a cough. Bible retreat? Evidently the teaching didn't take with Miss Wade. Her tongue on the ride in had bordered on tart. Of course, if she'd been a part of the gang long, by choice or as a prisoner, the men's language could've rubbed off on her.

Turner Reardon's mention of Miss Mamie's interrupted his train of thought. "We're staying there and can obtain the room next door to us for her. We'd vouch for her not leaving town." He glanced at Cole. "You're also rooming at Miss Mamie's, aren't you, Marshal?"

"Yes, that's right." Cole wasn't sure he liked Reardon's train of thought. From the stubborn expression on his prisoner's face, Miss Wade wasn't impressed, either.

"Perfect, then." Reardon turned to the sheriff. "Miss Wade would be closely supervised by Marshal Jeffers, Charity, and me."

Sheriff Cannon scratched his chin and rocked back on his heels. "Well, I don't know. 'Course, Miss Mamie wouldn't allow a woman dressed in men's pants in her place." He eyed Miss Wade up and down and then turned to Mrs. Reardon. "You think you could rustle up something for her to wear?"

"Of course, Sheriff. Clothes aren't a problem." She smiled up at him. "So, can we take her with us?"

"What do you think, Jeffers? Since you're the one

who'll have to stand watch over our prisoner, I'll leave the decision up to you."

The arrangement might be to Cole's advantage. He could keep Miss Wade under his thumb. She'd not leave the boarding house without him. He'd get the information he needed from her on the gang and track them down.

"I'll agree on one condition. Miss Wade will not leave the boarding house without me as her escort."

"What?"

Cole couldn't resist grinning. Now, here was the feisty woman he'd taken prisoner. She folded her arms across her chest and, eyes narrowed, frowned. "That's a bit extreme, don't you think?"

Cole shrugged. "That's the deal. Accept my offer to be your escort, or stay in jail."

****

The door to Miss Mamie's boarding house was opened by a plump, dimpled older woman just an inch or two taller than Dessa, who resisted a grin. Dessa bet this lady wouldn't be much of a jailer. That thought flew out the window when the woman grabbed her arm and led her to the stairs.

"I have your room ready, young woman. Marshal Jeffers informed me of the rules, and I assure you they'll be followed to the letter." She stopped before a door and looked Dessa up and down. "And you'll not be wearing that get-up in my home. Least ways, not the pants. Are we clear?"

"Yes, ma'am. Clear as a bell."

Mamie sniffed. "Good." She opened the door and drew Dessa in with her. Dessa looked around at her new jail cell. Clean and homey. A quilt covered the iron bed occupying one wall. Beside it, a table held a kerosene lamp atop a crocheted doily. The window stood open just a crack. Lace curtains moved to the breeze. A tall chest and rocking chair took up the opposite wall.

Dessa approached the bed and ran her hand over the yellow-and-purple handmade quilt. She draped the quilt she'd carried in with her over the iron footboard, noting the similarities in the pattern. Both had stars with eight points.

"This is a lovely room." Much nicer than she'd expected for the old days. Lordy, the fact she was in 1890 hadn't sunk in yet. Would it ever?

Mamie sniffed in an effort to hide her pleasure, but Dessa wasn't fooled. "Well, I run a quality establishment." She walked to the washstand beside the door. "Hot water is available in the kitchen in the mornings and evenings. If you want a tub bath, arrangements must be made in advance."

Oh, man, she'd love a bath. The thin set of Mamie's lips indicated Dessa better not ask tonight.

Charity walked in with an armload of clothes as Mamie left the room. She hung a dress on a peg on the wall and laid a nightgown on the bed. "Turner and I are right next door. Tap on the wall if you need anything. Mamie is on your other side, and Marshal Jeffers is across the hall." She grinned and winked. "I think the marshal is sweet on you, but he'll toss you back in that jail cell in a heartbeat."

Dessa glanced toward the open doorway. "The buffoon. He actually believes I'm connected with that gang of bank robbers."

"It's hard for him to deny what he saw. Give him

some time to sort things out."

Dessa didn't believe he ever would. She'd have to do the sorting herself.

"I know you're confused and full of questions, but I'll answer as many as I can in the morning." She squeezed Dessa's hand. "Try to get a good night's rest."

Dessa grabbed her arm as she turned to leave, and leaned in to hiss, "Morning's not soon enough. I need to talk to you now."

Fatigue etched Charity's brow. "I'm sorry. It'll have to wait."

"Oh, of course. I wasn't thinking. You're tired and need to lie down."

Charity smiled and rubbed her belly. "Yes, the little bugger wears me out. See you early in the morning." She turned to leave.

A cough came from the doorway. "And remember, I'll hear you if you try to leave." Marshal Jeffers leaned against the door jamb of the open doorway, entirely too sexy for Dessa's comfort and too sure of himself to boot.

"And just where would I go, Marshal, being as I don't know a soul in this one-horse town other than Charity here?"

He merely shrugged and tipped his hat as Charity left. He pushed away from the wall, turned, and walked across the hall, his boot heels ringing against the hard wood.

****

Dessa lay in bed, ensconced in the feather mattress, listening to the night sounds around her. Nine o'clock was too early to be going to sleep, but when in 1890, do as the locals do. They'd probably be up when the rooster crowed. Early nights and early mornings would take some getting used to. She didn't even have a book. If she did, she'd go blind trying to read by the soft glow from the coal oil lamp on her bedside table.

Faint snoring came from next door. The sound blended with a louder tune coming from across the hall. She snickered, and then her humor faded. Was the marshal sleeping with his door open in case she tried to leave? Rolling to her side, she inched her way to sit up on the edge of the bed. The springs creaked, and the noise across the hall stopped. Damn. Surely he'd not heard that. Trying to be quiet, she eased from the bed. The floorboards groaned under her weight. Still no snoring from her jailer, and damned if she didn't hear his floorboards creak. How could Cole Jeffers be such a light sleeper?

Disgusted, she lifted the lid on the chamber pot, dropped it with a clang, and then climbed back into the bed. She twisted and turned trying to disentangle her long cotton gown from around her legs. Settled, she waited for the snoring to recommence. It wasn't long.

Sighing, she turned to her side and breathed in the fresh fragrance of the sheets. She suspected they were sun-dried, something she'd not experienced before. It sure beat the smell of the fabric softener sheets she tossed in the dryer. She'd not slept in a featherbed, either. What would it be like to share one with a man— say, like the marshal? There'd be no way to prevent rolling toward him, unless she hung on to the edge. A grin stretched her lips. The possibility wasn't likely. No question the man stirred her sexually, but she also admired his integrity.

What was she thinking? Cole Jeffers believed her a

bank robber. He didn't like or respect her. Anyway, she'd go back to her time as soon as possible. She'd achieved her goal—found Charity Dawson. Yeah, but it'd be impossible to publish Charity's story. People would believe Dessa nuts if she wrote about her experience with time travel. At least she'd be able to give Mr. Dawson an update on his daughter.

The question was—could she get back to the future?

****

"I know it's hard to accept, Marshal, but I believe Charity and Dessa's stories. There's no other way to explain the things they know." Turner sat on the sofa, his arm around his wife. She smiled up at him. Miss Wade sat in a side chair, her baggy dress hanging on her body.

Cole didn't doubt Turner believed his wife. For himself, he couldn't accept the possibility of time travel so easily. He knew strange things were possible, but traveling from one time period to another? He didn't think so.

"I mean no offence to either of you, but I have faith in what I can see and hear. I found Miss Wade in the company of the Faraday gang, and I believe she knows their current location."

Miss Wade jumped up. "I do not." She sighed. "Look, I read part of a book on bank robbers of Texas while at the cabin in Fredericksburg. The Faradays were mentioned, but I can't remember any particulars."

"Think, Dessa," said Mrs. Reardon. She squeezed her husband's leg. "Name some landmarks around here, Turner. Maybe between you and the marshal you can spur her memory."

Thirty minutes later, Miss Wade dropped back into her chair. "None of those places ring a bell." She ran her fingers through her short hair. "I need to get back and get that book."

With a frown, Mrs. Reardon shook her head. "I'm sorry, Dessa, but that's probably not possible. I tried, and it didn't work."

"I won't give up without trying." Miss Wade stood, turned on her heel and walked from the room. A minute later they heard her door close upstairs.

****

"Miss Mamie?" Dessa called as she jogged down the stairs.

"In here."

Dessa drew to a halt just inside the warm kitchen and breathed in the yeasty fragrance of baking bread. "Mmmm, the smells in here are heavenly."

"Well, if it ever smells bad, I'll be out of business." Mamie threw Dessa a grin over her shoulder and then went back to stirring a pot of bubbling liquid on the range. "What do you need, Miss Wade?"

Martha, Mamie's cook, cut off the heel of a cooling loaf, slapped butter across the top, and handed the slice to Dessa.

Dessa mouthed a *thank you,* took a bite, and savored the sweetness of the warm buttered bread. She spoke around her mouthful. "Do you have paper and pen I can use? I'll reimburse you when I find a job."

"Writing supplies are in the desk in the parlor."

"Thanks." Dessa whirled and started for the door.

"Finish your snack before leaving the room, missy. I don't allow food to be eaten all over the house."

"Yes, ma'am." Dessa stuffed the remainder of the

bread into her mouth, wiped her fingers on a dishtowel, and hustled from the room.

Sitting at the small rolltop desk, she located the paper, a round cherrywood stick with a steel nib attached to the end, and a bottle of ink. She studied the nib, held the pen in her hand, and scratched on the paper, practicing. *This should be interesting.* She opened the ink and dipped the metal tip into the blue liquid. *Here goes nothing.*

Thirty minutes later, her fingers were ink-stained and the paper splotched. She abandoned the pen for a pencil. Rather than waste the sheet, she turned it over and used the back. The pencil, though similar to those in the future, was a tad fatter and had been sharpened with a knife. Once she started writing, the words flowed into the article. When finished, she sat back in the chair and sighed. Now to sell the piece to the *Prairie Gazette.*

****

Cole held Miss Wade's arm as they walked along the board walk. She stopped and peered in windows as if she'd never been to town before. This morning, a bonnet covered her short, spiky hair, and she wore her bright yellow sweater over her too-big dress, giving the garment some shape. Their mission today was to buy her a few clothes. To Miss Wade's credit, she'd argued with Turner about borrowing money, finally relenting with the promise to pay him back when she got a job. How she thought she'd work, he didn't know, but didn't comment.

At the Prairie Mercantile, he ushered Miss Wade inside and turned her over to Mrs. White, the shopkeeper's wife. Thrilled at being able to help outfit Miss Wade, Mrs. White ushered her behind a curtained-off area. She made numerous trips back and forth with dresses and petticoats. He only half-listened to their idle chatter until it turned interesting.

Miss Wade's voice rang out. "I can't breathe. I'll go without one."

A shocked gasp came from Mrs. White. "You can't, my dear. Not wearing the proper undergarments isn't an option. You'll be shunned."

"I don't care."

"Now, now, yes, you do. It won't be so bad once you get used to the restriction."

Cole hid his grin and turned to study the boots lined up against the wall. He needed new ones, but those he had on were comfortable. Hell, he might as well use this time to select a pair. He could break them in while in town guarding his prisoner, before going back out on assignment.

When they left the store, he had on his new boots, with the old ones wrapped up under his arm along with Miss Wade's large bundle. She wore a brown serge dress and a matching bonnet tied with a yellow ribbon.

"Your new outfit becomes you. The color brings out the yellow flecks in your eyes...like gold dust in a miner's pan."

Eyebrow arched, she studied him. As if deciding he wasn't mocking her, she nodded. "Thank you."

They resumed their walk back toward Miss Mamie's. His boots were already pinching, and he grimaced.

"Ah, new boots?"

"Yeah. Hate new ones."

"I hear you, but actually these button-up shoes are almost as comfortable as my tennis shoes."

Cole glanced down. The toes of her brown boots peeked out from under her skirt as she walked. Tennis shoes. He'd heard of the sport but didn't know they made special shoes for it.

She stopped and stared across the street. "Would it be possible to stop by the newspaper office while we're out?"

"What for?"

Nose in the air, she blurted, "I told you I'm a reporter, Marshal. I hope to write for the *Gazette*."

What could it hurt if she talked to them? He'd humor her, and writing would give her something to do while he decided if she was guilty or not. "All right, but don't take too long. Mamie likes folks to be on time for meals."

At the door, she stopped, hand on the doorknob. "Can I go in alone? I'm not going to run out the back door and escape."

If she tried to run, she wouldn't get far. "I'll wait for you out here."

She smiled and squeezed his arm. "Thank you, Marshal. I won't be long."

The woman was a charmer. Her smile could melt the hardest of hearts. It dang sure made his gallop in appreciation. Though he didn't believe her and Mrs. Reardon's time travel story, he did believe Miss Wade to be special in some way. She was different from the women he knew—wouldn't be afraid of being on her own with her husband away. Maybe she was a woman he could plan a future with.

The door opened, and Miss Wade stepped out. He pushed away from the wall and fell into step with her. "Marshal, would you take me back to where you found me?"

"Why would I want to do that? It'd serve no purpose."

"Look, I know you don't believe me, but I really am from 2010, just as Charity is from 2008."

"Now, just a minute." He stopped walking. "I know what Turner and his wife said yesterday morning. Mrs. Reardon did show up here under strange circumstances, but that doesn't mean I believe the story she traveled back in time. I sure don't believe you did."

"But you were there, concealed in the trees. Didn't you see me just appear all of a sudden?"

"I admit, it may have seemed like you did, but I don't believe in such. You had to be hiding somewhere, behind that quilt you took such pains to hang on to."

She raised her hand and swung, hitting him in the abdomen.

The air rushed from his lungs. Her swat hadn't hurt, but it irritated the heck out of him. He growled.

Eyes wide, she backed up against the building.

"Woman, the next time you hit me, I'll find a way to punish you."

Lips pursed, she muttered, "And how would you be doing that? Plan to beat me?"

"Of course not. I'll think of something. Your backhands are downright disrespectful and embarrassing." He took her arm. "Come on, let's get back. It's time for lunch."

She moved, but turned those big, brown eyes in his direction. "Please, Marshal. Take me back and let me look around, try to sort out what happened to me. Maybe something in the area will spark my memory, and I'll be able to remember some fact to help you catch the Faradays."

He mulled her comment over in his mind. Was she keeping something from him, or was it possible the scene could prompt memories? He wasn't about to avoid the chance to find out. Tomorrow he'd get a horse for her at the livery and take her there. Tonight he'd let her know. Stewing for a few hours would be good for her.

****

She eyed the horse the marshal had saddled for her. The mare seemed tame enough, but Dessa hadn't ridden much and hoped she was as gentle as he promised. He took her hand and led her forward. "Rub her head and talk to her, so she'll get used to your voice."

"What's her name?"

"Sugar."

Yeah, the name suited the brown-colored animal. "Hey, Sugar. You gonna give me a sweet ride today?" The horse nickered and tossed her head. Dessa giggled, pleased the mare appeared to like her.

Marshal Jeffers' chuckle surprised her. She glanced up to observe him smiling, a first in the two days she'd known him. Maybe he wasn't as stodgy as he'd led her to believe. Or he might be anxious to get out of town and enjoy a ride in the fresh air. Wouldn't it be lovely if she found herself riding back into the countryside of 2010?

After two days in 1890, she'd seen all she wanted to of chamber pots, corsets, and drawers. Today, she'd decided not to wear the restricting garments and donned her normal underwear, her tennis shoes, and the baggy dress of Charity's she'd worn yesterday morning, with her jeans underneath and her sweater over. Miss Mamie loaned her a straw hat to keep the sun off her delicate skin. If the older woman only knew how many times Dessa had gone out without a hat or sunscreen, she'd have a stroke.

"Can you mount by yourself?"

"Of course." She started to swat him to emphasize her answer, then thought better of it. She stepped in the stirrup and mounted the horse. He kneed his mount into a walk, and Sugar followed. "Have you decided what you're going to do if I hit you again—my punishment?"

He looked back at her, a huge grin stretching his handsome face. The man was too darn sexy for his own good—for her good, too. Her heart thumped in appreciation of his looks and the response he elicited in her.

"Yes. I'm going to kiss you."

Chapter Four

"Ha. That'll never happen. You're too stodgy."

He stiffened in the saddle, and then relaxed. His deep belly laugh echoed in the wind, and he winked. "Harrumph. You may think I'm dull, but you don't know me."

Stunned, the gesture and grin on his cocky face sent a coil of heat to form in her belly. *Whoa, Nellie, don't go there. You can't get attached to this man. You're not staying in the past, and anyway, you're his prisoner, not his sweetheart.*

Dessa frowned. He was right. She didn't know him. She cast a sideways glance his way. Could there be a passionate man under that armor of his? One who possibly desired her? She stifled a snort. Not bloody likely. If he kissed her, it would be strictly to embarrass her.

They left the grassland. The terrain changed as their horses stepped out of the winter wheat onto white caliche soil and rocks sprinkled with red cedars of varying heights. Patches of red dirt added color to the area. Dessa considered asking Cole how close they were to Amarillo, but decided she'd best concentrate on memorizing the way to the camp where he'd found her. If she could ever shake his company, she might want to come back by herself.

The trip seemed shorter today. Perhaps her state of

mind, not being in shock this morning, made time pass faster. No, a few days hadn't eased her situation, but she had Charity looking out for her. If she couldn't get home, Charity would help ease Dessa into a life in 1890. Charity seemed to have settled in nicely, actually happy with Turner. He was a good-looking guy and appeared to dote on his wife. Of course, if Dessa didn't clear her name, she might spend her time in some prison. She wasn't acquainted with women's prisons in the 1890s and frankly didn't want to learn about them by doing hard time.

The cedars thinned as they entered rougher ground filled with boulders and live oak trees. Within plain sight lay the disturbed logs of the fire the Faradays had built for warmth. She and Cole dismounted and tethered their horses to graze near a patch of grass.

Dessa picked up a stick and strode to the blackened remains. She stirred the ashes. Ah-ha, there they were, the remains of her cup, the yellow of the pottery barely visible through the dark film covering it.

She picked up a piece and held the shard out to Cole. "See? I told you I had a pottery cup. If I'd been with them, my cup would have been metal."

He took the chunk of glass from her and turned it over in his hand before stuffing it in his pocket. "Maybe. Maybe not."

She struck out in the direction she believed her bridge to be. "Come on. Let's see if we can find the stream."

"I'm telling you, no water is around here." But he followed as she stalked past the remains of the fire. He grumbled with each step—something about "women and their stubborn ideas."

Yeah, right. We'll see how your attitude changes when we get to the bridge. Dessa thrust her shoulders back and sucked in a deep breath. She'd show the man. She lengthened her stride and felt the pull of muscles in her buttocks. It had been days since she'd had an opportunity to jog, and her body missed the exercise.

Cole reached her side. They walked in companionable silence. The cold air nipped at her ears and nose. Cedar was strong in the air. Her eyes itched, and she sneezed several times.

Where was the darn bridge? They'd been walking almost an hour and still nothing. She stopped and allowed her eyes to travel the landscape. Her heart thumped rapidly in her chest. Her throat tightened. She wanted to weep but swallowed her emotion. Crying wouldn't help her situation. The only thing to help would be accepting her circumstances and developing a plan.

Cole stood, hands on his hips, his expression grim. "Are you ready to believe there is no bridge and water around here?"

Unable to speak, she nodded, turned on her heel, and started back toward the campsite.

Cole caught her arm to stop her. "I'm sorry, Dessa."

She yanked from his grip. "I guess I'm truly crazy."

"No. You're not—"

A crack echoed across the plain, cutting off Cole's words. A cry of pain escaped his lips. As if she were dreaming the entire scene, she watched as he reached for his head, pulled away his bloody hand, and toppled backward like a felled tree.

"Cole!" Fear stabbed Dessa in the chest. It was no dream. She dropped to her knees beside him and lifted his head to her lap. "Cole, Cole. Oh, God, please don't be dead."

Three riders broke from the trees and bore down on them.

She scrambled to reach the revolver strapped to Cole's leg. Her hand touched cold metal, and she pulled the gun from its holster.

Before she could raise the heavy weapon, one of the riders jumped from his horse and tore the gun from her hand.

Dessa lunged to retrieve it as the man shoved her. She hit the ground on her butt and scrambled to get up.

He raised a hand. "Stay down, missy, if you know what's good for ya."

She crawled to Cole. "He's hurt. I need to help him."

He peered down at Cole's wound. "It's just a scratch."

She snarled. "Are you a doctor?" Hands shaking, she tore a strip of cotton from her petticoat. "If he dies, they'll hang you without a trial."

He guffawed. "Have to catch me first. Now, you have a choice. You can come with us, or I can shoot the marshal in the heart."

"Surely, you don't—"

He cocked the revolver.

Could he be that cold blooded? Yes, the sneer on his ugly mug said he could. "Please, let me at least wrap this around his head."

"Make it quick." He turned to his men. "Go find their horses."

"What do you want with me?" She'd just slow them down.

"You'll find out soon enough." He nodded toward Cole. "Hurry up."

Fearing he'd yank her up at any minute, she wiped at the blood as she examined the wound. A sigh escaped her. The bullet had grazed his head, leaving a deep furrow in its wake. No doubt he'd have a terrible headache, possibly for days, but he wouldn't die. Thank God. She quickly tied the cloth around his head, placing the knot over the gash, to better absorb the blood.

At the sound of pounding hooves, she gently laid Cole's head against the hard ground. She murmured a quick prayer for his safety and then stood. She didn't want the man's attention to return to Cole. The marshal should regain consciousness in a few hours. Surely someone would come looking for him when they didn't return.

"Where the hell's the marshal's horse?"

"Sorry, Zeke. The gelding wouldn't let us get near him."

"Shit."

So, Zeke was the Faraday gang leader. He took off his hat and slapped it across his leg. Dust flew and settled on his already filthy clothes. Unlike the other men, who wore baggy dungarees with their loose wool coats, Zeke wore pinstriped pants with a duster.

The two men on horseback eyed her with caution and then turned to Zeke. "You want us to tie up the marshal?"

Dessa held her breath.

"Naw, he's not going anywhere for a good while." He nodded to Dessa. "Get on your horse, missy."

She hurried to do his bidding. The sooner they left, the safer Cole would be.

****

Something tickled Cole's ear. Buck huffed and blew, his lips fluttering. Cole shook his head to rid himself of the nuisance and groaned. His head throbbed. The pain sent bile rushing to his throat. He rolled to his knees and emptied the contents of his stomach in the dirt. What the hell happened? He reached for his gun to find his holster empty. Dread gripped him. Dessa. Where was she? Had she drawn him out here and hit him on the head, stolen his gun? No, he remembered hearing the report of a rifle. Moving his head slowly, he looked around for some sign of the woman.

She was gone. He knew in his gut that she'd not have left him wounded to fend for himself if she had a choice. He was a good judge of character, and in the short time he'd known her, she had proven to be caring. No, she would have tied him up, left his gun where he could reach it after working his way loose. Someone had shot him to get at her. But who would want to kidnap her? And why?

Fear gripped him. The pounding in his head echoed the thundering of his heart. He had to find her, make sure they didn't hurt her. He struggled to his feet and stood waiting for the trees around him to stop spinning. Buck nudged him. Cole caught hold of the saddle horn and laid his upper body across the saddle. He needed to rest for a minute and think. Deep gulps of air eased the pain and nausea. He rinsed his mouth with water from his canteen and spat it on the ground.

Concern for Dessa gnawed at his mind. Would they

abuse her, violate her? Instinct told him to go after her, but before he did, he needed to study the tracks. He'd have to wait for light. From the location of the moon, it appeared to be near midnight. Cole would try to rest. Tomorrow he'd get an early start.

Unsteady on his feet, his movements jerky and labored, he removed Buck's saddle and laid it on a level piece of ground. He always carried provisions and a bedroll. While Buck munched on a ration of oats, Cole located his hat a short distance away. He poured a small amount of water into it for Buck. With his animal taken care of, Cole collapsed on the ground and curled up in his bedroll.

Buck's nickers and pawing the ground at his back woke him. Something had spooked the animal. The horse had positioned himself behind Cole, putting himself between him and the source of danger. Still as death, pretending to be asleep, Cole rolled over and peered through his lashes into the dawning light, searching for a threat. Nothing but waves of swirling mist rushed toward them, covering the ground.

He rolled to his feet. "Oh, God." Hand to his head, he swayed and stumbled to a nearby tree for support. With his eyes still closed, he took deep breaths as he waited for the pounding in his head to lessen. The pain eased but didn't disappear. Buck whinnied. Cole moved away from the tree and strode to the horse.

He patted Buck's neck. "It's nothing but fog, boy." Cole bent to pick up his bedroll, almost hidden by the mist now. Odd. He'd never seen vapor so thick or swirling as this. Hadn't Dessa mentioned fog moving on the morning he'd captured her? Yes, the mist had been thick that morning. Cole remembered the phenomenon, something not common in this area due to the dry air in the region. The hair on his neck stood on end.

He saddled Buck, stored his bedroll and, leading Buck on foot, headed in the direction he and Dessa had walked yesterday. Twenty yards later, he stopped.

"Damn."

Just ahead, a small curved bridge spanned a creek.

Dessa hadn't lied.

****

Zeke pulled Dessa from her horse. Pain shot up her legs all the way to her butt when her feet touched the ground. She screamed at the shock. Her legs caved beneath her, and she crumbled. Zeke caught her under the arms before she fell to the dirt, and she cried out again. Her arms ached from holding onto the pommel with both hands tied all day. She gave in to the tears she'd held inside for the past four hours.

"Stop that sniveling now." He cut her bonds and pointed to a group of trees against the dark rock cavern. "You need to take care of business. Better get to it, else you'll have to hold your water 'til morning."

Using her skirt to wipe her tears, she stumbled over rocks as she hobbled to the area he'd designated. The sun had set, and light from the moon outlined the tall, cavernous walls around them. Thank goodness for the cold weather, so she didn't have to worry about snakes. At the moment, she didn't care if she encountered any other critters. She wanted to empty her bladder and fall into a coma. Dwelling on her precarious situation would have to wait until morning.

The minute she exited the bushes, Zeke took her arm and led her into a small, one-room cabin. The

45

savory aroma of cooked beef assailed her, and her stomach rumbled in response. He shoved her toward a filthy pallet on the floor, and she collapsed, not caring who or what had slept on the blanket before her. An old woman shoved a bowl of stew into her hands and set a cup of water at her feet.

"Thank you."

"She's a polite little thing, ain't she, son?"

Zeke snorted. "Her manners aren't important, Ma."

Dessa inhaled the food, surprised at its good flavor. She emptied the bowl and the cup, then lay down on the pallet and curled onto her side with her back to the fire. Zeke and his mother sat at the table while Zeke ate. Warmth invaded Dessa's body, and she closed her eyes and listened, hoping to gain insight as to why Zeke had kidnapped her.

"What do you mean by bringing a woman here, boy? You want to be hung? The law will run you to the ground like a rabid dog."

Through her lashes, Dessa saw Zeke look her way. She remained still, hoping he believed her asleep.

He whispered, "Ma, she's a witch or something. She appeared before me and the boys." He snapped his fingers. "Just like that." Leaning back in his chair, he crossed his arms across his chest. "She's going to teach me how to appear and disappear. Can you imagine how easy it'd be to rob banks that way?"

Ma shook her head and stood up. "I never took you for being a fool, Zeke. I expect you inherited more from your crazy grandmother than I suspected."

"I saw it with my own two eyes."

"You saw something, maybe something unusual, but that don't mean that mite of a girl can pop in and out of a place like you're wanting." She snorted. "Probably a trick of light or something."

The chair scraped across wood as he lurched to his feet. "We'll see about that. She could be my opportunity to get rich, and I intend to take it. You'll not be interfering with my plans. You hear me?"

"I hear you."

Dessa woke in the wee hours of the morning to find her hands and feet tied. Someone had thrown a wool blanket over her. The fire cast a warm glow over the room, just enough to make out her surroundings. Where had Zeke brought her? Yesterday he'd been closemouthed about their destination, and she hadn't recognized any landmarks. Could her life get any more complicated? A lump formed in her throat, and she sniffed. First she'd traveled through time, and now she'd been taken prisoner by a notorious gang.

Did Zeke really believe she could teach him to pop in and out of banks? She sighed. At least they didn't want her dead, or she wouldn't be here. An ugly thought entered her head. Would they try to molest her? The thought of being raped by Zeke or his men made her shudder. No, he'd not looked at her with lust in his eyes, and she didn't believe he'd let his men harm her. Of course if she couldn't tell him how she'd appeared before his campfire, he might become violent. She'd better develop a plan.

She hoped Cole was awake and able to follow their trail. Could he, with a concussion? He didn't seem the type of man to let a little headache keep him from doing his job. No, he'd be coming after her as soon as he could get on his horse.

Loud snores came from the bed against the wall.

Ma, she supposed. Evidently the men slept outside somewhere. Good. She relaxed and drifted back to sleep.

****

Cole hobbled Buck where he could graze and get to the water. Apprehension tightened his shoulders as he crossed the bridge into unknown territory. He certainly didn't believe he'd traveled forward in time, but this area wasn't supposed to be here. Hopefully he'd find answers to how Dessa appeared out of thin air in front of the Faradays' campfire.

He stopped to survey the area before striding up the small berm to a pond. A large cabin sat amid trees beyond the water. A silver contraption on four wheels sat beside it. A roar filled the silence. He stared as a black carriage, without a horse to pull it, whined to a stop alongside the silver object, slinging gravel.

He stumbled back a step. What the hell? Upon closer inspection, he realized the carriages were similar to the motor cars he'd seen last year in Dallas, but these were fully enclosed in shiny steel.

A woman exited the coach and waved. "Yoo-hoo. Hello there."

He looked behind him to see if he was alone. Was she talking to him? "Ma'am?"

"I'm looking for Miss Wade. Is she around?"

"Uh, no, ma'am. She's not." He walked toward the cabin.

The woman stepped away from the carriage. If he thought Dessa's mode of dress outlandish, this lady's was a close match. She wore an animal-skin jacket with denim pants. The big red bow that held her dark hair on top of her head matched the color of her painted lips.

She met him at the porch steps and waved at the two carriages. "Well, her car is here."

"Yes, ma'am." He couldn't tell this woman Dessa had been kidnapped. He hated liars, but... "Well, uh, she's gone for a walk."

She eyed him with suspicion, then noticed the star on his coat.

"Has she done something wrong?" Her kohl-painted eyes rounded in question and then turned to one of panic. She crossed her hands over her expansive bosom. "She hasn't disappeared, has she? Lands, I couldn't stand if one of my renters vanished again."

He yanked his hat off. "Oh, no, ma'am. I'm Marshal Jeffers, a friend of hers. She's out walking. Enjoys taking the morning air."

"I see." She offered her hand, and he shook it. "I'm Sarah Lawrence, her landlady." A smile crooked her lips as she looked him up and down. She mouthed something under her breath which sounded like, "Lucky girl."

A flush rose in his face, adding to his discomfort at lying to the woman about Dessa.

"Do you have any idea if Miss Wade plans to stay another week?"

"Yes, she does."

"Hmm. Okay then. Tell her I came by."

She walked across the rough ground, wobbling on shoes with high, skinny heels, her backside twitching with each movement. He expected one of the heels to break at any minute, but she reached her coach without mishap. The thing roared to life, lights came on in the front, a small one blinked, and the machine traveled backward down the drive. It stopped, and then traveled forward out of sight. He shook his head in wonder. She'd not even had to turn a crank to start the thing.

He walked up the steps and stood at the back door, gathering the courage to go inside. What would he find? If it was anything like what he'd experienced out here, he was in for more of a shock. He was tempted to turn and run, but Dessa had mentioned a book on bank robbers in Texas. If he was right and Zeke Faraday had taken Dessa, he might gain answers.

The screen door squeaked when he pulled it open, and the doorknob turned easily. Heart thundering, he stood on the threshold, listening to make sure the cabin was empty, and then entered. The place was fancier than anything he'd ever seen, but he refused to be distracted. He stalked from the kitchen into the parlor. Books littered a table. On top was the one he wanted. He grabbed the volume and quickly fled the cabin, making sure to close the door on his way out. The woman had slowed him down. He had no idea how this time travel business worked, but he wanted to get back to Buck before the fog fully dissipated.

When he reached the bridge, his heart dropped into his stomach. Buck was gone.

Chapter Five

A nudge to her back jerked Dessa awake. In the near darkness, panic gripped her. Where was she? A voice broke the gloomy environment.

"I'm gonna untie you so we can go outside and tend to business. Don't be doin' nothing stupid, or I'll hit you upside the head."

Dessa didn't doubt Ma could hold her own in any tussle. She didn't intend to test the older woman's words. As she pushed up off the pallet, Dessa groaned. Her muscles and bones screamed to protest their mistreatment of the previous day. Plus, she wasn't used to sleeping on the floor.

She limped along behind Ma, the cold air adding to her discomfort. Gradually her joints eased and the pain lessened. No doubt her legs, butt, and shoulders would be sore for a day or two. A pink glow rose behind the cliff bordering the cabin, casting enough light for them to make their way to the stand of brush and scrub oaks.

Back inside, Ma stirred the coals in the fire and added kindling. Within minutes she had a nice blaze going and the small room warmed up. She filled a big pot with water and oats and made a place for the pan on the fire. A huge coffeepot joined the oatmeal on the fire, and soon the brew boiled over. Ma moved it away from the heat to steep. Dessa sat on her pallet and watched the old woman's every movement.

The door opened and Zeke and his two cohorts entered. He glared at Dessa and then turned on Ma. "Why ain't she tied up?"

"I'm busy cooking for you and your sidekicks. Anyhow, she's not going anywhere."

Zeke snorted, kicked a chair out from under the table, and sat down.

Ma grabbed five tin cups off a shelf above the fireplace and set them on the table. "Pour the coffee, will you, son?"

Dessa expected the surly man to refuse, but he got up, grabbed a rag to protect his hand, picked up the pot, and filled the cups. He placed one on the floor beside her.

Heat rose off the aromatic liquid. She picked it up and quickly took a sip. Strong and black, the caffeine hit her system, and she blinked in shock. Sawbuck's had nothing on Ma when it came to coffee. Heat from the tin burned her fingers, and she set the cup down to let the brew cool.

Ma dished oatmeal into bowls, and the men each grabbed one, along with a cup of coffee, and carried them outside. Zeke handed Dessa a bowl before he started eating from his own.

Dessa stared at the sticky goo. Her stomach lurched. Oatmeal wasn't a favorite of hers—actually she barely tolerated the stuff—but she needed to eat to retain her strength. She took small bites, struggling not to think about the texture, and washed it down with a sip of hot coffee. Soon her bowl was half empty. Her spoon clanked against the crockery edge. She couldn't force down another bite.

"If you're finished, come up here and sit." Zeke

waved a dismissing hand at Ma. She rose and moved to sit on the bed.

Oh, boy, here it comes. If she told Zeke the truth, would he let her go? Not likely. He'd keep her with him. The thought of him and his cohorts traveling to the future, something she must prevent if at all possible, scared her. Somehow she had to escape before they reached the campsite. Cole would do all in his power to find her, but what if he was still unconscious? Surely someone from town would have come looking for them when they didn't return.

Dessa settled herself in the chair with her cup before her. The coffee wasn't as hot now, and she sipped at it.

"Now, missy, I want to know how you appeared before my campfire." He leaned back in his chair and laid his folded hands on his trim belly.

"I'll tell you, but you won't believe me."

"Quit stalling, Miss Wade." Zeke took a swig of his coffee and eyed her over the cup. "Let's have it."

"Let's have what?"

"Don't play me for a fool."

Ma snorted and mumbled, "Why not?"

Zeke either didn't hear his mother or ignored her comment. "How'd you pop into my camp"—he snapped his fingers—"just like that?"

"If I tell you, I'm afraid you'll think I'm nuts; you won't believe me."

From the bed, Ma quipped, "Just tell him, honey. If he's dumb enough to believe it..." She shrugged.

Zeke shot his mother a dirty look. "Mind your own business, old woman."

"This young woman is my business, whelp. This is

my home. You can remember that or get out."

They warred with their eyes. Zeke dropped his gaze first and then turned his attention back to Dessa. He drew a piece of paper from his shirt pocket, unfolded the sheet, and slid it to her.

She gasped. It was her article for the *Prairie Gazette*.

"And I want to know how you found out about my secret hideout."

"That's easy. I read it in a book published in 1992." Of course, she didn't remember the location. The hint was a teaser for her next article. That's why she needed the book, but she'd not be confiding her lack of information to Zeke.

Ma's chuckle turned into a round of cackles. She slapped her thigh and howled with glee.

Zeke merely stared at her, his expression unreadable.

"You see, I'm a time traveler. I traveled back in time from 2010."

****

"Buck!" Cole's voice carried across the meadow. A faint nicker answered his call from the receding mist. Cole broke into a run in an attempt to catch the fast-moving fog. Fear at being left behind in the future spurred him forward. When his boots disappeared in haze, he didn't slow his pace. Minutes later, breathing hard, he caught up with Buck, reins dragging in the dirt, stomping in agitation as he waited for Cole.

Cole gathered the reins in one hand and patted Buck's neck. "It's okay, boy. We're not going to let a little fog spook us, now are we?"

Buck snorted and butted Cole's chest.

"Yeah, I know how you feel, partner." Cole took deep gulps of air and willed his heart to slow its rapid pace. He wished he could say he'd dreamed the entire experience, but the book clutched in his hand prevented such an explanation. Flipping the volume open, he searched for the print date: October, 1992.

Hoofbeats rapidly approached. He stuffed the book in his saddlebag, mounted Buck, and rode him into the trees. Without a weapon, he was at a glaring disadvantage. If the riders were a threat, his only chance was to outrun them.

Sheriff Cannon and Turner Reardon rode into the small clearing. Cole squeezed with his knees, and Buck bolted to join them. All three animals skidded to a halt.

Elijah whipped off his hat and used his sleeve to wipe the sweat from his brow. "Thank God, Cole. We've been beside ourselves with worry."

"Where's Miss Wade?" Turner swiveled in the saddle and searched the trees.

"I'm sorry, Turner. I think Zeke Faraday took her." He pushed his hat back and winced as he touched his wound. It was sore as hell. "Shot me and took her."

"Holy hell. Charity is already worried sick. We need to find her." Turner jumped off his horse and searched the ground for signs. "Was she taken here?"

"Yes. They rode in from the northeast, but I was out cold when they left." He and Elijah dismounted and joined Turner as he squatted on the ground. "We'll find her, Turner." She was his responsibility, no longer a prisoner but a woman he cared about, cared more than he wanted to admit. He couldn't figure out why Zeke would take her—if it was Zeke. The thought of her being held captive by an unknown band of outlaws

55

caused his gut to clench. To his knowledge, Zeke had never kidnapped a woman and abused her, as some miscreants were known to do. God, he prayed she was unhurt, wherever she was.

"Here," yelled Elijah from the trees west of the clearing.

Heart pounding, Cole hurried over to see what Sheriff Cannon had found. Sure enough, hoofmarks littered the ground. He traced one in particular. "This is Sugar's hoofprint. She needs a new shoe." With his finger, he traced the slight indentation left by the iron shoe, a half diamond on the inner rim. He stood. "Let's go."

They rode alongside the trail, stopping from time to time to re-examine the tracks. Four hours later, dust rose from several miles away. They stopped.

"Looks like four riders," said Turner, eyes squinted as he peered across the wide expanse of red prairie land.

Cole swung around in the saddle and removed binoculars from his saddlebag. He put them to his eyes and looked. Relief pumped through his veins, and he relaxed in the saddle. "It's Zeke. He's leading Dessa's horse, but her hands aren't tied. Two men are following close behind."

"Odd, they're coming back this way," said Turner.

Cole feared he knew why. Zeke wanted to know how Dessa had popped into his camp undetected.

"You'd think they'd be hightailing it out of this area." Elijah glanced at Cole. "Especially knowing you'd be after them. Don't reckon they thought they'd killed you?"

"Naw." He touched the strip of Dessa's petticoat

wrapped around his head. "They let Dessa patch me up, so I expect they knew I'd live."

Elijah spit a stream of tobacco into the dirt. "Whaddaya think, Cole? Do we lay low and wait?"

Turner's nod and jutting chin indicated he agreed with the sheriff's suggestion.

"Yes. Let 'em come to us. When they're close enough, we'll fire off rounds at the ground in front of their horses to spook 'em."

"Hold on a minute," Turner sputtered.

"Don't worry about Dessa. I'll ride in for her."

"She could still get hurt."

"Yes, she might. You have a better plan?"

"We could shoot them."

Sheriff Cannon guffawed. "Yeah, son, we could, but we won't if we can keep from it."

"They sure as hell didn't have trouble shooting the marshal, here."

Cole had to admit, Turner had a point. "Dessa is our first concern. We'll take Zeke and his boys alive if we can. What I can't understand is why they'd want to take her hostage in the first place."

Elijah's eyes rounded. "Hell, son, didn't you see this week's *Prairie Gazette*?"

Oh, hell, what had Dessa done? He knew she'd written an article about Zeke Faraday and his gang, but he'd had no idea the paper owner had actually printed it. Now he thought about it, Dessa had hidden something from him when he entered the parlor yesterday morning.

"No, I didn't."

"Her article was right there on the front page. Said next week she'd reveal the location of Zeke's secret hideout.

****

Zeke led them down an incline into a valley. They must be getting closer to where they'd left Cole, as the territory was familiar. At the thought of Cole, a lump formed in Dessa's throat, and she struggled to push it down. She prayed he was okay and searching for her.

Shots rang out, their report echoing across the valley floor. Horses squealed in distress, Sugar included, but she wasn't dancing and rearing like the others. One of the boys hit the dirt and scrambled to catch his horse's reins.

Cole. Her heart thumped with joy. He'd come for her. Bent low over the saddle, Cole rode toward them. She leaned forward and grabbed the lead rope Zeke had tied around Sugar's neck. She yanked, trying to free it, but Zeke had the other end around his saddle horn. He grinned maliciously at the futility of her struggle.

I'll show you, you jackass. Dessa jumped off Sugar's back and broke into a run. She hated to leave Sugar, but Zeke wouldn't mistreat the animal.

Zeke growled and rode to grab her. More gunshots erupted. One winged Zeke. He tottered in the saddle but managed to turn his horse and run.

"Cole!" Dessa ran to meet him as he and his big horse barreled toward her. Her hat flew off, but she didn't bother trying to catch it. Skirts tangling about her legs, she stumbled but righted herself and lifted the fabric above her knees. Thank goodness she'd worn her tennis shoes, though she was so grateful to see Cole she'd have run barefoot through hell and not slowed down.

Cole was off his horse and caught her against his

chest before she could slow down. He stumbled back a couple of steps but didn't loosen his hold on her. Arms around his neck, her legs dangled above the ground as she buried her face against his neck. She breathed in his scent, not caring he'd not bathed in several days or that his beard growth scratched her skin. Heck, she didn't smell too good, either.

His breath rushed past her ear, causing gooseflesh to rise on her body. "Sweetheart, are you hurt?"

Sweetheart. The endearment brought tears to her eyes. "No, they didn't mistreat me."

He set her on her feet. His big hands cupped her face, and then slid down her arms as if making sure she had no wounds. Each touch seared her with longing. She wanted him to kiss her. Couldn't he see the yearning in her eyes?

Frustrated, she slapped him on the chest.

One arm circled her waist and lifted her up to meet him eye to eye. Voice husky, he growled, "What the hell was that for?"

She grabbed his face and pulled him closer. "So you'll kiss me, Marshal."

His eyes blazed with a need her soul echoed. "Why didn't you just say so, Sweetheart?" His words brushed against her ear. "Happy to oblige."

Dessa shivered in anticipation.

Cole kissed her neck and nuzzled his way around to the side of her mouth.

"In fact, I've dreamed of tasting your lips, your skin."

She turned her mouth to meet his.

His lips scorched hers as he took possession of her mouth, molding his over hers, drawing her deeper in sensation.

A groan rumbled from his chest and he broke away, set her back from him.

Her legs wobbled and threatened to drop her in the dust.

"Come on, we need to get back to Sheriff Cannon and Turner."

He mounted his horse and lifted her to sit across his lap. One arm clasped her to his chest as he kicked Buck into a trot.

They'd almost reached the other men when the sound of hooves and a horse's whinny alerted them to company. They turned to find Sugar quickly approaching.

Cole chuckled. "Guess Zeke didn't want to add horse thieving to his crimes."

At least Zeke had some smarts. Horse stealing was probably still punishable by hanging.

When Sugar pulled to a halt beside them, Cole grabbed the lead rope and led her along behind them.

Sheriff Cannon and Turner were busy setting up camp near a shallow creek in a small grove of trees. The sheriff blew on the smoking flames of the makings of a camp fire. Turner walked toward him carrying a coffeepot.

Cole dismounted and lifted Dessa to the ground. Both men approached. Turner reached for her and pulled her close, his eyes taking stock. "You all right, Dessa?"

"I'm fine. They didn't hurt me." She grinned. "Now, I must admit I'm rather sore from all the riding to and fro."

Turner sighed. "Thank God. We've been worried

sick."

"How's Charity?"

Turner beamed. "She's wonderful. Delivered a healthy baby boy yesterday."

Dessa gasped. "You should be with her, not here."

He snorted. "She kicked me out, said, 'Find Dessa and don't come back without her.'"

She hugged him, grateful to have folks in this foreign time care about her. "I'm so happy for you both. I can't wait to see him."

Sheriff Cannon took Turner's place in front of her. Hands clenched at his sides, he sputtered. "What were you thinking, to write that newspaper article, girl? You just invited them to come for you."

"I never dreamed they'd get a copy. I just wanted to sell newspapers."

"Well, you sure stirred up a hornet's nest. First the article, then riding off with Cole. The women in Prairie are fit to be tied about you being out all night with the marshal—alone. They're running around fussing like a bunch of old hens, squawking like a fox got in the coop and stole all their chicks."

He shook his finger at both Dessa and Cole. "Best be prepared to dance to their tune when we get back."

Cole's tanned complexion paled.

Dessa turned on Turner. "What on earth is he talking about?"

Turner flushed and coughed. "Uh...they intend for Cole to make you an honest woman by marrying you the minute you return."

Chapter Six

Cole restrained his groan, but Dessa sputtered, "That's ridiculous. I spent the night with Zeke's Ma in her little hut, with the men who kidnapped me outside all the time." She jabbed her fists on her hips. "No way am I getting married, especially to Cole. He's totally innocent in this matter."

"From your scraped and rosy cheeks, I wouldn't say *totally*, Dessa." Turner grinned and arched a brow at Cole. Elijah leaned in to look closely at Dessa. Face flushed, she whirled and stomped over to stand before the fire.

Cole resisted the urge to rub his hand over his two-day beard. Instead he removed his hat and wiped his brow on his sleeve. Turner joined Dessa at the fire. He squatted and moved the coffeepot off the hot coals.

"Why set up camp, Elijah? If we set out now, we can be in Prairie before dark."

"Figure you two might need some time to adjust to the idea of getting wedded." His expression sympathetic, Elijah added, "'Course, when the women find out she's been in the hands of the Faradays and spent the night with his ma, they'll probably relent." He cocked his head. "That is, unless you two want to get married."

"Naw, you heard the woman. She doesn't want to get married. Least ways, not to me."

Elijah snorted. "Could've fooled me. The way you two were wrapped around each other down there, thought we'd have to fire off a couple of rounds to get you to come up for air."

"Not many women would want to marry a man like me, one away from home most of the time. A woman needs a husband to stay around and protect her."

"'Pears to me Miss Dawson ain't like most womenfolk we know. She held up just fine under this ordeal. Most ladies would be hysterical, whining, and carrying on. But nope, not Miss Dawson." The sheriff guffawed. "Bet it wouldn't take her long to learn to handle a gun. Pity any man on the receiving end of the barrel, if she does."

Cole chuckled at the mental picture. Yup, Dessa was a spitfire, all right. Elijah didn't realize how true his words about Dessa were. No doubt about it. She was from the future. His early morning trip and the book in his saddlebag proved it. Guess they raised 'em up different in that time period. Of course, he knew a few women as outspoken as Dessa. They were much older and not near as pretty. He sighed. Might as well get things in the open before they headed for town.

The reality saddened him, as had her refusal to marry him. He'd grown attached to her. Had he harbored thoughts of a future with her? No way to deny his attraction. Their kisses in the valley floor had him hard and wanting to make love to her. His desire wasn't just physical; his heart and soul longed for a woman in his life, one to call his own, have children with. Her aggression in initiating the kiss pleased him. She desired him too. Of that he was sure. But she'd be returning to the future, and his life was here and now.

No need to dwell on what couldn't be.

"Let's get us a cup of hot coffee." His stomach rumbled. "Got any grub? I haven't eaten since yesterday morning."

"You bet." Elijah went to his horse and removed a bundle and his cup.

Cole retrieved his own cup and the book before joining Dessa and Turner, both sitting on the ground and sipping hot coffee. Turner poured Cole some coffee. "Thanks."

Dessa's gaze landed on the book. Her mouth dropped open. "How—"

"Later. Let's enjoy our coffee and eat first."

Elijah set the bundle on the ground and unfolded the cloth to reveal the victuals. Cole's mouth watered at the sight of the baking powder biscuits. He picked one up and broke it open, then layered two pieces of bacon between the pieces and wolfed the bread and meat down in two bites. The others ate sparingly, so he finished off the pile and washed the morsels down with coffee.

Dessa stood and approached him. "Let me take a look at your wound."

He laid his hat on the ground, and she removed the strip she'd tied around his head. Turner handed her a cloth and his canteen. She poured water on the rag and dabbed at the wound. He winced.

"Sore, huh?"

"Yep."

"Headache?"

"Not too bad today. Hurt something fierce last night when I woke up."

"I don't suppose you have any aspirin or powders

for pain, do you?"

Aspirin or powders? Cole glanced to Turner. He shrugged. Elijah shook his head.

"Guess not," Dessa muttered as she tied a clean strip of cotton around his head. It appeared Turner had come prepared for the worst with supplies to treat wounds. "That ought to do it until you can visit the doctor." She went back to her rock and picked up her cup.

"Nope. Doc might give me laudanum, but I'd have to be half dead to take a dose of that stuff." He shuddered at the thought. The medicine made a man crazy. "A little headache's nothing."

"Can I see the book now?"

Cole handed it to her. She flipped the volume open and scanned the pages until she found what she wanted. "Okay, here we go. 'Federal Marshal Cole Jeffers located Zeke Faraday's hideout in Pala Duro Canyon in November of 1890. Zeke and two gang members gave themselves up peacefully. Zeke had been wounded a week earlier and died from those wounds in the Prairie jail before going to trial.'"

Sheriff Cannon blustered. "How can a book know something before it happens? Never heard of such. And where is this Pala Duro Canyon? No place by that name around these parts, leastways that I know of."

"It's near where Mrs. Faraday lives, I think. The terrain resembled the pictures I've seen of the Pala Duro Canyon State Park." Her forefinger tapped the page. "Hmm, what was it I read about the canyon? Oh, yes, it's where Charlie Goodnight has his ranch, in this time period." She looked around at them. "I bet you guys know him, right?"

"Know of him, Miss Wade," said Elijah. "Everybody in the Texas Panhandle knows of the man. He's a legend in these parts. Let me see that book." He reached for the tome, and Dessa handed it over. He reread the section she'd tapped with her finger. Then he flipped through the pages, ran his fingers over them, feeling their slick texture, casting her suspicious glances as he did so. "Never seen a book so fine before."

"Look at the copyright date, Sheriff."

Elijah read the copyright patent and, eyes narrowed, muttered, "Nineteen-ninety-two? This is a hoax. What are you up to, missy?"

"I tried to tell you, when Cole brought me in, that I was from the future. This proves it."

He tossed the book to the ground. "It doesn't prove a thing. You're trying to play a trick on us." He turned on Cole. "Where'd you find this book?"

"In the future. At the cabin Dessa mentioned. I suppose it was in 2010, like she said."

****

Dessa smiled at Cole's description of her landlady's car. At least the men had heard of automobiles, but not like the modern ones he described. Sheriff Cannon's and Turner's shocked expressions were comical to see.

Turner grinned. "Man, Cole, I wish I could have seen it with you. The things Charity talks about..." He shrugged. "Unbelievable."

"'Course it's unbelievable, 'cause it ain't true." Sheriff Cannon turned on Cole. "Son, you got shot in the head. I suspect you dreamed all that nonsense."

"I wish that were true, but what about the book? I

didn't have it when we left Prairie yesterday, and now I do." He shook his head. "Dessa told me she was from the future, but I couldn't believe it. In fact, I thought she was nuts. When the kid I wounded said she just popped out of nowhere, I still didn't believe it but had made up my mind she wasn't a part of Faraday's gang. Turner and Mrs. Reardon tried to convince me the day after her capture, and still I doubted." He shook his head and smiled at Dessa. "After this morning, I can no longer deny your story."

Dessa breathed a sigh of relief. His believing meant a lot to her. She returned his smile. "What did you think of my time period?"

He grimaced. "Scared the bejeepers out of me. I wasn't there long—maybe fifteen minutes—but I hightailed it out of there as fast as I could. The mist started receding and took Buck with it. Seeing my horse disappear lit a fire under me, I tell you. I ran to catch him."

"You didn't want to stay awhile and see what the future was like?"

He shook his head. "All I could think about was finding the book you'd mentioned and getting back here to find you."

"I knew you'd come for me. Though you were wounded, I didn't doubt for a minute you would find me."

Warmth spread through Dessa. Their eyes locked. The heat of his gaze seared her as his kisses had earlier. Her heart galloped in her chest. The air between them grew palpable. Dessa wanted to be in his arms.

A cough broke their trance.

Turner had picked up the book, and from his

expression of interest, it appeared he hadn't noticed their exchange. Sheriff Cannon, on the other hand, speared her with his eyes, his bushy eyebrows drawn together in a vee. "Why was Zeke bringing you back here? He have a change of heart all of a sudden?"

"Nope. He had a copy of my newspaper article."

He nodded. "Figured that's why he took you."

"Partly, but the main thing he wanted was for me to show him how to pop in and out like I did at his campfire. Of course, I had no control over showing up in his camp, and I told him so, but he had it in his head I could show him how to pop into a bank, rob the place, and pop out. I'm not sure Zeke is too bright." She snickered. "You should've heard his ma. Called him a fool and said he took after his crazy grandmother."

The men chuckled.

Sheriff Cannon scratched his chin as he studied her. "So if you couldn't teach him what he wanted to know, why was he bringing you here?"

"To travel forward in time."

"Lord, have mercy. Guess that means he'll come for you again after he's healed—if he survives." He turned to Cole. "Better watch her close, then."

Cole nodded.

Sheriff Cannon stood and poured the dregs of his coffee into the fire. "We better head back." Cole and Turner followed suit, so Dessa did the same. Turner carried the now-empty pot and stowed it in his saddlebag while the other two men kicked dirt onto the fire and dispersed the remaining coals.

Dessa stood by Sugar until they finished. Rather than mounting his horse, Cole approached her. One arm rested across Sugar's rump as he bent his head close to hers, his expression serious. "Do you want to try to go back to the future? If so, now is the time."

When she'd first arrived, that's all she could think about. Now she wasn't so sure. "I don't know."

"Why not? I thought you'd jump at the chance. What does this time period hold for you?"

His comment hurt and irked her. She bristled and prayed her face wasn't red. "I thought maybe it held love and possibly a family." She'd certainly not found a man worthy of commitment and happily-ever-after in the future.

"You got someone in mind? You sure as hell don't want to be hitched to me. Made that mighty clear a few minutes ago. Downright refused to marry me."

"I did not." She raised her chin. "Anyway, you didn't ask me."

He snorted. "Didn't have to. The womenfolk in Prairie did it for me."

"I wouldn't want a man who was forced into marriage. When I marry, it will be for love and passion."

"Well, we sure as hell have the passion."

That they did.

"I guarantee, Miss Wade, no one forces me to do anything I don't want to do. Not even Miss Mamie."

Dessa grinned at the idea of the little old woman herding Cole down the church aisle with a shotgun.

"'Course, I'm not particularly good husband material."

"Why not? Do you drink to excess, chew tobacco, chase women, or gamble all your money away?"

His grin and chuckle made her heart lurch. He exuded masculine appeal and wasn't egotistical like

69

many men in her era. No denying the sexual attraction between them, but did she love him? Better yet, did he love her?

"No, Sweetheart, I'm not guilty of those vices, but my job takes me away from home for days at a time. A life with me might be lonely."

There was that endearment again. "Am I your sweetheart, Cole?"

His blue eyes darkened with a force eager to consume her. Voice gruff, his words washed over her. "All I know is I've never wanted a woman like I do you. But it's not only passion. When I woke to find you gone, my heart stopped in fear for you. Even before then, I thought of you day and night."

Sheriff Cannon's voice boomed across to them. "Ya'll gonna yammer all day?"

The sheriff and Turner were mounted, waiting for them. Cole called over his shoulder, never breaking eye contact with her, "We'll catch up."

Cole stroked her chin as he waited for her to respond. His fingers trailed down the cord in her neck, blazing a trail of gooseflesh as he went. She loved his touch. She wondered if he knew how this simple gesture inflamed her.

"I'm not some simpering little woman needing constant attention, Cole. I'm not afraid to be alone, and my work would keep me busy."

He lowered his head to hers. Mouth a hair's breadth from hers, he asked, "How do you feel about me, Dessa?"

Her breath hitched at his closeness and the fire in his eyes, the heat of his body so close to hers.

"I burn for you, Cole."

His lips captured hers in a possessive kiss. When his tongue touched hers, she opened her mouth wider and moaned into his, "Cole, Cole."

He cradled her close, stroking her back, urging her hips closer to his. "Do you want to be asked, Sweetheart?"

Oh, jeepers, did she? If they were in her era, she'd say yes in a heartbeat, but they weren't. She was in 1890, a time totally unknown to her. No, that wasn't true. She'd always enjoyed history, especially U.S. and Texas history, so she knew more about Cole's time than he did hers.

Interesting, that he wasn't curious about the future, didn't want to explore. He'd made it clear he didn't want to know more about 2010. She didn't blame him for not wanting to get stuck in the future. What kind of profession would he have in her time? Not that he couldn't handle any law enforcement job, after training and getting up to speed on technology, but many lawmen in the future had college degrees.

Yes, adapting to the past would be easier for a person than acclimating to the future. If they wanted to be together, she'd have to stay in the past.

"I might."

He arched a brow.

"I need to sort through some things first." *Like, can I be happy giving up the life I know—my career as an investigative reporter.* She didn't have much family. Her parents had died in a car crash five years before. She didn't stay in touch with her one aunt and uncle, or several cousins. It'd be a year before they realized she was missing.

Her friends and colleagues were a major concern.

They'd worry and scour the Fredericksburg countryside looking for her. Poor Mrs. Lawrence, her landlady— she'd take a beating from the press and folks in town if another renter came up missing. Dessa hoped it didn't turn into a witch hunt.

Chapter Seven

"Take all the time you need." He cupped her cheek and ran his thumb over her bottom lip.

Dessa's insides quivered. Did he know what his simple gesture did to her libido? From his expression, no, but his eyes indicated what she did to him, a fact that gave her pleasure.

He turned her to face Sugar. "We better catch up with Elijah and Turner."

The sun slipped over the horizon as they rode into town and stopped in front of the stable. The men removed their saddlebags before the stablehand led their horses inside.

As Cole took her arm, he turned to Sheriff Cannon. "See you in the morning, Elijah."

He guffawed. "I'm tagging along. Think I'd want to miss the fireworks at Miss Mamie's?"

They'd no sooner stepped inside the boarding house than Miss Mamie came bustling from the kitchen, wiping her hands on her apron. She took one look at Dessa's bedraggled state and rushed forward. "Lands, child, are you all right?" Dessa hadn't seen herself but guessed she was a sight, covered in dirt and with her dress torn. She looked down at her once-yellow sweater, now a dingy brown.

Mamie shot Cole a heated glance and then noticed the bandage around his head. She grabbed his arm.

"You come with me, and let's take care of that wound." Her voice carried as she marched off with Cole in tow. "The rest of you might as well come too. I ain't going to bed 'til I hear what's happened and decide whether we'll be having a wedding tomorrow."

"I'll be back down in a minute. Charity will be wanting news." Turner ran up the stairs.

Dessa didn't doubt he was anxious to see his wife and newborn baby.

She and Sheriff Cannon sat at the table with Cole. "Don't believe you need to visit Doc," Mamie announced when she had cleaned the graze on his head and liberally doused it with carbolic acid. She smoothed on some type of salve. Cole winced. "Sorry. This ointment stings a mite at first, but it will soothe the pain in a minute."

Cole gingerly touched his head. "Thanks, Mamie. The soreness is better already."

Turner returned, a big grin on his face. "Charity wants you to stop by before going to bed, Dessa. She wants to observe for herself that you're all right." He draped an arm around Mamie's shoulder and squeezed. "Any chance you have any food left over from supper?"

"Of course I do, young man." She gathered her medical supplies and placed them on top of the Hoosier cabinet. "Sit down while I get you something."

Dessa stood. "Can I help?"

"No, young lady. Sit down and tell me what happened out there, and don't leave out one thing." She glared at Cole. "Not one."

"Yes, ma'am."

The sheriff and Turner grinned. Cole didn't fidget under the older woman's stare, just smiled.

Dessa relayed Cole's getting wounded and her being hustled off by Zeke and his boys to spend the night in Ma's cabin.

Mamie snorted. "Least Zeke had sense enough to take you to Mrs. Faraday. Keeping you overnight with no woman would have ruined your reputation for sure."

Dessa bristled. "Surely the folks in this town wouldn't blame me for what I had no control over."

"The good ones wouldn't, but some of those snooty women who call themselves living in the godly spirit would turn their noses up and ostracize you."

"Well, what if they had abused me?" She looked from Cole, to Sheriff Cannon, to Turner. They dropped reddened faces.

Mamie didn't miss a beat. "We'd find you a husband."

Dessa couldn't believe it. "And a husband would make me clean again?"

"No, but acceptable."

"That's the most barbaric thing I've ever heard."

Cole cleared his throat. "Why fuss over something that didn't happen? If Miss Wade's honor came into question, I'd marry her myself. She was my responsibility."

"I'd never marry to preserve my honor."

"I know that, Sweetheart, but I'd flatten any man who questioned it and scorch the ears of any woman who snubbed you."

Mamie's eyes rounded. Dessa watched as the older woman glanced at Cole, then at Turner and the sheriff. All three grinned broadly.

****

Dessa couldn't take her eyes off the baby. She

stood over his cradle and marveled at the perfection of his little fingers, his tiny nose, and his vivid blue eyes. He whimpered and tried to stuff both fists in his mouth, sucking greedily.

"He's hungry, Charity."

Charity grinned and scooted up in the bed. Mamie wouldn't let her get up yet—a common practice in this time period. "The little bugger is always hungry. Hand him to me, will you?"

Would she? She couldn't wait to hold the infant. "Sure." She lifted him to her shoulder and breathed in his sweet scent.

He rooted around and started sucking on her neck.

She giggled. "That tickles, young man."

She placed him in Charity's outstretched arms and Charity placed him at her breast and smoothed his hair, radiant happiness reflected on her face.

Dessa sighed. Until recently, she'd not given much thought to motherhood. An only child, she'd had little experience with children, especially infants, but she liked them. Now, for some reason, she longed to have a baby of her own. It was Cole's fault, no doubt. Caring for the man had put all sorts of ideas in her head—love, marriage, home, children.

The decision of whether to go home or stay here had plagued her half the night. She needed to make a decision soon. If she returned to the future, she'd be beset with dreams of Cole, regrets at leaving him. No doubt about it, the man held her enthralled. What would she give up if she stayed here? A lonely, rarely used apartment, friends she saw on occasion, people in the industry, travel, money, and her writing. How important were those things when compared to Cole—his love, his children, and a home? She could write here. Maybe not the same type and caliber of writing as she was used to, but she could make her way, put her stamp on this era.

"Dessa...Dessa. Earth to Dessa."

"What? Oh, my mind was elsewhere."

"Duh. No kidding." Charity grinned and winked suggestively. "That handsome marshal wouldn't be the recipient of your thoughts, would he?"

"Yeah, he would."

"The man's in love with you, Dessa."

"No, he's not. He likes me, desires me, but love's not in the picture—yet."

Charity snorted, giggled, and covered her mouth with her free hand. "Lands, I'm developing some bad habits. I never snorted until coming here. Get it from Turner's Aunt Ruby, and Mamie does it, too." She lifted the baby to her shoulder and patted his back. He released a loud, healthy burp and in moments was sound asleep.

"What are you going to name this precious bundle?"

Charity glanced up at the question and handed the sleeping boy to Dessa to lay in the cradle.

"We're going to name him Buford Dawson Reardon after my daddy. Poor kid. But I hope Daddy will look us up and see his namesake."

"I can help with that. I've been trying to come up with something I can do for the newspaper to keep me busy. I'll write a weekly column about weddings, births, and social events of the area." It wasn't investigative work, but perhaps she could be happy. "Plus, I think I'll write a book about Prairie. Maybe include some pictures, so your daddy can see your children and how happy you are."

Charity bit off a sob and reached for Dessa's hand. "If you can do that, I'll be forever grateful."

The door opened and a tall, homely woman rushed in. "Where's my baby?"

"Aunt Ruby." Charity held her arms out. The woman embraced her and then turned with longing to where the baby slept. "Oh, my, he's just adorable." She sniffed and wiped the tears from her cheek with a thin hand. "My great-nephew. I'd about given up hope of having babies in the house, and now I have this precious boy."

"Ruby, this is Dessa Wade. She arrived under the same circumstances I did."

Dessa wasn't prepared for the woman's welcoming embrace, but gave in and returned the gesture. Ruby's frame, though bony, exuded comfort. "Child, you are welcome here, and we'll do everything we can to help you settle in." She patted Dessa's cheek. "You call me Aunt Ruby, just like everyone else in this family."

Dessa spoke around the lump in her throat and smiled. "Thank you."

Ruby glanced at Charity. "You reckon we'll be having another woman pop up every two or three years?"

Charity's laugh bounced off the walls. "Lordy, I hope not."

The baby fussed at the commotion, and Ruby scooped him from the cradle. Tears ran down the grooves of age in her face. "Law, he's the most beautiful thing I've ever seen."

A knock sounded on the door.

"Just a minute," called Charity as she straightened the bedcovers.

Dessa rushed to the door. "I'll get it and leave you three alone for awhile."

Cole—tall, lean, and handsome—stood propped against the wall across the hall. He pushed away when she came out. "Have time to go for a ride with me?"

"Sure. Can we stop by the mercantile before we go? I need a coat of some kind."

"No need. Got you a warm cape on my way back from the stables. It's in your room."

His gesture delighted her. She smiled up at him. "Thank you. That was thoughtful of you."

"That yellow thing you wear needs a good wash. I hope it survives. Sorta gotten used to you looking like a canary."

"It'll clean up just fine. Modern fabrics are much easier to care for."

He waited at the door while she retrieved the cape. Laid with it were a brown felt hat to protect her skin and a pair of brown leather gloves.

"They're beautiful, Cole."

The cape was the same color as the hat and gloves. "Thought the color would bring out the yellow in your brown eyes." She ran her fingers over the fine leather of the gloves and sniffed. This man was a treasure. Thoughtful and kind.

"Here, let me help you." He draped the cape over her shoulders and set the hat on her head, angling it just so. It had a leather tie, and he slid the knot up under her chin. "Perfect."

"You'll let me repay you for these."

"No need."

"It's not proper to accept such personal items from a man." In this time period, anyway. No need to add more fodder to the gossip lines in Prairie.

"It is if we're betrothed."

"We're not—"

He bent down and captured her mouth in a kiss. Before she could voice her objections, he hustled her out the door.

Mamie was dusting furniture in the parlor when they passed through. She smiled her approval. "Y'all have a good time."

They'd just about reached the stable when they passed a couple of ladies on the street. Dessa smiled at them, and Cole tipped his hat. The women backed up against the storefront and brushed their skirts aside as if Dessa were still covered with dirt. Cole stopped, anger tensing his body.

Dessa squeezed his arm and whispered, "It doesn't matter, Cole. They mean nothing to me."

"It damn well matters to me." He turned to face her and smiled. "Sweetheart, let's go pick out that wedding ring now."

The women gasped, but neither he nor Dessa turned to acknowledge them.

"What!" Dessa shrieked.

He chuckled, and Dessa wanted to swat him but didn't need him kissing her in front of the old biddies.

"Yes. Why wait? It may need sizing or have to be ordered. I don't want anything to put off our wedding."

She hissed, "We're not getting married."

"Maybe. Maybe not."

He took her arm and hurried her along the boardwalk, leaving her with no choice in the matter.

Inside the mercantile, the proprietor greeted them. "Can I help you folks?"

"Yes, sir, Mr. White. We'd like to see a wedding ring."

Dessa resisted the urge to pinch Cole. He could at least lower his voice. Everyone in the store watched them and grinned.

The man beamed. "Right this way." He lifted a tray of wedding bands from a case.

Rather than draw more attention by resisting, Dessa selected a gold band with filigree flowers etched into the surface. It was beautiful and fit her perfectly. Cole paid for it but left it there for the time being.

****

Dessa didn't say a word until they were out of town. She'd been huffing and puffing the entire way, no doubt anxious to voice her opinion. Nothing quiet and mousy about this woman. He loved her that way.

"You just wasted your money."

"Maybe, maybe not."

"Dadgummit, Cole, you keep saying that."

"Now, Sweetheart, let's not argue and ruin the day. I know you've not decided yet, but I couldn't let those women shun you like that. It was either the ring or boxing their ears." He'd come close to telling the old dames what for, but doing so wouldn't have helped.

"I guess. As long as you understand we're not getting married."

He nodded. "I do." But if he had his way, they'd be getting hitched before the week was out.

They turned toward a large live oak tree sitting atop a small hill where the view spanned the countryside all the way around. Mostly prairie grass, dead now in the throes of autumn, but the one tree provided shade from the blazing sun. He helped Dessa dismount and hobbled the horses to graze. Before leaving the boarding house, he'd yanked a quilt off his bed. Hopefully Mamie wouldn't skin him alive for using it on the ground. He spread it out and motioned for Dessa to sit. While she did so, he placed food items on the blanket.

"A picnic? You're full of surprises, Marshal. Where'd you get the food?"

"From the café this morning."

"Mmmm, looks delicious. I love fried chicken."

"Me too. One of my favorites." He studied her while she ate. Evidently she liked deviled eggs, too, as she ate several. "Can you cook, Dessa?"

"If you mean can I pop TV dinners in a microwave oven, I sure can, but anything else, I'm hopeless."

"What are TV dinners?" Heck, he had no idea what a microwave was, either.

"Prepared meals that come in a box. You put them in a microwave, turn it on, and in three to four minutes it's ready to eat."

He shuddered. "Sounds awful."

She laughed. "Actually some are rather good, but nothing like this chicken." She smacked her lips. Her tongue flitted out to lick the grease and crumbs away.

Desire curled in his stomach. He leaned in and kissed her mouth. She didn't push him away; instead she grabbed his shirt and pulled him closer. Arms wrapped around her, he lay back and pulled her down on top of him. His hands moved to her hips molding them to his arousal as their lips met, tasted, and took from each other. Their groans mingled into one.

"Dessa, honey. I want you." He shoved the remains of their picnic lunch aside and rolled, placing her under him. "So much."

She pulled his head down to hers. "Then take me, Cole."

Stunned, he looked down at her. "Then you'll marry me?"

"No. People in my time have sex without marriage."

"And how many people have you had sex with, *Sweetheart*?"

She frowned at the sarcastic emphasis on his endearment. "Not many."

He jerked away from her. "I'll not see you going back to your time carrying my child."

"Cole, in my time women use a birth control method. They get pregnant only when they plan to."

The idea of her having sex with another man, more than one man, didn't sit well with him. He wanted to be the only one to touch her, love her. "And you can't get with child right now?"

"No." She tried to kiss him, but he pulled away.

"How long has it been, Dessa?"

She sighed. "Over a year."

"Why then are you still doing this...birth control thing?"

She twisted the fabric of her dress and wouldn't meet his gaze. She shrugged. "Habit, I guess. Being prepared in case I ever met someone I wanted to have a relationship with." She clutched his arm. "I'm not promiscuous, Cole. I promise. But I see nothing wrong with us having sex. We're both consenting adults and won't be hurting anyone else."

"Ah, hell, Dessa, I want to marry you, make a life together, make love to you every morning and night. Not have sex and watch you leave me."

"Well, why the hell won't you ask me, then?"

"Ask you to marry me?" Hope bloomed in his heart.

She slapped his chest. "Yes. If you want me to commit, you have to ask. What do you think I've been waiting for, Marshal Jeffers?" She batted her eyelashes at him. "A girl needs the words."

He whooped, pushed to his knees, and tugged her up to join him. "Dessa, Sweetheart, I can't promise you a lot, but I swear I'll protect you and care for you every day of my life." It hit him suddenly and he brought her hands to his heart. He loved this woman. He released a sigh of relief and hope. Could she love him, too? "I'm not good with words, but I love you, Dessa. Will you marry me?"

Tears pooled in her eyes, and his hope dropped like a rock to his boots. "You love me?"

He nodded, misery clouding his ability to speak.

Her hands framed his face and she kissed him, tears salty on her lips. "I love you, too, Cole. Yes, I'll marry you."

Chapter Eight

Dessa came up for air. Cole held her tight, backed into the corner of Buck's stall. She didn't want him to go, or at the very least not to go alone. "Why won't you take Sheriff Cannon with you?"

He nuzzled her neck and whispered between nibbles, "Sweetheart, Elijah is a busy man...this is my job...I usually work alone."

"But, you'll be one against three." She brought his head up to hers, and hope flared. "I could go with you."

Eyes narrowed, he shook his head. "You will stay here and be safe." Voice husky, he spoke against her mouth. "I need to know you're here, Dessa. Promise me you'll not follow."

She didn't want him to worry. Having to keep her safe would put him in danger. "I promise. Don't you dare get hurt or..." *Heaven forbid, killed.*

"Nothing is going to happen to me, Sweetheart." He hugged her close, smoothing his hand up and down her back. "You've got to have faith in my ability to perform my job."

She sagged against him. He was right. If she continued in this vein, she'd be a nervous wreck every time he went out. "Of course, you're right."

"I'll be back in two to three days." He tilted her chin and grinned down at her. "You be ready to march down the aisle as soon as I get back."

"Getting anxious, are we?"

"Darn tootin'. I want you to carry my name, woman." He wiggled his eyebrows. "And be in my bed." He placed a chaste kiss on her lips and tweaked her nose. "Now, come on. Let's get you back to the boarding house, so I can get out of town."

She straightened her hat and took his arm. In front of Mamie's, he mounted Buck and studied her keenly for a minute. His intense gaze of promise stopped her heart. Then he winked and rode off.

Dessa released the breath she hadn't realized she was holding, grinned, and went inside the boarding house. She could hardly wait until tomorrow, when her article about the Faraday gang would come out in the *Prairie Gazette*. The editor was excited, too. The newspaper's readership had doubled after her first story, and he'd agreed to let her write a weekly column highlighting events in town. Her first feature was due tomorrow. The article announced the birth of Turner and Charity's son, several other births, and Cole and Dessa's upcoming wedding.

The parlor was full of luggage and Dawson's baby paraphernalia. The Reardons were going home to their ranch.

Charity burst through the kitchen door. "Oh, good. There you are. Did Cole tell you he'd bought our little cabin just outside of town?"

"No, he didn't." Dessa wasn't sure if she should be excited or mad. It would be nice to have a place of their own, but she would have liked to have a say in where they lived. She guessed it was a man thing, especially of this era. Cole probably thought she'd be thrilled. She would reserve judgment until after she saw the cabin.

"If you want to ride out of town with us and see it, we'll take Sugar along for you to ride back."

"Sounds good to me."

Thirty minutes later, Turner helped Charity and Ruby into the wagon while Dessa held the baby. She handed him up to Charity and mounted Sugar. There wasn't enough room for Dessa in the wagon unless she rode in the back. Sugar was more comfortable.

She urged the mare into a walk alongside, visiting with the women. Charity chattered about the cabin. "You're going to love it, Dessa. When we have time, I'll tell you how Turner's wranglers burned the original one down." She bumped shoulders with her husband.

Turner beamed down at Charity and added, "It wasn't a cabin, Dessa. It was a shack." He threw an arm around his wife and squeezed her as he smiled at Charity. "She made me build her a new, pretty one to replace that pile of sticks."

"That was the deal, darling. You owed me."

"Yeah, I did."

Dessa laughed at their banter, glad to see them so happy. "Won't you miss having a place to stay nearer to town?" She hoped they had sold their place willingly, rather than feeling obligated so she and Cole would have a home of their own.

"No. Now that we have Dawson, I won't be able to come to town and work at the law office very often." Charity shifted on the wooden seat. "Unless I could get Aunt Ruby to come in with me."

The older woman huffed. "We've already discussed this, young woman, and you know my answer. You'll not be dragging this baby all over the country."

87

"I know, Ruby. I'm just ragging on you."

"You're doing what?"

"Teasing you. When Dawson gets older, I might come in and stay with Dessa and Cole for a day or two and work if I want. By then Cole will have built on another room or two."

Ruby snorted. "By then you'll have another baby at your hip."

Charity gaped at the woman, her mouth open.

Dessa hid her smile. *Guess Charity didn't think about the lack of birth control options here.* Maybe she'd be able to talk the doctor into providing condoms. If Dessa remembered correctly, the Comstock Law prevented the sale or distribution of condoms or other birth control paraphernalia in the nineteenth century.

Her smile wilted. The situation wasn't humorous, especially since she was in the same position. She didn't want to have a baby every year. The matter required some serious thought.

"We're here," said Turner. "Take a look down the road, Dessa. There sits your new home." He turned the wagon onto the lane leading up to a small cabin. At least, it looked small from this distance.

As they drew nearer, Dessa noticed the structure was well kept with some type of shrub planted on each side. A railed porch ran the full length of the front. The door, with windows on each side, sat off-center. A barn stood thirty yards behind the house.

Turner halted the wagon and jumped down from the seat. "What do you think, Dessa?" He turned to help the two women down.

"I love it." And she did.

Charity took her arm and propelled her forward.

"Wait until you see inside. It's only two rooms right now, but expansion will be easy."

Inside, one room encompassed the living area and kitchen, including a sink, a black antique stove, and a Hoosier-style cabinet. A small sofa, with a rag rug in front, sat against the left wall. A table and four chairs occupied the middle of the room. To the right a door led into the bedroom, which held an iron bedstead, a chest, and a washstand. A privacy screen stood in one corner.

"Isn't it beautiful?" Charity ran her hand over the quilt on the bed. "I'll be taking this cover with me. It traveled through time with me, and I'd like to keep it."

Odd. Dessa had brought one through time, too. She glanced around. "You mean you're leaving everything else?"

"Of course. You need furniture, and if you later want to replace what's here, you can bring these pieces back to the ranch. We really don't need them, though."

"Come in here, ladies." Turner called from the other room. "Cole sent a gift for Dessa."

"A gift for me?" Dessa couldn't imagine. He'd already given her the cape, hat, and gloves. She hoped the man had saved some of his money for living expenses. Maybe he had plenty.

Dessa followed Charity through the door and watched her friend take a stand beside the table, a big grin on her face. There sat a typewriter, the oldest model Dessa had ever seen—a Remington Standard 2. It even had a shift key. Wow, she knew this era had typewriters, but not one that would be this functional. Of course, she hadn't given it a try yet. It would take some getting used to, but Dessa was up to the challenge. A box of paper sat beside the machine.

"Oh, my, this is the best gift I've ever received. Isn't that Cole the sweetest man?" No doubt he'd gone to a lot of trouble. How many men would even think of something so suited to her needs?

She ran her hand over the machine, anxious to get to work. There was next week's article to compose, and she wanted to start on a book—one about the citizens of Prairie. She resisted the urge to rub her hands in glee.

"Ladies, we'd better leave. I want to be home before dark." Turner took the baby from Ruby's arms and started for the door. He stopped and turned back. "Dessa, please get back to the boarding house before dark, or Mamie will send out a posse."

"I will. Promise."

Ruby followed Turner out the door. Charity hung back. "Are you sure about your decision, Dessa, to stay in this time period without even trying to go back?"

"I am." Dessa embraced Charity and pulled back. "Don't worry about me. You're happy, right? I can be happy too. I know it."

Voice choked, Charity said, "I'm so pleased you're staying. I need a friend who's been through what I have." She enveloped Dessa in a tight hug.

Dessa patted Charity's back, alarming thoughts racing through her mind. Had she made the right decision? Was Charity regretting hers? "You are happy, aren't you?"

"Oh, yes." Charity released her and smiled through her tears. "Deliriously so, but it's hard not having some connection with my past."

That made sense to Dessa. She doubted she'd have been willing to stay if she'd not had Charity to ease the way for her. Fear rose in her chest and left her gasping.

"I'm scared, Charity. I want a life with Cole, but I wonder if I'm up to the challenge."

Charity reached out and squeezed her hand. "You'll be fine. If you ever need to talk, you know where to find me." She sniffed, and then put an arm around Dessa's waist. "Walk me out."

Dessa swallowed the lump in her throat. "You're right, girlfriend. We need one another." Arms linked around each other's waists, they bumped hips as they strode out the door to the waiting wagon.

****

Bone-tired and filthy, Cole walked quietly up the stairs of Mamie's boarding house, hoping not to wake anyone already asleep. It was nearing ten o'clock. He wanted a bath and then sleep for ten hours straight, but all he could think about was Dessa and kissing her sweet lips. While on the trail, he'd thrust all thoughts of her to the back of his mind. Daydreaming about a woman would sign his death warrant. He was home now, his prisoners locked in Sheriff Cannon's jail.

His breath quickened when he noticed a faint streak of light under her door. He looked down at his dirty clothes, rubbed his hand across his two-day-old beard, and hesitated before knocking. They were getting married. She'd see him like this many times in the future. If she rebuffed him tonight, she wasn't the woman he thought she was. He knocked softly.

The door opened a crack, with only Dessa's head peeking through. Her brown eyes lit with happiness, and his body warmed in response. Before he could speak, she opened the door wider, grabbed his shirt front, and pulled him inside.

"Cole! You're back." She wrapped her arms

around his neck and kissed him.

He pulled her closer and breathed in the sweet fragrance of her hair and skin, then set her aside. "I'm filthy, Sweetheart, and smell like a sty." Her long, filmy, white gown left her toes bare. His eyes strayed to her breasts pushing against the semi-transparent fabric. He swallowed the groan rising in his throat and averted his eyes.

"I don't care." She tugged him over to the bed. "Sit down. Tell me. Did you get Zeke?"

He dusted the seat of his pants before sitting down with her beside him. "I did. And that book was right. Zeke is in bad shape. Doc's with him now, but I doubt he can save him." The man deserved prison, but his crimes didn't warrant death. Zeke had walked down the wrong road and now paid for his mistakes.

"I'm sorry. His mother will be heartbroken."

"I expect she knew he'd come to a similar end." He reached out and stroked her cheek. Her skin was soft, pale against the dark strands of her hair. It was a little longer, but nowhere near long enough to cover her neck. He struggled to keep his eyes from drifting lower. "Let's not talk about Zeke. I want to know if all is planned for our wedding tomorrow."

"With every woman in this town in on the event, I don't see how a thing could be missed." She took his hand and kissed his palm. "Thank you for the typewriter, Cole. It's the most romantic gift I've ever received."

He couldn't resist a grin. How many women could find joy in such a mechanical device? Only his woman. "I'm glad you like it."

"I love it, and the cabin is perfect." She linked her

fingers through his. "Are you sure we can afford all this stuff you're buying?"

"We can, Sweetheart. Until now I've not had anything to spend my salary on. I've always wanted a small ranch, and the land on either side of the one hundred acres with that cabin might be obtainable, in time."

His eyes strayed to her breasts. Unable to resist, he cupped one in his palm and watched her eyes darken with passion. He kissed her as he ran his thumb over the taut peak and captured her moan in his mouth.

"Ah, darlin', just one more day." And it couldn't come soon enough. She was a passionate woman, and he longed to make her his.

****

Dessa clutched Turner's arm as he walked her down the aisle toward Cole. Her soon-to-be husband stood tall, appearing a bit like a preacher, dressed in a dark suit and white starched shirt. His cowboy boots shone from a recent polishing. Even at his wedding the ever-ready six-gun hugged his leg, rawhide holding it in place. No matter. Dessa wanted this man—the entire package.

When his eyes met hers, his smile stole her breath and every coherent thought. Her feet moved of their own volition, as if his magnetism pulled her forward, her heart beating in time to her movements. All doubts she might have had fled. This man was her destiny.

The ladies of the community had outdone themselves—from the flower-festooned church to the groaning tables loaded with food at the reception and dance. Dessa would have felt guilty except the women derived so much pleasure from the event. Their enjoyment reminded Dessa to cherish the moment even more than she would have otherwise. Life in the past was simpler but much more personal. When a community accepted you, you became part of the family.

She danced with every man in town before Cole claimed her for the ride home. Their place sat just west of town. The setting sun drifted behind the horizon, stealing its warmth away. Dessa pulled her cape closer around her shoulders, glad to see the cabin come into view.

At the front porch, Cole helped her untangle the long skirt of her wedding dress and dismount. He lifted her into his arms and carried her up the steps and across the threshold. "Welcome home, Sweetheart." He let her feet touch the floor, pulled her into his arms, and bussed her cheek. "It'll only take a minute to bed the horses down." He lifted her cape from her shoulders and draped it across a chair before turning back to run his fingers lightly over her shoulders, down her arms. "Reckon you can get out of this contraption by yourself?"

She turned around to present her back. "It might help if you undid the first ten buttons."

"Hmmm, let me see." He fiddled and cursed. "How you women manage these tiny things, I'll never know." His breath on her neck warmed her. Each touch of his fingers on her skin increased her heart rate. His breathing sped up. At last he had the dress open to her waist. Cool air touched her back. Rather than leave her, he spread his palms across her shoulders. His lips touched her neck, and she shuddered.

He jerked back and muttered something like,

"Damn horses," and stomped to the door. "I'll be back in a minute."

When he returned, Dessa sat in the bed, her feet tucked beneath her, waiting. He eyed her with appreciation, his gaze taking in the scooped neckline of her nightdress. She hoped he didn't miss the sheerness of her finely woven cotton gown.

She watched his every move as he stripped, baring his lean body to her gaze. Her breath hitched in her throat. Her skin flushed. Beautiful. Every inch of him was sculpted muscle—a model of perfection, his desire for her obvious. She opened her arms, anxious for him to come to her.

"I want to see you, too, Sweetheart."

Blood pounding in her ears, she scooted off the bed and stood to face him. She lifted her arms above her head. He reached for the hem of her gown and, in one movement, whisked the garment from her body and tossed it over the end of the iron bedstead.

Dessa waited while his eyes drifted from her shoulders to her feet and then back up again. Then he touched her, his hands following the path his gaze had roamed. Tremors started in her legs, and she reached to clasp his waist.

He caught her to him and whispered against her lips. "You are lovely, Dessa—more beautiful than I'd imagined." He lifted her in his arms, laid her on the bed, and then blew out the lamp.

When he joined her, she moved into his arms, hers wrapped around his neck, their bodies flush. Cole sighed against her collarbone and traced kisses across it. "Guess I won't have to worry about you being shy in the bedroom."

She snorted. "Not hardly." She nibbled his earlobe. "Not ever with you, love."

"Good." His hands stroked her back and dipped to glide across her buttocks. "You are so soft—just like a baby's skin."

"Yours is soft in places, too..." She drew her hand over his hip and then pressed her belly against his erection. He groaned and jerked her closer. "And hard in others."

He kissed her hungrily, thrusting his tongue inside her mouth and drawing hers inside his. Their hands roamed, stroked, stoking the fire that burned within them.

Cole settled between her legs. "I want you, Sweetheart. Are you ready for me?"

"Oh, yes. I've been ready since I met you."

****

Fredericksburg, Texas, 2012

Buford "Bull" Dawson stood staring out at the small pond behind the cabin where Charity and Dessa Wade had disappeared. It had taken him two years to set his plan in motion. He'd sold his apartment in New York. Most of his assets were in the control of Jacob Reardon, Charity's great-great-grandson, to be equally distributed among her descendants—those of Charity and Turner Reardon.

He'd kept out just enough money to buy this cabin and the surrounding land, plus supply the gold coins stowed in a money bag he wore at all times.

He sat down on the step and looked, for the hundredth time, at the book he'd brought along with him—*Nineteenth-Century Life in Prairie, Texas.* Published in 1898, it had been written by Dessa Wade

Jeffers, the investigative reporter who'd visited him in the fall of 2010. Somehow it had appeared in the law firm vault, wrapped in brown paper held together with string and addressed to him. Receiving the volume had been one of the happiest moments in his life, and it sealed his fate.

He flipped the book open to a marked page. Charity's face smiled out at him. His namesake, Buford Dawson Reardon, a chubby cherub of an infant, sat in her lap. A lump grew in his throat, threatening to choke him. A grandson. His chest expanded. He'd never dreamed of having a grandchild. Tears of humility pricked his eyes. He sniffed and brushed them aside. Charity's strong husband stood behind her with a hand on her shoulder. Another page showed a picture of Dessa Wade Jeffers and her husband. Of course there were other families in the book, but it was these two who meant so much to him—his daughter and the woman who'd decided to discover what happened to her.

Thank God, Dessa Wade had gone looking for clues to Charity's disappearance. Dessa had devised a way to let him know his daughter was well and happy. No doubt the book, though a boon to the community, had been for his benefit. Yes, Charity had said in her earlier note to him that she was happy and not to worry, but seeing it with his own eyes meant the world to him.

He'd be damned if he'd stay here. He wanted to see his daughter, watch his grandchildren born and grow up. If the two women could travel back in time, so could he.

Daddy is coming, Charity.

A Love
of
His Own

by

Linda LaRoque

Dedication

Thanks to my husband Larry
for reading my work over and over again.

Chapter One

New York, November 1, 2012

"Are you sure this is what you want, Granddad?"

Pride rose in Buford "Bull" Dawson's chest. A warm glow of contentment filled him. His grandson, the young man he'd met less than a year ago, was in fact his daughter Charity's great-great-great-grandson, Jacob Reardon.

Bull closed the book and stood. With the tome under his arm, he walked around the desk and laid a hand on Jacob's shoulder. "I'm sure, son."

The younger man nodded. "It will be as you say. You have my word."

Throat clogged, Bull struggled to keep tears at bay. He'd come to love Jacob and wished he could stay in New York and watch him prosper, but Texas, with Charity and her son, called to him.

"I know you will." He sniffed and wiped at an errant tear. Damned if old age wasn't making him soft. "I'm proud to have known you, boy. Just check Texas history to see I made it and am happy."

Jacob grabbed Bull in a tight embrace. "I'm grateful I got to know you and will do my best to make you proud."

Bull patted his back and stepped away. "Remember all I taught you, and you'll be fine. Find a way to share with your relatives. Family is everything."

****

Fredericksburg, Texas, November 30, 2012

Bull kicked the kitchen chair under the table. "I'm getting damned tired of this garb, toting around extra weight day and night." Wearing jeans, boots, sheepskin coat, and a flak vest carrying thirty pounds of gold wore him out. He had to admit each day became easier, and he'd lost weight. Not that he was excessively overweight, but at his age, extra pounds were dangerous.

Everything he owned he'd signed over either to Jacob or to charities. He'd taken ten thousand dollars and converted it into gold bars that weighed five ounces each. One hundred bars were sewn into the flak vest he wore under his jacket. The gold would allow him to make a fresh start and help Charity and her husband if needed. His Winchester and the knife in his boot offered protection from hostiles, and the jacket and hat protected him from the elements.

After a week of wearing it all the time, he'd grown accustomed to the brown felt hat perched on his balding head. The rifle never left his hand, even when he was on the john. He didn't have a clue how this time travel business worked, but he didn't want to be caught without his rifle or anything else he needed for the life he planned with Charity's family. He chuckled. Hell, he didn't want to be caught with his pants down, either. If he didn't get to take a shower soon, he'd drive away anyone he met, but he feared taking his clothes off. It'd be his luck to end up in Prairie, Texas, in the buff.

He snorted and stomped out the door of the cabin, the same one from which his daughter, Charity

Dawson, and the journalist Dessa Wade had disappeared—Charity in 2008 and Dessa in 2010. Both women had landed back in the Texas Panhandle town of Prairie—Charity in 1888 and Dessa in 1890. Thank goodness for Dessa's book, *Nineteenth-Century Life in Prairie, Texas*, published in 1898. One look at the picture of Charity, her husband, and their son (and his namesake), Buford "Bull" Dawson Reardon, and his fate was sealed. The desire to share in his grandson's life propelled him toward his goal. He'd plant his feet at this cabin until he traveled back in time or died, whichever came first.

Bull settled his hat firmly on his head and stepped off the porch, intent on enjoying the moonlight sparkle on the pond before turning in. He stopped. An idea froze him in motion. Maybe being in the cabin prevented his goal. Hell, he'd sleep under the stars tonight. He stomped back inside and retrieved one of the quilts and a pillow off the hall closet shelf. So what if he got them dirty? He'd bought this place and everything in it for an exorbitant price. The owner, Mrs. Lawrence, didn't want to sell. He upped the price until she couldn't see past the dollar signs. She'd thrown up her hands in surrender and walked away a rich woman.

He strode across the creek to the small clearing just beyond, lay down on the quilt, and rolled to his side, pulling half of it over him. Afraid he'd wake up in 1892 without his rifle, he cradled it in his arms and clutched the brim of his hat with his right hand. A rock bit into his hip. He shifted and rolled to his back and gazed up at the stars. Tonight the sky was cloudless, its inky darkness dotted with thousands of celestial bodies. As a child he'd known the names of many clusters, but since then a multitude of other information had shoved the names to folders in his mind now too difficult to retrieve.

Interesting that regret didn't nag at his conscience—regret to be leaving what he'd worked so long for. Perhaps it was because his reason for happiness no longer lived in this time period. Yes, he'd known Charity would leave him, travel to the past. He'd learned of her destiny shortly after his wife's death when Charity was a girl. That's why he'd tried to keep her on a short leash and by his side. Evidently the decision wasn't his to make.

So much for his diligent efforts. Look where that got him—alone. Oh, well, maybe it was karma. If only God had the same fate planned for him. Bull couldn't imagine life without his daughter. The past four years had been hell, worse than if she'd died. Knowing she lived yet not being able to see her and her family singed his heart. Hell, he should have remarried a long time ago, had more kids. Would children have eased the hole in his soul? No, he didn't think so.

He gazed up at the huge expanse above him. *Lord, if you're up there, take pity on me. Please send me back to 1892 to my daughter and grandchild.*

Would he like the man Charity had married? Did it matter if he did or not? No, it didn't. His daughter had rebuffed many men in New York, ones who were after her inheritance and wanted into his good graces. Oh, there'd been relationships, but none that turned permanent. Turner Reardon had to be a special man for Charity to marry him. No doubt Reardon and Bull would find common ground, forge a bond.

Bull closed his eyes, a smile stretched his mouth,

and he chuckled. He couldn't wait to see the surprise on Charity's face when he arrived. In years past, their relationship had rocky spots. Now he'd make up for his past domineering ways.

Sometime during the night, he woke to find the stars overhead had disappeared. He blinked several times to focus, but nothing changed. *Must be clouds rolling in. Hope it doesn't rain.*

Cramped from lying on his back, he sat up to change positions. As he did so, his head popped up out of a mist. Odd, he'd never noticed the vapor before, but he'd not been out this late, either. He glanced around. Moonlight gently illuminated his surroundings. Nothing was changed. Disappointed, he lay back down on his side and pulled the quilt up to his ears.

****

"Whoa, boys." Dipsey pulled the wagon to a stop and set the brake. She hopped down, her leather boots hitting the road with a thud. Sam, the lead mule, had been favoring his right front leg the past few minutes. She'd better take a look before he went lame.

"Let me see, Sam." She lifted the mule's big hoof and held it between her knees. "Ah, a rock. No wonder. Hurts, doesn't it?" With a small twig, she flipped the stone out. "Now, that'll feel better." She let his foot drop and patted his neck. Joe snorted and butted her shoulder, so she turned and gave him a pat, too. The brothers were jealous, each afraid one would get more attention than the other. They were the same when it came to feeding time. She had to separate them lest they try to horn in on each other's grub.

Dipsey walked back to the wagon and placed one foot on a spoke of the front wheel to climb into the wagon. A snorting sound from behind her made her pause. Grabbing her rifle from under the seat, she whirled and peered into the field of winter wheat gently waving in the cool morning air. Sunlight glanced off the stalks, giving the field a slight iridescence, but no movement caught her attention.

The noise stopped, then resumed with a loud bleating resonance. If she didn't know better, she'd think Thomas was asleep in the wheat field, but she'd buried her husband two years past. Who trespassed on her land?

Rifle cocked, she stepped in the direction of the snoring. Thomas always said she could sneak up on Satan himself. She hoped her skill served her well today.

Lying on her precious wheat, flattening it and breaking the stalks so it was unsalvageable, was a big, burly man. Wrapped in someone's finely stitched quilt, he had a brown felt hat over his eyes. One arm lay across his chest, the other cradled a newfangled model Winchester, so new the shine hadn't yet worn off.

She snatched the rifle from his arm. The dang fool didn't open his eyes. Dipsey thumped him on the shoulder with the butt of his weapon. He farted and rolled to his side, exposing a muscled butt and legs encased in denims. She stumbled back a few steps. *Disgusting man!*

She fired off a couple of bullets, sending wheat flipping into the air two yards above the man's head. Darn it. More of her precious crop damaged. If the waste continued, her animals would go hungry this winter, and she didn't have the money to buy feed.

The man lurched to his feet. "Holy hell." He started

toward Dipsey. "What the hell are you doing, woman?"

She cocked the rifle. "Stay put, mister."

He halted and eyed her weapon before turning his gaze to her. His stare traveled from her boots, past her worn, brown wool dress to her face; his eyes widened when they landed on her scar. She expected to see aversion. Most people shunned her because of her past profession. If they didn't know of her life as a whore, the ugly scar on her forehead caused them to look away. The man didn't appear put off. He actually smiled before his expression sobered.

"Could you lower your rifle?"

She snorted. Did he think she was crazy? "Who are you and what are you doing on my land?"

"Your land? I'll have you know..." He turned in a slow circle while taking in his surroundings. He stopped in front of her, whooped, and clutched his head. "I did it, I actually did it."

He reached out to her, and she stumbled back. "Stay put."

Head bobbing up and down, he asked, "Tell me, what is the date?"

Keeping the rifle aimed at his gut, she pondered his question. Some folks couldn't keep up with the days, especially people like her, who worked on their land day in and day out. Maybe he was lost and needed help finding his way. She looked him up and down. Tall and thickly built, he didn't appear to have missed a meal. Not that he was fat, mind you. No, he carried muscle. Under his coat, she couldn't tell if the thickness was fat or layers of clothes.

His eyes were clear, not glazed over like the man she'd seen in town several years ago. The sheriff had to send him away to some asylum, as he wouldn't keep his clothes on and scared folks with his raving. No, this man, though his elation was odd, didn't appear deranged. He was well groomed and his clothes clean, though from the faint odor that reached her nose she figured he'd been wearing them for several days.

What hair remained on his head appeared from this distance to have been dark at one time. Blue eyes pleaded with her for an answer. For an older fella, he was handsome, a quality she'd not noticed in a man for a while and shouldn't be noticing now.

"It's the first day of November."

"The year, lady, what's the year?"

"Why, it's 1892."

He jumped into the air, clicked his heels, and yelled, "Hallelujah!"

Chapter Two

Bull stopped mid-jig at the open-mouthed gape of
the woman before him. Her long blonde hair fell in twin
braids down her back. A thick, jagged scar on her
forehead marred her lovely pale skin but didn't detract
from her beauty. Lovely blue eyes perused him. She
probably thought he'd lost his mind. Her hold on the
rifle, and the direction of her aim, left him little doubt
of her apprehension.

About twenty yards behind her stood two large
mules hitched to a wagon. How he'd slept through their
approach he had no clue. No matter. As long as she
didn't shoot him, nothing mattered.

"I'm sorry, madam. Please excuse my exuberance.
I'd explain, but it's a long story." His heart thundered in
his chest. "Could you tell me if we're near the town of
Prairie, Texas?"

She nodded. "Town's about eight miles from here,
just beyond that hill."

Eight miles. That wasn't far at all. At last he'd see
Charity and his grandson. He'd done it. He'd traveled
back to 1892. Lightheaded, he swayed and his legs gave
way. He stumbled backward, but caught himself before
hitting the ground.

The woman lurched forward, then stopped. No
doubt she feared him. "Are you sick?"

"No, no, I'm just excited to have arrived and am

anxious to see my daughter."

She cocked a brow wrinkling the puckered scar on her forehead. "Who is your daughter? Does she live in Prairie?"

"Charity Reardon." He couldn't avoid the boast of pride. "I have a grandson I've not seen. Actually, I've never met my son-in-law."

For the first time, she smiled. "The Reardons are my neighbors. The turnoff to their place is just a short ways up."

Bull couldn't believe his good luck. "Will you give me a ride? I'd be happy to pay you for your trouble."

Her brow furrowed. "Where're you from, mister? You sound different, not like folks around here."

"New York." He extended his hand. "I'm Buford Dawson, ma'am."

She glanced at his hand, tentatively placed hers in his for a second, and then pulled it back. "Dipsey Thackson." Her face twisted as she thought, the scar on her forehead moving as her expression changed from doubt to acceptance.

"I'm headed to town to pick up supplies. If I make a detour and take you directly to their place, it'll put me past dark getting home. I could drop you at the turnoff. It's a two-mile walk to their house from there." She turned and strode through the wheat. He grabbed up his hat and the quilt and hurried to catch up. At the edge of the road, she stopped. "You're welcome to ride along to Prairie, if you'd rather. I can drop you at the Reardons' on my way home."

Darn. He'd prefer to see Charity immediately, but perhaps time in town would be good. He could deposit his money and buy some clothes. "Thank you. I'd be most grateful."

"Climb aboard, then."

She tucked both rifles in the corner passenger box of the wagon, lifted her skirts to reveal well-worn brown leather boots, and placed one foot on a spoke of the wheel. He tossed the quilt over his shoulder and then gripped her upper arm to help her up. Muscles bunched beneath his hand. She yanked from his grip and snarled, "Don't."

"I'm sorry. Just wanted to help you."

She nodded. "Not needed."

He rounded the vehicle and tried to emulate her method of boarding. His boot slipped on the spoke and hit the ground with a loud thump. Determination overrode his embarrassment, and he made it up on the second try.

Before his rump had settled firmly on the seat, she jiggled the reins. "Step on, boys."

The wagon lurched forward, slamming Bull against the backboard. He grabbed his hat with his left hand, the seat with his right, and hung on as the mules ate up the miles. Learning to ride a horse hadn't been near this bad. It had taken practice to adjust to the horse's gait, but he'd finally been able to keep from bouncing in the saddle. He had no time to adjust to the rhythm of the buckboard. Just when he thought he had, he was thrown into the air again. The woman beside him ignored his discomfort as her dainty derrière didn't budge from the seat.

They'd not gone far when Mrs. Thackson nodded toward the left. "That's Turner and Charity's place."

Three long poles formed a gate. A sign attached with rawhide swung from the top. "Reardon Ranch" had been burned into the sign.

Before he could respond, they hit a large rut in the road. He swallowed a groan as a most private part of his anatomy slammed down on the wood. It was a good thing he didn't plan to father children in the near future.

Finally they crested the hill and the town stretched out before them. Few trees protected the community from the wind, but the surrounding grassland most likely cut down on the amount of dust. He marveled at the vintage establishment. It reminded him of a movie set plunked down in the middle of a prairie.

His heart thundered with excitement. He'd made it. He'd traveled back in time to 1892. It was crazy, and if he was nuts, he didn't care. He'd be with his daughter and grandchild. As soon as he put his gold somewhere safe, he'd buy some clothes and a horse.

"Is there a bank in town, Mrs. Thackson?"

"Yes, across the street from the sheriff's office." She glanced his way. "I 'spect you'd best check in there first. Sheriff Cannon likes to know who comes and goes in town."

Made sense to Bull. If he were responsible for the safety of these people, he'd feel the same way.

As they entered town, people stared at him and then quickly turned away. They were snubbing Mrs. Thackson. Why? Surely it wasn't because of the scar on her forehead. His face burned with anger and embarrassment.

They passed the sheriff's office just as a big man with a star on his chest walked out. He watched them drive by. Mrs. Thackson pulled to a stop in front of the mercantile.

Bull stood and tried to maneuver his way off the

wagon. He wanted to help the lady, but his bones screamed in protest at his own descent.

The sheriff appeared, a big smile on his face for Mrs. Thackson, and helped her down. The man grew in Bull's esteem. Here was a self-assured man.

"Thank you, Sheriff."

"You're welcome, ma'am."

He turned his attention to Bull. Piercing eyes studied him from the toes of his new boots to his brown felt hat. "Don't believe we've met, mister."

Bull extended his hand. "Buford Dawson from New York City, Sheriff. I'm here to see my daughter, Charity Dawson Reardon."

Brows furrowed, the sheriff scratched his chin. "You don't say."

"Mr. Dawson, I'll be about my business," said Mrs. Thackson. "Will a couple of hours give you time to tend to your business in town?"

"Yes. Thank you. I'll be ready."

She nodded and walked into the mercantile.

The sheriff clapped him on the shoulder. "Come over to the office. I have some questions for you."

"Sure, let me get my rifle."

"It'll be safe where it sets. Folks respect others' property in Prairie." He turned and strode down the sidewalk. Bull hurried to catch up.

Inside, a tall, dark-headed man came through the lockup area. Sheriff Cannon chuckled. "Hey, Cole, look who's here. Charity's daddy." He slapped his leg. "Haw-haw-haw. Got us another time traveler."

Bull stopped in his tracks. They knew? He'd wondered how Charity and Dessa explained their sudden appearances.

Cole also had a star on his chest. A smile split his handsome face as he strode forward, hand outstretched. "Pleased to meet you, Mr. Dawson. I'm Marshal Cole Jeffers, Dessa's husband."

"You mean those two girls told you about their experiences and you didn't think they were crazy?"

"'Course we thought they were nuts." He shrugged. "Things happened, making us believe them."

"Elijah, I'm going over to the newspaper office to get Dessa. She'd have my hide if I left her out of this meeting." He turned to Bull. "Don't say a word until I get back."

"All right."

Sheriff Cannon waved at a chair against the wall and sat down behind his desk. "Pull up a seat, Mr. Dawson."

Bull pulled the chair closer to the desk. "Call me Bull. My name is Buford, but I acquired the nickname in college."

"It fits you." He grinned. "Fits your grandson, too, but they call him Dawson. He's one little determined kid. Don't take 'no' quietly."

"I expect he got that from his mama. She was a terror for a few years there."

The door flew open, hitting the wall. Bull turned in his chair to see Dessa Wade. Her short, dark, spiky hair had grown to shoulder length, and her yellow dress emphasized her brown eyes and beautiful complexion. Her mouth gaped open as she stared at him. Bull stood and opened his arms. She flew into them.

"I can't believe you're here." She pulled back and looked up into his face. Tears gleamed in her eyes. "Charity will be so happy to see you."

He hardly knew this young woman, but she'd given him a glimpse of his daughter's life in the past. From that glance, he'd planned his trip back in time to be with her and his grandson. He owed her and would be forever in her debt. She was now part of his family.

****

Before he knew what was happening, he was the proud owner of a sorrel mare, had several changes of clothes, including a black suit wrapped in brown paper, and gifts for Charity, Reardon, Aunt Ruby, and little Dawson. Cole had helped him pick out the horse and clothes. Dessa scoured the mercantile for just the right gifts for Bull to choose from, and they both escorted him to the bank to deposit his money. When he'd unloaded the gold from the vest, he felt light enough to fly. The banker shot Bull suspicious glances until Marshal Cole Jeffers assured him the gold was genuine and not stolen.

Bull stood just inside the mercantile door and waited for Mrs. Thackson to finish her transactions. He couldn't help but overhear her conversation with the proprietor.

"Mrs. Thackson, I'm sorry, but this is the last time we can let you purchase on credit. We have to pay our bills."

"I understand. I thank you for your kindness to me. The sale of Mr. Thackson's land will pay my bill and see me through the winter."

The older woman patted Mrs. Thackson's hand and smiled. "You're more than welcome, dear. I hope your property sells soon."

Bull held the door as she strode through it and offered him a nod. Her cheeks were flushed. Most likely discussing her financial business with others in earshot embarrassed her.

"Is there anything I can load for you, Mrs. Thackson?"

"No."

He rushed to help her up. She stared at his hand a moment, then took it and let him help her into the wagon. "If you don't mind, I'll ride the horse Marshal Jeffers helped me select."

She eyed the sorrel. "A nice animal, Mr. Dawson."

"She has a nice, easy gait. A lot more comfortable than that wagon seat."

Her lips twitched as she tried to hide her grin. "I 'spect so, Mr. Dawson." The expression transformed her face. It had been lovely before, but with her eyes sparkling with humor, she was beautiful.

His admiration must have caused discomfort. The smile wilted. She turned away, released the brake on the wagon, and flicked the reins. "Gee, boys."

Bull watched in fascination as the mules made a tight left turn.

"Walk on."

The pair of animals pulled the wagon out into the traffic on the road out of town. Bull followed behind until they got outside of town. The used saddle he'd purchased cupped his buttocks comfortably, but it would take lots of riding before his backside fully adjusted. Plus, his anatomy still ached from the earlier wagon ride.

At the outskirts of town, he eased up beside her. The clomping of the mules and the movement of the wagon made a terrible racket. How he'd slept through their approach this morning, he didn't have a clue. He spoke loudly to be heard. "I hear you have some land to sell."

"Yes, one hundred acres."

"Where is it located?"

"It is a strip between Mr. Thackson's land and the Reardons' ranch." She leaned forward and called, "Trot on, boys." The mules increased their speed and further talk ended.

Bull studied the landscape as he rode. Belle, his horse, did indeed have a nice gait. He was able to quickly adjust to her movements. The terrain changed the farther they were from town. It was rougher, with less grassland. To the far right, trees dotted hills. To the left, the wheat field went on for miles.

Some miles outside of town he noticed a cabin far down a road to the right. It was a neat place with a large barn. A dog barked in the distance but didn't leave his post near the house.

"Whose place is that?"

"Dessa and Cole Jeffers. They bought it from Charity." She chuckled. "You'll have to ask her to tell you the cabin's history."

"I'll do that." He wanted to know everything about her arrival in Prairie.

An hour or so later, Mrs. Thackson pulled the wagon to a stop by the Reardons' ranch entrance.

His heart lurched to his throat. In a few minutes he'd be seeing his daughter. It'd been four long years, in which he'd thought never to see her again. Losing her had almost killed him, especially since he'd known for years she'd disappear. To be able to join her meant everything to him. Charity's mother had died shortly after Charity's birth. To lose both of them was unthinkable.

"Just follow the road. You can't miss the house. It's a big one."

"I can manage, but I'd like to talk to you about your land. I need a place of my own. If Turner thinks it's a good investment for me, I'll be over to talk with Mr. Thackson in a day or two."

"Mr. Thackson died two years ago. Have Turner bring you over. If you like the property, the land agent in town will take care of the details."

"I'm sorry for your loss. Thank you for your assistance today."

She nodded. "Tell the Reardons hello. I must get home to my son."

Before he could reply, the mules had broken into a trot and were leaving dust in their wake.

A widow, huh? With a son. No wonder she was in debt. He'd buy her land whether it was any good or not. He nudged Belle into a trot. He snorted at the horse's name. Not a very manly name for a man's horse, but hey, the transportation was good.

As dust flew up behind him, his attention focused on his future—his daughter and grandchild were at the end of this road.

Chapter Three

Dipsey pulled the wagon into the barn. Her son, Joshua, stepped from a stall and helped her down. Before she could speak, he turned away and started unhitching the mules. He kept his head down, his straight brown hair falling forward to cover his face, a sure sign he'd been fighting at school again. She sighed, her heart sagging. He fought because of her. Most of the womenfolk who knew her history shunned her, but they weren't cruel. Though the men might have been nicer, they dared not for fear of their wives' reprisal. Only one man despised her with a vengeance and wouldn't let her forget. That hate only grew stronger when she'd married Mr. Thackson.

Maybe she shouldn't have married Thomas, but then she'd not have Joshua. He was the one joy in her life. She sighed. When her husband had been alive, life had been simple. He took care of business and she rarely went to town. Of course, the townsfolk knew he'd taken a soiled dove to wife, but they didn't have the guts to talk about her to his face. He'd beaten more than one man for making crude remarks. A few showed kindness—Sheriff Cannon and his wife, the Jefferses, and the Reardons. Why this was so, she didn't know. Perhaps the lawmen could see the failings of their own people. Maybe their Christian beliefs encouraged forgiveness.

There was something different about Mrs. Reardon and Mrs. Jeffers. Everything about them spoke to a mysterious presence. Much like the aura she'd felt around Mr. Dawson. The man puzzled her. How had he made it to her field without passing her house?

She wanted to go to her son and smooth away his hurts, but her attention wouldn't be welcome. He rebuffed her shows of affection. He'd become a man too soon. She missed the little boy he'd been. All the rejection she faced in town couldn't take away the joy she'd found in being a wife and mother.

Dipsey unloaded the supplies she needed in the house and carried what she could. Joshua would bring in the remainder when he came in.

"Supper will be ready shortly. Remember to wash up."

"Yes, Ma."

****

Charity lived in a large white farmhouse with a wraparound porch. Several dogs barked in the yard. *Guess no one can slip in unnoticed.* A man, Turner Reardon, Bull suspected, stepped out onto the porch, a shotgun propped on his hip. Bull couldn't see his face until he stopped on the top step. The setting sun cast him in yellow light. Tall, his son-in-law appeared relaxed, yet Bull knew without a doubt Turner Reardon could turn deadly in an instant, a fact evident in his stance, the way he held the gun, and the eyes that took in every detail. He presented a sturdy, resolved front. Bull instantly liked the man who protected his home and family.

Bull saw activity at the windows. Did his daughter hold a gun on him too? The idea made him chuckle. No doubt she'd picked up life here just fine.

He removed his hat. Now that he'd arrived, he wasn't sure what to say. When had he ever been at a loss for words? Never. *Get on with it, Bull.* "Mr. Reardon, I'm Bull Dawson, Charity's father. I've come to see her and my grandson. Course, I'm pleased to meet you, too."

Turner stepped off the porch and walked toward him. Bull stepped down from the horse and bent his legs a couple of times to ease his aching muscles. The younger man looked him over, and then grinned.

He slapped Bull on the shoulder. "Howdy, Mr. Dawson." He transferred his gun to his left hand and used his right to shake Bull's outstretched hand. His dark blue eyes shot shards of steel gray. "You can't take her back with you. She has a life here now."

"Never. I've seen how happy she is. I'm staying here with you guys. I want to be part of my grandson's life."

Turner nodded. "Well, then, I 'spect we best let Charity know you're here." He turned and hollered into the house. "Charity, put that rifle down and come on out. We've got company."

The door opened and Charity stepped out. She stopped on the top step. A long blue dress protected by a white bib apron brought out the blue of her eyes. They crackled with curiosity. Her hair had grown, and she'd piled it up on top of her head. "Who is it, Turner?"

Turner held out a hand to her. "Come see for yourself. He's come a long way to see you and make Bull's acquaintance."

She smiled and started toward them. Halfway there, she stopped. Her hand went to her throat.

"Daddy?"

Bull opened his arms.

She squealed, "Daddy," and ran into his embrace.

****

Bull sat in the rocker, his grandson sound asleep against his chest, the soft rhythm he'd set comforting to both Bull and the boy. Without a fearful bone in his body, the child had launched himself at Bull and squeezed him around the neck. By dinner time Bull had become "Gampa."

"Mercy me, Buford, how many more folks you think we need to expect from that cabin in Fredericksburg?" Ruby, Turner's aunt, had difficulty calling him Bull, so he guessed he'd have to answer to Buford around her.

"None." He turned to his daughter. "I bought the cabin, its contents, and the land. The house will be dismantled, the land cleared, and a large pond built. Your great-great-great-grandson Jacob Reardon took over the firm for me, honey. He's taking care of everything in Fredericksburg."

Charity grabbed Turner's hand. "A descendant of ours?" Turner put his arm around her. "Oh, Turner! Imagine."

"Bound to happen, sweetheart." He grinned and winked. "After all, we've got a second baby on the way."

She swatted at him. "You're not supposed to tell, yet."

"Bull won't tell anyone."

Bull's heart swelled with thankfulness. Charity was happy. She'd married a good man, and now they had another child on the way. He'd made the right decision to locate them.

He noticed the quilt he'd carried in, lying where he'd left it across the back of a chair, and nodded toward it. "That's the only item I brought from the cabin. Well, other than my clothes, rifle, and knife. The weapons are vintage, supposed to be authentic to 1892."

His daughter's brows drew together in thought. She ran her hand over the beautiful quilt. "You know...Dessa and I had quilts with us, too." She turned to her husband. "Do you think the quilts might be significant, have something to do with our time traveling?"

Reardon shook his head. "I don't think so. Remember, Cole traveled forward without one. 'Pears to me it's that mist ya'll have mentioned."

"Whew! Had me worried there for a minute." The baby squirmed against Buford's chest. Oops, he'd stopped rocking. He pushed against the floor with his foot and set the rocker in motion again. "That cabin was filled with old quilts. I suppose Jacob will either sell or donate them to charities for auctions."

Charity stood and, for the second time, bent over the chair to take Dawson. Bull hadn't been ready to give him up earlier. "I've got to take him, Daddy." She smoothed her hand over the baby's back. "He'll be spoiled rotten and want you to rock him every night."

Buford sighed. "Yeah, I know. He's kin to his mother."

"Let me take him, honey." Turner carefully lifted Dawson into his arms. The baby fussed for a second and then snuggled against his father's neck. "Sit here and visit a while longer."

"I'll be up in a minute."

"No rush."

She sat on the settee and Buford moved from the rocker to join her. "I'm sorry I tied you to New York, Charity. You tried to break away several times, but you see, I knew what would happen if I let you go, that you'd travel back in time. The book you sent me, informing what happened to you, I accidently found when you were just a child."

****

Dipsey strained the milk into the crockery jug, then covered the jar with a fresh dishtowel and carried it outside, across the back yard, and to the spring house. Inside, she set it on a shelf and placed the cold metal lid on top to keep out rodents and bugs.

Her breath misted in the chilly air. Snow clouds dotted the sky. She dreaded the heavy blanket of white that often covered the plains in winter. It made her work harder, hers and Joshua's. She worried about her son on his travels to and from school. He carried a heavy burden for one so young. Each morning he milked the cows and gathered eggs before mucking out the stalls and laying fresh hay. If not for the bullies at school, his studies were a joy for him. He was smart. If only she could find the money to send him to college, but they did well to eat and feed their animals. He rode his horse to school each day. She smiled at the picture Joshua presented atop the paint his father had given him on his twelfth birthday. With Joshua bent over the horse's neck, they moved as one, graceful like the wind brushing past the prairie grass.

An hour later, her chores done in the house, she strode to the barn to saddle her horse, Mazie. She rolled fence posts and a shovel in a tarp before attaching it behind the mare's saddle. With wire cutters, a hammer, and nails stowed in her saddlebags, she mounted the horse and rode west toward the Reardons' place. Her fences along their joint property line needed mending. Turner usually took care of them, but she wanted to do her share.

She was tired of trying to take care of this place by herself, but she couldn't quit. It was Joshua's legacy, and she had to preserve it for his future. If only she had the money to hire help. But she didn't, so no need to fret over it. She'd learned to take one day at a time. 'Twas the only way to survive.

Her field of wheat didn't cover near the acreage Reardon's did, but what she had in the ground thrived. Thank goodness. She and Joshua had tilled the land and planted it themselves. It'd been hard work. Every year since Thomas's passing some of Reardon's hands showed up at harvest time to help out. They were a godsend.

Two riders appeared in the distance. She withdrew her rifle from its scabbard and laid it across her lap. Most likely some of Reardon's men, but it never hurt to be careful. She squinted against the sun. Why, it was Turner Reardon and Mr. Dawson. Looked like the older man had made it to his daughter's just fine. After his rough ride on the buckboard and then on the horse, she wasn't sure how he'd manage. She grinned. It was obvious the man hadn't been born to the saddle as most folks around here were. A New York City man. Most likely he rode around in a carriage.

"Howdy, Dipsey." Turner waved as they neared.

"Hello, Turner, Mr. Dawson. What're you gentlemen doing out this way?"

"Good morning, Mrs. Thackson." Mr. Dawson was wearing some of his new clothes. He shoved the hat back on his head, his grin crinkling the skin around his eyes. "We've come to take a look at the land you have for sale. Since I'm from the city, Turner here will advise me."

"Well, if you decide you want it, the agent in town can handle everything." *Please, Lord, I pray he buys the land.* She shoved the rifle back into its scabbard. "I'd invite you up to the house for a cup of coffee, but I have a lot of work to do today."

"Charity said to tell you hello and to invite you and Joshua to church and Sunday dinner with us." Turner and Charity wouldn't give up on getting her to church with them. They asked her about once a month. Didn't they understand how she felt when people stared at her scar and snubbed her?

"My thanks for the invite, but we'll be busy doing chores during church. We'll be at your place by lunchtime. Joshua wouldn't forgive me if we missed one of Ruby's meals."

"I could send a couple of men over to help, Dipsey."

"I'll not be going to church, Turner. You know my feelings on the subject." Before he could respond, she turned her mare and kicked her into a trot. She waved and hollered, "See you Sunday."

****

Turner's scowl voiced his displeasure. Evidently he didn't approve of Mrs. Thackson's decision to not attend church. Bull hadn't attended much in his lifetime, but believed in the old adage, "When in Rome, do as the Romans do." If the Reardons attended church, then Bull needed to do the same. It'd be good for him to get on a better footing with his Maker.

"What does Mrs. Thackson have against the church?"

Turner turned his head and spat, the spittle hitting the leaves of Mrs. Thackson's wheat. "It's them damn fool old biddies in town. They won't welcome her, nor will some of the men. She was a prostitute before Thomas Thackson married her." He shook his head in disgust. "She's one of the most honorable women I know. Yes, she sold herself, but I believe when a person tries to change, they should be given the chance."

Bull agreed. She seemed a nice lady, one who worked hard to provide for herself and her son. He'd seen the way people treated her in Prairie. "How'd she get the scar?"

"A drunken customer thought he'd carve her up. He was found dead a couple of days later." Turner scratched his chin. "I've always wondered if it wasn't Thomas Thackson that killed him. Not long after, he married Dipsey and took her to his farm."

"She's a beautiful woman."

"You takin' a shine to our neighbor, Bull?"

"Maybe. Would anyone object?"

"Nobody I know. Charity would be tickled pink."

As they rode over the land for sale, Bull made up his mind. Turner assured him the land was a good investment. The location was perfect. He could ride over and see his grandchildren every day if he wanted.

Bull made another decision. As soon as he finalized the purchase of Mrs. Thackson's land, he'd be courting the widow lady.

Chapter Four

Bull chuckled as he walked from the land agent's office. The man had stuttered and hemmed and hawed when Bull said he'd be paying five dollars an acre rather than the two dollars Mrs. Thackson had asked. He could afford to be generous. Now the lady would have some of the money she needed and Bull would have a plot of land. He rode out of town with a sense of accomplishment lightening his mood.

Shouts off to his right drew his attention. A group of boys were huddled around two kids fighting. The smaller kid, at least a foot shorter than his opponent, screamed, "You take that back, Billy Gifford." He barreled forward and head butted his opponent.

Billy laughed, grabbed the kid's long brown hair, and pulled him back, holding him at arm's length. "You just don't never learn, do you, Joshua. I told you to stay away from school. We don't want your kind here." Then his large fist hit the kid in the mouth. Blood spurted as the smaller boy stumbled back, landing on his butt.

Bull looked around. Would no one step in and stop them, at least to keep the smaller kid from being beaten to a pulp? Their teacher stood at a window of the schoolhouse, watching and doing nothing. Heat rose in Bull's face. He kicked the mare into a trot and pulled her up in the middle of the group crowded around the fight.

A young girl tugged on Billy's arm, and screamed, "Stop it! You're hurtin' him bad."

Billy shoved her to the ground, growling, "Get outta the way, Beth," and yanked the kid up and pummeled him again.

Bull jumped off the horse. "Stop it."

The smaller boy was almost unconscious, and the bigger kid kept punching. Bull grabbed Billy by the scruff of his shirt and shook. "I said, stop it!"

Billy tried to break free, but Bull didn't let go.

"You're not my pa."

"No, I'm not, or you'd not be beating up on someone smaller than you. That's a coward's way of doing things."

The prissy teacher rushed out the door. "What's going on out here?"

Bull rounded on the scrawny man in the ill-fitting black suit but kept a firm grip on the kid. "You know exactly what, mister." He nodded toward the schoolhouse. "I saw you watching from the window and not doing a thing. Get over there and tend to that boy, and if he's seriously injured you'll be held responsible."

The man's mouth opened and closed like a fish's, but no words escaped. He rushed to the boy, dropped to the dirt, and tore off a piece of the kid's shirt to wipe away the blood.

Beth, probably ten years old, wiped tears away with the sleeve of her dress. As she looked down at the fallen boy, her fragile shoulders shook. Bull touched her gently on the back with his free hand. "Do you think you could get some water to help clean him up?"

She nodded and rushed to the well beside the school.

Bull directed his attention back to his hostage. Before he could say anything, he was grabbed from behind, loosening his hold on the boy, and whirled around. "Get your hands off my boy."

"You his father?"

"Sure am. Name's Brodie Gifford." A barrel of a man, he didn't boast an ounce of fat and stood several inches taller than Bull. An abundance of long dark hair stuck out from beneath his worn, limp, suede hat.

Bull released the boy. Billy smirked and puffed out his chest as he moved to stand beside his father. "Happy to know you're here to reprimand him for beating up kids smaller than him."

Brodie Gifford snorted. "That Thackson kid had it coming. He ain't nothing but a whore's son. Shouldn't be here with the children of decent folk."

How dare he talk about Mrs. Thackson that way? Bull hissed. "And I suppose you consider yourself decent folk."

Gifford threw out his chest and growled, "You saying I ain't?"

"I might be."

Brodie studied Bull from his new boots to his hat and chuckled. "What's your name, mister? Where you from? I like to know the name of folks I whip, 'specially when they talk all fancified, like you."

"Bull Dawson from New York City."

Gifford spit a stream of tobacco. He patted his son on the back and grinned. "Move out of the way and watch how it's done, son. I'm gonna clobber this Yankee feller."

Bull positioned himself with one foot in front of the other for balance, both fists at the ready in front of his face.

Brodie stared, then threw back his head and guffawed. "Ain't that a sight, Billy? We got us one of them pugilists."

"Sure is, Pa. You can take him, though, can't ya?"

Gifford snorted. "Ever seen a man that could whip me, boy?"

"No, sir, don't reckon I have."

"Quit your stalling, Brodie, and get on with it. I've things to do this afternoon."

Brodie's brows drew together in a menacing frown. He rushed Bull and swung. Bull ducked. The miss angered Gifford. He swung again and again, Bull easily stepping out of the range of his fists. Bull popped him three times in the face in rapid succession. Furious now, Brodie howled and charged. Bull put more force into his swing and hit Gifford hard, twice, once in the nose and once on the jaw. Blood spurted, and Brodie fell to the ground, stunned. He struggled to rise.

"Stay down, Gifford."

Bull turned to find Sheriff Cannon taking in the situation. He fixed Bull with a glare. "Not in town two days and already in trouble fighting. Can't have that, Mr. Dawson, no-sir-ree."

Bull couldn't think of a suitable comment so kept his mouth shut. He'd not been in a street fight since a young teen. His behavior today shocked him.

The sheriff's gaze traveled from the boy rising from the ground to Billy. "So, Billy, I see you didn't heed my advice. Been picking on the younger kids again, or is it just Joshua Thackson you like to torment?"

Billy's chin jutted out and muttered, "Joshua started it, Sheriff."

"That's a lie, Billy Gifford." Beth's blond pigtails bounced as she shook her fists. "You're mean. You're a bully." She turned to Cannon. "He scares all the little kids, Sheriff. Calls Joshua's mama a 'hor.'"

Joshua blushed scarlet. He laid a hand on the girl's shoulder. "It's okay, Beth." He shot Billy a glare. "One day I won't be smaller than you."

Billy smirked. "If you live that long."

Sheriff Cannon whirled. "Shut up, you two." His expression brooked no argument. "I've had it with you, Billy. Next time you take your fists to someone smaller than you, I'm locking you up for a week."

He kicked Brodie's booted foot. "Get up, Brodie. If Joshua needs to see Doc, you be prepared to pay his bill." Eyes narrowed, his gaze swung between Brodie and Bull. "And if I catch you two fighting again, you can spend a night in jail as cell mates."

"Well, prepare a cell, because if Mr. Gifford here slanders Mrs. Thackson again, I'll be cleaning his clock." Bull didn't like Gifford and especially resented his allowing his son to bully her son.

"Best keep your threats to yourself, Mr. Dawson." The sheriff's eyes landed on Gifford. "I'll be taking Mr. Gifford to task for his mistreatment of the Thacksons."

Brodie ignored the comment and dusted off his pants. "Ain't right for me to pay for the boy's doctoring. It's his ma's responsibility."

"'Pears to me it ain't right for your son to beat up kids, either." He lifted Joshua's face and looked at the bruises. "You okay, boy? Dizzy or anything?"

"I'm fine, Sheriff. I just wanna go home."

"Good, good, but I'd feel better if you'd let Mr. Dawson ride along partways with you to the Reardons' cutoff. He's new here and might get lost."

The boy eyed Bull, then seemed to make up his mind and nodded. "I'll get my horse and be right back, mister."

"No hurry. I'd like to have a little word with the schoolteacher before we leave."

"Glad that's settled. I feel better the boy won't be alone." Cannon grinned and nodded to the nervous schoolteacher. "You'll keep your fists to yourself while speaking with Mr. Turnbo there."

"Violence won't be necessary." Bull approached the teacher, who stuck out his hand.

"Pleased to meet you Mr. Dawson. Name's Otto Turnbo."

Bull ignored the offered hand. Voice low, he bit out, "If I ever see or hear of you ignoring a fight again and allowing a child to be beaten in that manner, you'll be getting a taste of my fist."

****

The ride across to the Reardons' place took only thirty minutes when the horses moved at a trot, a pace the yeast bread she'd prepared could handle. Dipsey rode alongside Joshua. He always enjoyed visits to their neighbors, but today he seemed particularly anxious to arrive. Perhaps it had to do with anticipation of seeing Mr. Dawson again. Dipsey's heart rose to her throat, tears threatening to choke her. Mr. Dawson's defense of Joshua affected her like nothing else had in a long time. Her boy needed a man's interest.

She hated violence, but the news that Brodie

Gifford had gotten his comeuppance filled her with satisfaction. He needed to be taken down a peg or two. Who would have known Mr. Dawson would be the one to do it? Gifford's slanderous words hurt her, but not near as much as his son's mistreatment of Joshua. She'd be forever grateful to Mr. Dawson. She'd sensed him to be a good man; now he'd proved it.

She still reeled over the price he'd given her for her land. Five dollars an acre when she'd only asked for two. His generosity alarmed her. Was he possibly hoping for something in return? She'd never go back to her old ways, and the idea that Mr. Dawson wanted personal favors of that kind from her didn't sit well. She'd get him alone for a talk today and try to return the additional money. She didn't want to be in his debt.

Would she ever be free of her past? Maybe in time the community wouldn't continue to shun her, but she feared Gifford's hate would only die with her death. The scar on her forehead throbbed, and she resisted the urge to rub it. The horrors of that night often visited her in the night. Lance Gifford had hit her again and again. Then he'd pulled out his knife. Her screams had brought help before he added more scars to her face. The next night Lance had been found dead in the alley behind the house where she worked. Dipsey suspected Thomas had killed him, but he'd never admitted it to her. In truth, she didn't care who did it, but Brodie Gifford, Lance's brother, did.

Chapter Five

"Mi...ghty...good pie...Miss Ruby."

"Joshua, don't talk with your mouth full." Dipsey tried to keep a straight face. Her son was on his second piece of apple pie. Ruby always baked two when they came over, because she knew how much the boy liked them. For some reason Dipsey's pies never turned out as good as the older woman's. Maybe when she was her age they would.

He wiped his mouth on a napkin and bowed his head. "Sorry, Ma."

His look of contrition didn't fool Dipsey. He was too excited to be sorry. Normally his manners were good, but when Mr. Dawson and Turner mentioned teaching him to fight, he'd turned downright boisterous. Guilt nagged at her conscience. She should've thought about getting Turner or another man involved in the boy's dilemma sooner. Not that she approved of fisticuffs, but he needed to be able to defend himself.

Another man? What man did she have to call on if need be? Yes, Sheriff Cannon and Marshal Jeffers would help her, as well as Turner, but that was it. She glanced at Mr. Dawson. He'd asked her to call him Bull, but she hadn't been able to lower her defenses yet. To her, he was still Mr. Dawson. Maybe after she knew him a little better she could drop the surname. He called her by her given name and grinned every time he said it. She didn't take offense. He wasn't poking fun at her, but for some reason her name appeared to tickle him. It was unusual. She'd inherited it from her great-grandmother, who'd acquired it as a nickname because she dipped snuff.

"I'm glad you enjoyed it, Joshua. If we can keep these two men from eating a third slice, there'll be some to take home with you."

Young Dawson waved his hands, slinging apple bits on his mother, and yelled, "Me pie, too, Josa."

Charity laughed. "Hey, squirt, let's clean your hands."

He pushed out his lip. "Me no squt."

Joshua leaned over and tickled his chin. "Yes, you are."

Dawson howled and wiggled. "Down. Play with Josa."

"If you're finished, will you take him for a minute, Joshua?"

"Yes, ma'am." He waited while Charity cleaned the squirming baby and then lifted him down. Joshua took his hand. "Let's go find your rocking horse."

Charity smiled at her. "He's a good boy, Dipsey."

Turner rubbed his full belly and added, "His daddy would be proud of him."

She nodded. "I appreciate you and Mr. Dawson taking him under your wing like this."

"If I'd known he was having this much trouble, I'd have seen to it sooner." He stood and clapped Bull on the shoulder. "Just glad we know about it now." He chuckled. "Sure wish I could have seen Brodie get a dose of his own medicine."

"Daddy, I never knew you to be a violent man, one

to get into fights."

He pushed his chair back and stood. "Well, honey, you didn't know me back in my younger days. I didn't go to private school in New York like you did. I was around some pretty tough customers, and I had to learn to fight to survive. In college, I took boxing and ended up on the team."

Dipsey didn't know what a boxer was supposed to look like, but she suspected Mr. Dawson packed more than a few muscles, even if he was creeping up on sixty. She eyed his broad chest and shoulders. He glanced her way, and she started and flushed at being caught studying him before she averted her eyes. But as she stood and started gathering dishes, her thoughts remained on him. *No doubt, there's more to the man than meets the eye.*

"Why didn't I know that? Have you been going to the gym, sparring all these years?" Charity asked.

"How'd you think I kept my weight down?" He patted his thick waist. "Not that I couldn't afford to lose more."

Though he was thickset, Dipsey didn't consider him fat. The man was solidly built. Her Thomas had been tall and lean, sometimes on the bony side. She liked a little flesh on men.

Turner called from the kitchen. "Come on, Bull. The boy's chomping at the bit to get started."

****

Bull asked Ruby to sew two canvas bags in preparation for Joshua's training. She had one of those Singer treadle sewing machines, and with one leg rocking, she sewed the bags in no time at all. He and Turner had filled one with dirt, pulled the top together with twine, and hung it from a rafter in the barn.

Turner stood to the side, grinning like a jackass, as Bull demonstrated bouncing and stepping on the balls of his feet. "You need to move fast, son, and stay out of the reach of your opponent's fists."

"Looks mighty sissified, if you ask me," muttered Turner. "Just duck when you need to, take aim when you get the chance, and swing."

Bull couldn't resist a challenge. He faced Turner, and, fists up, bounced from foot to foot. "Come on, let's see if my technique is worth learning."

"You're on, old man." Turner shrugged out of his jacket and tossed it across a hay bale.

Bull couldn't resist a snort. The "old man" comment didn't sit well with him. He didn't like to be reminded he was beginning a new life so late in years. He'd just have to make the best of the time he had left.

He posed in front of Turner, fists up. Turner smirked and swung. Five minutes later, Turner still hadn't landed a blow. Turner's temper flared, his eyes narrowed with determination as he planned his strategy. *Best to put an end to this before one of us gets bloody.* Bull popped Turner in the nose, trying not to use too much force. Charity would have his hide if he messed up her husband's pretty face.

Turner growled and swung. Bull blocked the blow and shouted, "Enough. I don't doubt you're a worthy opponent, Turner, in a fight with your peers. If you learned a few boxing moves, you'd be deadly." He nodded toward Joshua. The boy stood wide-eyed, waiting to see what happened next. "Joshua doesn't have the brawn yet, so he needs the technique to stay out of Billy's way, let him wear out, and hopefully get in a few good licks. You're strong enough and smart enough to take out probably any man in a fight. The boy doesn't have that advantage yet."

Chest heaving, Turner nodded. "I concede your point, but it's damned embarrassing—getting whipped by an old man." He laughed and slapped Joshua on the back. "I'm going to tell Charity you popped me in the nose, son. Can't have her thinking her old man whipped her husband."

Joshua frowned. "What about Ma? She'll whup me for sure, Turner. Can't we tell her you fell?"

"He's pulling your leg, Joshua." Bull looked closer at Turner's nose. "It's not swelling too badly. Maybe Charity won't notice. If she does, I'll take the heat."

"Take the heat?" Joshua looked at Turner.

He clapped him on the back. "It means take the blame. He and Charity are from New York. They have some strange expressions."

"Turner, if you don't mind, I'd like to talk to Joshua alone for a minute."

Turner cocked a brow. "Sure. If that's all right with Joshua."

The boy shrugged. "I guess so."

Bull waited until Turner closed the barn door. He motioned to a hay bale. "Have a seat. This won't take long."

Joshua sat, brow furrowed.

"I realize you're the man of the house now that your father is gone."

The boy sat up straighter; his chest expanded slightly.

"I admire your mother and would like your permission to court her."

Joshua jumped up, hands fisted. "My ma is a good woman. Don't be thinkin'—"

"Whoa. I assure you my intentions are honorable and include marriage, if she'll have me." He rubbed the back of his neck. "She's not very receptive to me. I think it's because the townsfolk don't accept her, something I intend to change." He intended to talk to the new preacher about the situation. He wasn't a church-going man, but he knew enough about the Bible to know the congregation wasn't following its teachings.

"You better not hurt her."

Bull's heart twisted. This child had seen a world of hurt in his short life. Yet he shouldered it well, and his defense of his mother was admirable. Bull cared for Joshua and would like to be a father to him. The thought of teaching him how to be a man appealed to him. Heck, the boy would probably have to teach Bull how to do many things.

"I promise not to hurt her, but you're going to have to help me out and not let her take a gun to me when I come calling. Think you can do that?" Bull put his hand out.

Joshua took it and grinned. "Yeah."

Chapter Six

Dipsey pulled her buckboard in line with the others. "Whoa, boys." She set the brake and hopped down from the wagon. The house-raising was well under way.

The sounds of hammers hitting nails and men shouting directions and jests to each other echoed through the area. Children played chase in a cleared-off area, while babies crawled on quilts under the watchful eyes of a few older girls. The big oak tree thirty feet in front of where Bull Dawson had chosen to erect his house provided just enough shade to protect the little ones from the sun.

She spotted Joshua carrying a bucket of nails for refills for the men's bib pockets. Bull clapped him on the shoulder, said something to him, and nodded in her direction. Joshua waved and hollered, "Be there in a minute, Ma."

Dipsey nodded and returned her son's greeting.

On Sunday she'd caught Bull alone to talk about the price of her land. Offended she'd think his generous offer carried strings, he'd assured her it didn't. "But why pay more, Mr. Dawson?"

"Because I have more than enough money to be generous when I so chose. Plus, I happen to know land will increase in value soon."

How on earth could he know that? She studied him

and again noted how different he was from the men around Prairie. It must have to do with being from New York.

Bull saw her watching them, smiled, and waved. The man had been attentive the last several weeks, but she didn't want to encourage him. She didn't want to be rude, either, so she nodded and directed her attention to the women.

A middle-aged woman, one she'd not seen before, broke away from the group of ladies bustling back and forth, carrying drinks to the men and food to the makeshift table of boards atop sawhorses.

"Hello. Mrs. Thackson, isn't it?"

Dipsey stiffened. The women at these gatherings never approached her.

"Yes."

The lady extended her hand. "I'm Mrs. Booker."

Dipsey placed her hand in Mrs. Booker's, confused by the woman's friendliness.

"My husband is the new pastor in town."

"Oh, my, Mrs..." Dipsey tried to pull her hand away, but Mrs. Booker held tight and patted it gently.

"Now, now, I know what you're thinking." She frowned and turned to glance at the other women, who quickly looked away. "My husband got wind of the way the townsfolk have been treating you and your boy. He won't have his parishioners behaving in such an unchristian manner, no sir-ree. Gave them the sermon on 'casting the first stone' on Sunday."

She embraced Dipsey. Dipsey froze, but when the woman didn't release her, she relaxed and hugged her back. Tears gathered in her eyes, a lump rose in her throat, and though she struggled to say thank you—

anything—only a croak came out.

"Oh, here's that young son of yours." She released Dipsey and turned to Joshua. "Why don't you unhitch the mules for your ma, son. We'll get the food."

"Yes, ma'am." Concern etching his brow, Joshua glanced at Dipsey. She smiled and nodded. He grinned and rushed to do Mrs. Booker's bidding.

Mrs. Booker lifted Dipsey's basket of rolls while Dipsey took the fried chicken from the back of the wagon. "You've done a good job raising that boy. He and my son Aaron got acquainted last week in school. I think they'll be good friends."

Dipsey glanced at Joshua. He'd not mentioned having a friend. Come to think of it, he'd been happier this week, but she thought it had to do with Bull coming over, with their work in the barn. He'd not come home once with fresh bruises, either. Why hadn't she noticed? Was it because she'd been wrapped up in her own enjoyment of Bull's visits?

She found her voice and managed to say, "Joshua needs a friend."

"We all do, dear."

****

Bull picked the last morsel of meat off the chicken leg with his teeth and tossed the bone to the dog waiting patiently a few feet away. Seemed people in the nineteenth century didn't fear feeding their dogs chicken bones as they did in his time. Afraid they'd choke to death, he'd never given one to any of the dogs he'd had through the years. Table scraps were these animals' daily fare, supplemented with any critters they caught.

He rubbed his full belly. Dipsey sure knew how to

fry chicken, and her yeast rolls melted in his mouth. He watched her, from where he sat on the ground with several other men, and sipped his coffee. She smiled shyly when another woman spoke to her. Bull's heart twisted at the insecurity in her eyes, as if she expected them to change and shun her at any minute. She looked over and caught him watching her. He smiled and touched the brim of his hat. She flushed but returned his gesture. Elated, he winked. Her mouth dropped open. She snapped it shut and turned her back. He chuckled.

"How about a piece of my buttermilk pie, Mr. Dawson?" Mrs. Booker stood over him, brow raised.

"I'd love one." He held up his plate. She dropped a large slice on it. He took a bite. The buttery, creamy custard pleased his taste buds. "Mmmm, mmmm, this is delicious. My first taste of buttermilk pie."

She jerked her chin back. "Where're you from, Mr. Dawson?"

"New York," he said around a mouthful of the concoction.

"That explains it, then. I expect you're more used to fruit pies."

"Yes, ma'am."

She fisted her free hand on her hip. "I noticed you makin' eyes at Mrs. Thackson."

"She's an attractive woman and a good cook."

Mrs. Booker drew herself up to her full diminutive height and sniffed. "What are your intentions, Mr. Dawson? The woman has received enough poor treatment from folks around here." Agitated, her voice rose in volume. The men near him stopped talking. They tried to pretend disinterest, but Bull knew they were all ears. "The preacher and I'll not be having you showering her with dishonorable intentions."

"Don't worry, Mrs. Booker. I aim to convince the lady to marry me." He looked at each of the men. "And I'll not have any man treating her with anything but respect. Have I made myself clear?"

"'Spect so, Bull."

"Yep."

"I'm hearin' you."

Mrs. Booker's frown stretched into a delighted smile. The color in her pink cheeks deepened. "I'm pleased to hear it." She winked. "If you need some hints on courting the lady, come by the parsonage. Mr. Booker and I'll be happy to give you some pointers."

****

Bull stood in the twilight drinking a cup of coffee as he surveyed his new home. The mongrel dog who'd adopted him sat on his haunches at his side. A soft glow emanated from the front room, where he'd left a coal oil lamp burning. Its simplicity beckoned him, reminding him of his changed circumstances. The fact he'd traveled back in time still amazed him. Sure, there were inconveniences, but none outshone being with his daughter and her family. Life was good.

He'd considered trying to farm and raise cattle to make a living, but after spending some time with Turner and his men, he decided he was better suited to being a lawyer. He'd talked with Jonas Bailey, the lawyer Charity worked with, and he'd agreed to sponsor Bull while he read for the bar. Bull would take the exam in June. He didn't expect to have any difficulty passing, but he needed to brush up on laws pertaining to today, especially those in Texas.

Bull smiled with satisfaction. He was with his

daughter and grandchild, had a home, friends, and a potential job. Yes, life was good.

After the house-raising, it had taken him, Turner, and some of Turner's hands several days to add the finishing touches. A wide porch ran the full width of the house, complete with two rocking chairs for those nice evenings. From now on he'd be stargazing or reading a book. No more television for him. So far, he hadn't missed it.

He strode up the three steps, into the house, and closed the door behind him. His hand hovered over the lever lock on the door and then fell to his side. Old habits were hard to break. Turner had teased him about installing a door lock. Said the dog and his Winchester were the only security devices he needed.

The main room had dividers to separate the kitchen from the living room. Warmth from the wood cookstove located in the far back corner of the kitchen met him as he entered the room. He'd prepared a pot of coffee earlier and now poured himself another cup. He sipped the brew as he surveyed the room. The metal sink stood against the back wall, with wooden cabinets on either side. A hand pump was attached to one. The icebox sat near the back door, an extravagance for sure, but he wanted his home to be the best. The cupboard and sturdy long table finished off the area. The coal oil hanging lamp cast a warm glow on the polished oak. He turned the wick down until the flame went out. With a match, he lit the lantern sitting on the cabinet and then carried it with him into the living area.

His sofa faced the large fireplace, which had vents to also warm the master bedroom. On each side of the living area were two bedrooms—the master and one he hoped would be occupied by Joshua.

Tomorrow his courtship of Mrs. Thackson would officially begin.

Chapter Seven

Dipsey peered into the mirror and smoothed, for the third time, stray wisps of her blonde hair against her head. She'd pulled it back into a bun. Perhaps it was too severe a style for the occasion, but it fit her mood. With a finger, she traced the scar on her forehead. If only she could do something about the disfigurement, maybe she'd fit in with the rest of the women. Well, no use wishing about something that couldn't be helped. She plopped the bonnet on her head and tied the ribbons under her chin. It was her best one and went well with her only good dress—a navy-blue serge with white piping. She twisted her hands and then ran them down the skirt of her dress. Why had she agreed to allow Bull to pick them up? Because she didn't want to disappoint her son, that's why.

"Ma!" Joshua's voice vibrated through the bedroom door. Did he think she'd lost her hearing? "You ready? Mr. Dawson is here."

She drew in a deep breath to still her nerves and then opened the door. Bull stood in the living room, a gift box in his hands. He smiled and handed it to her.

Blood rushed to her face. Was the man courting her? She looked at her son. Did he mind? He didn't appear to, or maybe he didn't realize Mr. Dawson's intentions.

Joshua grinned. "Take it, Ma. See what's inside."

She took the box. "Thank you, Mr. Dawson."

"You promised to call me Bull."

"Yes, I did. I'll try to remember." Dipsey pulled the pink ribbon and the bow easily came undone. It would be perfect to dress up a bonnet or dress. She laid the box on the table and lifted the paper to reveal a label reading "French Chocolates." Oh, my, she loved sweets, and never in her life had she had a piece of chocolate candy, much less one from France. She lifted the lid to expose a dozen pieces.

Joshua bent over to get a closer look. "Wow, Ma. They're shaped like little hearts." He sent Bull an admiring glance. The man had the gall to wink. So he'd already talked to Joshua, and it appeared her son approved of Mr. Dawson's courting his ma.

She stifled a groan and prayed to drop through the floor. The heat in her face intensified. Her heart hammered against her chest. How did she feel about being courted? She was flattered, of course, but were his intentions honorable? Time would answer her question. Right now, Bull and Joshua waited for a response from her.

"They're beautiful, almost too pretty to eat."

"They'll spoil if you don't eat them." Bull chuckled. "Try one."

"Let's all try one, then." She lifted a piece and popped it into her mouth. When her teeth broke the chocolate shell, cherry crème oozed over her tongue. The sweet flavor exploded in her mouth, causing it to water at the sensation. She closed her eyes and groaned. Startled by the sound, she blinked and met Bull's amused gaze. "It's delicious."

He put a piece in his mouth and chewed slowly, his

gaze never leaving hers. "Indeed, it is."

"Can I have another piece, Ma?" Joshua's comment broke their gaze. Seeing his hopeful expression, Dipsey couldn't deny him the treat.

"One more, and then we'd best leave." She didn't want to be late arriving for church and have everyone turn to stare as they walked in.

Joshua snagged another piece. Dipsey put the cover on the box and carried it to the pie safe to store. She didn't intend to share with any mice or other vermin determined to taste the sweet concoction. Thank goodness it was winter, and she didn't have to deal with ants.

****

Bull held the door while Dipsey stepped out on the porch, and he closed it behind her. The near-indigo dress showed off her rounded figure and brought out the blue of her eyes. She was a beautiful woman. He'd like to see her hair down. Maybe he could get Charity to convince her to wear a less severe hairstyle.

He breathed a sigh of relief. His gift had been well received. Desire had shot through his body with her moan of pleasure at the taste of the chocolate.

Dipsey stared at Bull's new buggy. Her mouth rounded in surprise. Joshua ran ahead and whooped.

"Wow, Mr. Dawson. She's a beauty." He turned to his mother. "Ain't this fine, Ma?"

"Yes, son, it sure is. Bull, you're full of surprises today." She arched a brow. "I hope this is the last. Joshua might not be able to handle any more excitement."

Bull took her arm and guided her down the steps. "Well, I do have one more, if it meets with your approval."

She stopped walking. "What now, Mr. Dawson?"

"I thought we'd have dinner at the café after church. Then I'd like to show you and Joshua how I've fixed up my place."

"We'd love to see your home, but aren't Charity and Ruby expecting us for the noon meal at their place?"

He ushered her toward the buggy. Joshua already sat in the back, waiting for them. "That was our original plan. I hope you don't mind I made other arrangements."

She chewed her bottom lip. Bull hoped he hadn't pushed too far. Today was her first visit to church.

"I suppose that will be fine, but it seems an extravagance, a waste to pay for someone to cook our meal when Charity and Ruby have plenty."

"True, but I want today to be special for you."

She didn't respond, but ducked her head, either to avoid his comment or to ward off the cold breeze, and proceeded to the buggy. He held her arm as she stepped up into the carriage, and let her settle her skirts around her on the seat. "Hand me one of those blankets, Joshua." He'd brought along several to guard against the cold air. He shook one out over Dipsey's lap. "Wrap up back there, Joshua. It's pretty cold this morning."

He climbed into the driver's seat, slipped his gloves on, and clicked the reins. Belle broke into a gentle walk.

"Aren't you cold, Bull?"

"I'll be fine."

She spread part of her blanket over his knees. "We can share."

****

"Good morning, Bull, Dipsey." Turner slid down the pew and made room for them.

Charity smiled and reached for her hand. "I'm so glad you came."

Dipsey nodded and returned their greeting. Heads had turned when they entered; some peered at them and dipped their heads or smiled in welcome. Others merely looked, raised their noses in the air, and swiveled their heads back to face the dais. Not everyone forgave easily. She understood their hesitancy. Hopefully in time their attitude toward her would soften. At least they weren't putting their heads together to gossip. The tension eased from her back and neck somewhat as she settled in the pew.

"Ma, can I go sit with Aaron and his ma?"

She glanced toward the preacher's wife in the front pew. Mrs. Booker, her face alight with openness, motioned for Joshua to join them.

"Mind your manners, then." Her heart surged with joy that her son was welcomed by this gracious woman and accepted by her son. Billy Gifford sat two rows up with his parents and sister. His gaze followed Joshua's path, an expression of longing altering his usually brooding countenance. Her mother's heart twisted in pity for the boy. Brodie turned. His eyes met hers. She stiffened in preparation for a sneer, but instead he slightly tilted his head before turning back and placing his arm around his daughter.

"Are you all right?"

"I'm fine." She smiled at Bull, but lowered her eyes. "Thank you for talking me into coming to church today."

"You're welcome."

The service was long, but Dipsey drank in every word. Pastor Booker didn't shout or pound his Bible on the pulpit, but his eyes met those of his flock and held them as he made his points. The only sounds, other than his voice, were those of fretting babies, impatient children, and the quiet whispers of their parents. She glanced at Joshua. He too listened intently. Her heart swelled with gratitude for the arrival of the Bookers and their true Christian charity. She leaned against the arm behind her on the back of the pew. Perhaps some of her gratitude should go to Bull Dawson.

****

Before Bull drove the carriage into his yard, he noticed the horse tied to the hitching post out front.

"Wonder who's here?" Getting used to visitors making themselves at home in his house was hard for Bull to adjust to. He knew it wasn't uncommon for company to go inside and get comfortable to wait, but he didn't know anyone in the area other than the Reardons and the Jefferses. He'd never seen the bay before.

"You know that horse, Joshua?"

"No, sir."

"Hand me the Winchester." Joshua passed it to the front. Dipsey took the rifle and laid it across her lap. Bull pulled the buggy to a stop, handed the reins to Dipsey, and hopped down, taking the weapon as soon as he reached the ground. "Stay put until I see who it is. If there's trouble, I expect you to go to Turner's."

The expression on Dipsey's face said otherwise, but she nodded in agreement.

As Bull strode up the steps with the rifle cocked, he

tried to be quiet, but his boot heels rang against the wood. Not that it mattered. Surely whoever was inside had heard them drive up, but why hadn't they come out?

He opened the door and stepped inside.

A man sat on Bull's new horsehair sofa, his feet propped on the ottoman that matched the chair in the corner. Dressed in a black suit with a striped vest underneath, his arms were flung back and hugged the back of the couch. He smiled up at Bull.

"Howdy, mister. Sure is a nice place, ain't it?"

"Yes, I'm very proud of it. Who are you?"

The man unfolded his long-limbed length, stood, and offered his hand. "I'm Stephen Thackson. Sure appreciate you building this nice place on my land."

Chapter Eight

Dipsey stood in the main room of Bull's cabin. Fists on her hips, she stared at her brother-in-law, her brow knitted in scorn, her distaste for the man obvious. "This is not your land, Stephen."

"Ahhh, Dipsey, mouthy as ever. Guess that comes from your whoring roots."

She stiffened and gasped. Joshua launched himself at the man, swinging his fists. Hand on the boy's head, holding him away from him, Stephen merely laughed.

Bull pulled Joshua to his side. "Let me take care of your uncle." He pushed him toward his mother, who put an arm around his shoulders.

"Let's take this outside, Mr. Thackson. No need to mess up my furniture."

Stephen chuckled. "So, she's spreading her legs for you. Maybe she will for me, too, after I move in. She can pay for her and the boy's keep."

Bull shoved him outside and down the steps. "Okay, let's get something clear. If you say another ugly word about Mrs. Thackson, I'll beat you to a pulp."

"Hee-hee." Grin filthy, the man shrugged out of his jacket and tossed it across the porch rail. "Got it bad, huh?"

He circled, eyeing Bull. He feinted and charged, his blow catching Bull on the chin. Bull stumbled back a step. Good. Stephen Thackson had struck the first blow. That should satisfy Sheriff Cannon's edict about no more brawling.

Thackson snickered. "Come on, big man. Let's see what you've got."

His taunt added fuel to Bull's simmering anger. How dare this twisted man come waltzing into Bull's home and, with his ugly words and assumptions, wipe the smile off Dipsey's lovely face. Her day had gone so well. She'd laughed at the café and joked with him. Now this.

Dipsey and Joshua had stepped out onto the porch. Stephen jeered, "Now watch a real man in action, Dipsey. I'm sure I can pleasure you more than this old man."

Through the roar in his ears, Bull heard her gasp. He swung and connected with Stephen's face again and again. When the man went down, Bull grabbed his shirtfront, yanked him into a sitting position, and continued to pound him. Rage consumed him. How dare this piece of scum treat Dispey so? He was evil. Bull had seen plenty of people like him in his fifty-five years.

"Stop it, Bull!" Hands pulled at his coat. "You'll kill him." Sobs broke through the haze before his eyes, and he stopped. His lungs hurt and he drew in deep breaths of air.

"Okay...okay...you're right." He released Stephen and turned to Dipsey and the boy. She was sobbing openly, and Joshua's chin trembled. He put an arm around each of them. "I'm sorry. I didn't mean to be so harsh, but he has such a foul mouth. He'd better learn to control it."

Joshua blurted, "He deserved it. He's mean." He looked up at Bull, his eyes filled with admiration. Bull cringed, guilty at allowing his rage to surface. "Someday I'm going to be able to whup bullies like that."

Bull laid a hand on the boy's shoulder. "Violence is not always the answer. A man tries to solve his problems peacefully, but I couldn't allow him to talk about your ma that way."

Stephen groaned, and they all turned toward him.

"We better get him on his horse."

Bull pulled Thackson to his feet. The man wobbled for a few seconds and then gained his balance. His bloodied eyes leveled on Bull.

"I'll get you for this."

"You do that, Stephen."

"Who are you, anyway? What are Dipsey and the boy to you?"

"I'm Bull Dawson, new to Prairie, and I intend for Dipsey to be my wife."

Thackson snorted and laughed. "Think you're marrying a rich widow, huh? Hate to disappoint you, but this land and everything on it is mine."

"We'll see about that, Stephen."

"I've got papers to prove it."

"Fine. Take them to the judge in town. I'm not sure, but I believe Mrs. Thackson has a will."

****

Two days later, Dipsey arrived at Jonas Bailey's law office to find Bull, Charity, and Mr. Bailey poring over several documents.

Charity rushed forward, hugged her, and led her toward a chair. "Have a seat. We'll be ready to walk over to the courthouse here in just a minute." She patted her hand. "You are not to worry. Stephen Thackson will not take your land."

"It's for Joshua, not me. I know Thomas wanted his son to have the land. How could Stephen think otherwise?"

Bull's gaze landed on her, warming her with its sincerity. "We know that, Dipsey. Stephen is greedy and trying to steal it for himself."

"Thomas told me Stephen sold his part of the farm to him years ago, long before he married me."

His expression hopeful, Mr. Bailey asked, "Do you have a copy of the deed of sale, or know if Thomas filed it with the county?"

Sick at heart, she shook her head. Why hadn't she asked more questions when Thomas was alive? When he'd gotten sick, he'd dictated a will to her. Turner and Aunt Ruby came over to witness his signature, but Stephen was claiming his parents' will left the land to be divided equally between Thomas and himself.

She shuddered at the thought of having to share with her brother-in-law, of having him live nearby. Every time he'd ever visited he made advances toward her and called her a whore. Thomas hadn't believed her until he'd caught his brother trying to rape her. Stephen had taken a terrible beating that day, and Thomas had told him to never step foot on the farm again.

Mr. Bailey shrugged into his coat and set his hat on his head. "I'm going over to the county clerk's office to look for the deed. I'll start back twenty-five years. Do you think that's far enough back, Mrs. Thackson?"

She thought for a minute. "Yes, Thomas married me fourteen years ago.

"Thanks, Jonas," said Charity. "We'll go to lunch and meet you at one o'clock. Would you like us to bring you something to eat?"

"No, I had a big breakfast. I'll be fine 'til supper."

****

Promptly at one o'clock, Judge Howell pounded his gavel on the sound block, the bangs resonating off the walls. "Mr. Jamison, I see you're representing Mr. Thackson. Let's see what you've got."

Charity had filled Bull in on the pompous Mr. Jamison. He was in full form today, posturing before the judge and the few observers in the courtroom. Bull swallowed his laughter.

"I have here, Judge, a copy of the original will of Mr. Thomas Thackson, Senior. It clearly states that the land in question was to be divided equally between his two sons—Thomas Thackson and Stephen Thackson."

"Hand it over, Jamison."

The judge studied the paper. "It's dated January 18, 1855. Do you have a copy of the original deed?"

"Yes, indeed, Judge."

"Well, let me have it, then."

The man approached again and laid the document in front of Judge Howell. He glanced over it and put it with the will before turning his attention to Dipsey. His eyes darted from her to Charity to Bull. "Where's Mr. Bailey?"

Charity stood. "He's at the county clerk's office, Your Honor."

"Mrs. Reardon, we've been over this more times than I can count. You cannot practice law in my court. Now, if Mr. Bailey doesn't appear in five minutes, I'll have to rule in favor of Mr. Thackson."

"Yes, Your Honor, I do understand, but I'm hoping you'll allow my father, Mr. Buford Dawson from New York City, to argue in Mr. Bailey's absence."

Judge Howell peered over the top of his glasses at Bull. "What do you have to say for yourself, sir?"

Bull stood. "Your Honor, I'm licensed to practice law in the state of New York, but not in Texas. I'm serving as an apprentice to Mr. Bailey and plan to take the Texas bar exam in June."

The judge nodded. "Proceed, then."

Jamison jumped up. "Your Honor, I object. This man isn't licensed in Texas."

"Sit down, Jamison. This is my court, and I'll run it how I see fit." He nodded at Bull. "Proceed."

"Thank you, Your Honor." Bull approached the judge and placed Thomas Thackson's will on his desk. "This will was dictated to Mrs. Thackson by her husband as he lay ill and dying, just over two years ago."

After looking over the document, Judge Howell asked, "Are the witnesses here today?"

"Yes, Your Honor."

"Stand up, you two." Evidently the judge knew Turner and Ruby. "Do you both vow that when you witnessed this will Thomas Thackson was aware of what was in the document and of sound mind?"

"Sure do, Judge," quipped Turner.

"I do," replied Ruby.

Judge Howell gave a dismissive wave. "Sit down, then."

"Your Honor," howled Jamison, "I'd like to cross-examine them."

"I bet you would, but denied." He turned his gaze

on Bull. "Unfortunately, Mr. Dawson, this document only insures that half of the land be passed down to Joshua Thackson. Legally the other half belongs to Mr. Stephen Thackson."

"Yes, Your Honor, but it's common knowledge Stephen Thackson sold his half to his brother Thomas some years ago."

Stephen jumped to his feet. "That's a lie. The whore is lying."

The sound of Judge Howell's gavel hitting the desktop rang through the room. "Shut your ugly mouth, Mr. Thackson. You'll not be talking to a woman in my courtroom in such a manner. Either apologize to the lady, or I'll collect a fifty-dollar fine from you."

For a moment Bull thought the fool would pay the fine, but he finally said, "I'm sorry."

"You'll stand up and look at the lady."

Face red, tendons straining against his neck, Stephen stood and faced Dipsey. "My apologies, Mrs. Thackson." Back rigid, she nodded.

The back door flew open and Jonas rushed down the aisle waving a piece of paper. "I found it. I found the deed." He slid in to stand beside Charity. "May I approach, Your Honor?"

"You may."

"This deed states that Stephen Thackson sold his half of the land to Thomas Thackson on August 1, 1874."

Judge Howell turned to Thackson. "I'm afraid you don't have a leg to stand on. The land belongs to Joshua Thackson in its entirety and will be managed by his mother until he comes of age." He hit the sounding box once. "Court's adjourned."

Chapter Nine

Dipsey sat with Charity while Bull and Jonas talked with Jamison. The minute the proceedings were over, the other attorney had leaned over and said a few words to his client. Then he joined his opponents to chitchat. Evidently the lawyer held no hard feelings. She wished the same were true for her brother-in-law.

Stephen remained seated for a moment, his hands folded in front of him on the table. He slowly rose and turned to Dipsey. His gaze never leaving her face, he walked to stand before her. Dread inched up her spine.

Rage and hate transformed his handsome features. He spat out, "You'll pay for this, bitch. You and your brat."

She jumped to her feet. "Don't you come near me or my boy."

His lip curled as he rocked back on his heels. "Or what?"

She trembled but clenched her fists to steady herself. "I'll kill you if I have to, that's what." And she would. No one would hurt her son. He'd suffered enough.

Charity put an arm around Dipsey's waist. "Stay away from them, Mr. Thackson. It's not her fault you sold your share of the property." She called, "Daddy, Mr. Thackson needs to be shown out."

"Is that so?" Bull approached, face stern, and

cocked a brow at Stephen.

Stephen slammed his hat on his head and glared at Dipsey. "I'm leaving." He walked down the aisle and out the door. Each thud of his boot heels echoed doom. Dipsey feared he wouldn't let things go easily. They'd hear from him again, and he'd use more than words the next time.

"Are you okay?" Bull's blue eyes bored into hers. This man truly cared about her and her son. She'd never dreamed to see such concern from a man again. How had she been so fortunate?

"A little shook up, but fine."

He rounded the table and pulled her into his arms. "I'll not let him hurt you or Joshua."

Dipsey melted into him, her head against his chest. She inhaled his male scent, the fragrance of freshly laundered and starched shirt, and his spicy aftershave. He rubbed her back, the motion soothing the tension along her spine. Could she trust this man with her life? With Joshua's life? Yes, she believed she could. Could she trust him with her heart? Did it matter? Probably not, as she'd already given it to him. He cared, yes, but did he love her?

"I don't trust Stephen. I don't think it's safe for you and Joshua to stay by yourselves. What if I stay with you?"

Dipsey stepped back. He dropped his arms.

"Daddy, that wouldn't be proper. Remember, things are different in this day and age."

What on earth did Charity mean by that—different in this day and age? They'd always been that way. An unmarried man and woman didn't stay in the same house unless they were chaperoned.

"They can stay with us. Dawson will love having Joshua, and Aunt Ruby and I will enjoy having Dipsey to visit with." She clapped her hands together in glee. "It's just a few days until Christmas. Won't it be fun to all be together on Christmas Day? We'll have Cole and Dessa Jeffers over, too."

Sharing the holiday with friends and family sounded like a dream come true to Dipsey. But it wasn't possible. "I can't leave our place unattended. Stephen could burn it down."

Charity grabbed up the papers on the table and stuffed them into a folder. "Don't worry about your farm. Turner will send a couple of men over to stay and see to things."

Tears pricked Dipsey's eyes. "Ya'll are so good to me, Charity. How'd I get such good friends and neighbors?"

"By being one yourself, that's how." Charity grinned. "Come on, now. Let's get to the parsonage and pick up Dawson. He'll have run Mrs. Booker ragged by now."

****

Dipsey settled into the Reardons' spare room. Their house was bigger than her own, and nicer, but hers was comfortable enough for her. She hung a couple of dresses on a peg on the wall and put her underthings in one of the empty drawers.

The door was open, and Charity bustled in. "Can you come downstairs? Daddy and the Jefferses are here. We want to share something with you."

"Be right with you." She followed Charity down the stairs. Bull met her and escorted her to the settee, where she sat beside Dessa. Cole stood behind his wife, one hand on the couch back. Charity moved to sit on the arm of Turner's chair, her arm around his shoulders. Bull sat in the one remaining chair in the room.

Dipsey couldn't imagine what this was about, but from their expressions, it was serious. Fear and dread inched up her spine. Was their friendship all a sham?

Bull coughed. "What we have to share with you is unusual, and you may have difficulty believing it."

Turner chuckled. "Yeah, though I believed Charity, Cole's experience erased any doubt I might've had."

Cole grinned. "Sure made a believer out of me."

What on earth were they talking about?

Bull leaned forward and studied her intently. "You see, Dipsey, Charity, Dessa, and I are from the future. We traveled back in time—me from 2012, Dessa from 2010, and Charity from 2008." Bull's hands waved around as he described his frustration at not knowing how to trigger events to send him back. She followed their movement up and down, out and back, her mind numb with shock. She shook herself to focus. He was saying that his last night in the future, he'd lain down on that quilt, out under the stars, and woken in 1892. She remembered how he'd whooped for joy, the morning she found him, when she'd told him the date.

Dipsey couldn't speak. Her eyes sought those of the others, waiting for them to deny what Bull had said. She didn't want to call him a liar, and she didn't want to believe he was crazy.

Her desperation must have shown. "Now, Dipsey," Charity reached for her hand. "I know this sounds crazy, but it's true." She described her arrival in Prairie, her shock and disbelief.

Dipsey had heard about Turner's trial, how Charity

had married him to save him from hanging, and the commotion when Charity proved it was the banker who'd killed the widow and those other women. But she'd not known all the details of Charity's arrival in Prairie, nor Dessa's.

Dessa explained her appearance in the middle of the outlaws' camp and then handed Dipsey a book titled *Outlaws of Texas*. "This was published in 1992. Cole didn't believe I was from the future, but the outlaws who kidnapped me wounded him and left him near where I'd appeared." Face animated, she glanced up at her husband and smiled. "He got caught up in that mysterious mist and ended up in 2010 at the cabin where I'd been staying."

"The same one where Daddy and I stayed, too," piped Charity.

"Talk about a shock, Dipsey," said Cole. "I'd never seen such outlandish things in all my born days. I grabbed the book Dessa had mentioned and hightailed it back to the fog as fast as I could. I didn't want to chance having to stay in the future with all those newfangled things."

Charity stood. "Well, we'll leave you with Daddy now. We know this is a lot to take in, but know this— Dessa and I ended up here accidentally, but we chose to stay because we fell in love with these two wonderful men. I got word to Daddy in the future about what had happened to me and that I was happy. Daddy came back to 1892 intentionally, to be with me and Dawson, his family."

With a parting smile, Charity strode to the door, and everyone in the room but Bull followed her out the door.

She must have appeared cold-cocked.

Bull's face scrunched with concern as he peered down at her. He patted her shoulder. "You stay put. I'll be right back." He returned with a glass. "This is brandy. Strong stuff, so take small sips."

Small sips? After what she'd heard? She took a large swallow and gasped as the fiery liquid ran down her throat to warm her belly. It wasn't like the watered-down whiskey she'd drunk at the saloon years ago.

Bull sat down beside her on the settee. "You're wondering why we told you all this, aren't you?"

"Yes."

"Do you believe us?"

To delay answering, she raised the glass and took just a sip of the beverage this time. It went down much more easily. Her eyes met his eager face and tried to answer without hurting him. "I'd be lying if I said yes, but I believe *you* believe it."

"It's true, I promise." He sat back and took her free hand. "Do you think I'm crazy?"

Though the thought had entered her mind, if he was nuts, that meant the Reardons and Jefferses were, too. She'd known them long enough to know they were some of the sanest people around. From the first time she'd met Charity and Dessa, as well as Bull, she'd sensed they were different, but it wasn't something she could explain.

She squeezed his hand. "No, I don't."

He released a breath. "Thank God." He took the glass from her hand and drained it before setting it on the table beside him. "Do you care for me, Dipsey?"

Her heart thumped in her chest and sent blood rushing to her face. "Yes, I do, Bull. Very much."

He smiled and moved closer, his arm around her shoulder. His lips close to her ear, he whispered, "I'm going to kiss you. If you object, you'd better say so now."

She giggled and tilted her face to his, anticipation setting butterflies loose in her stomach. Shocked at her forward behavior, she decided to avoid brandy in the future.

He lowered his head, touching his lips to hers. They were hard, but gentle. He increased the pressure and Dipsey, hands gripping his coat lapels, met him as each searched and found the response they desired.

Flames, hotter than the ones resulting from the brandy, lit in Dipsey's limbs and traveled up her body, the one she'd believed dead to passion. His kiss stoked the fire until she pulled back with a gasp, seeking air.

Bull dropped his forehead to hers. "Ah, darling, I never thought to love again, but I love you. Will you marry me?"

"Yes, Bull. I love you, too."

Chapter Ten

Saturday morning, Bull waited for Dipsey in the parlor. Today they'd ride into town to pick out wedding rings. Joshua had spent the night with Aaron Booker, so they'd pick him up before they returned this afternoon.

Footsteps on the treads alerted him to her arrival, and he walked to meet her at the foot of the stairs. Lovely as usual, today she was radiant. Her hair in a loose bun, tendrils of blond curls gently framed her face, and freshly cut bangs covered her scar. The mar on her forehead hadn't bothered him, but from her smile of self-confidence, he could see covering it did wonders for this wonderful woman's sense of self.

"Dipsey, you are beautiful."

She blushed and touched the hair covering her forehead. "How do you like my bangs?"

"I like them. They suit you, as do those curls around your face, but you'd be lovely bald."

She swatted him playfully on the arm. "Oh, you."

This woman had smiled and laughed more in the past few days than she had in the months he'd known her. Her happiness warmed him.

"I've never thought of such a style, but Dessa and Charity said many women in your time wear them."

"Yes, they do, and I bet the ladies in Prairie will be copying your new style in the weeks to come."

She blinked at him in shock and then laughed.

He grabbed her hand and pulled her forward into his arms. "Give me a kiss, darling."

She tilted her face to his and kissed him. Aunt Ruby's snort as she entered from the kitchen caused Dipsey to jump back.

Ruby chirped, "You two best get to town before the stores close. And best get that new preacher to marry you before you jump the gun and have the honeymoon before the wedding."

Dipsey squealed, "Ruby! What a thing to say."

Bull laughed and slipped Dipsey's cape over her shoulders. "She has a point. Let's go."

Their first stop was the mercantile. They pored over rings. He wanted to buy her a band with diamonds, but she resisted. "I'd have to take it off while I worked. I want one to wear all the time and not have to worry about losing stones in the garden or the dishwater."

They settled on matching gold bands. Before they finished shopping, he planned to buy her a locket with diamonds. Christmas was three days away.

"While I'm looking at suits, pick out a wedding dress and a couple of church dresses. A new bonnet, too."

"I don't need—"

"I want you to have them. Humor me, okay?"

Her face lit with a smile. "All right. Will you pick out a suit for Joshua? His old one is too small." Before he could answer, she was weaving her way toward the bonnets displayed against the wall.

He enjoyed seeing her happiness selecting new things. No matter the century, women did love to shop.

While she tried on dresses, he slipped back over to the jewelry case and picked out a locket. The proprietor, Mr. White, wrapped the trinket in festive paper, and Bull placed the small package in his pocket while Mrs. White helped Dipsey with dresses.

They left the store loaded with packages. Bull stowed them on the floor in the back of the buggy. "Let's go eat lunch before going to the Bookers."

Dipsey's brow puckered. "You're spending a lot of money today. Don't we need to be frugal, save for next winter?"

Her worry was touching. Their lives were so different, but he wanted to spoil her a little.

"We can afford it." He took her arm and guided her down the street to the café.

As they ate he described, in low whispers, the vest he'd had on the morning he'd arrived and how much gold he'd carried inside.

Eyes round, she chuckled. "I thought you were rather thick around the middle."

"Thought I was fat, huh?"

"Well, maybe not fat, but I think stocky is more the word."

He snorted. "Sounds like fat to me." He tried to sound hurt but wasn't successful. She grinned, and he winked.

They finished their meal and drove to Pastor Booker's home beside the church. Oblivious to the cold, Joshua, Aaron, and Billy Brodie played ball in the front yard. Bull and Dipsey exchanged glances. Her face lit with a smile. It was good to see the boys had made peace.

Bull helped Dipsey from the buggy, and they walked up to the porch to be met by Mrs. Booker, her rosy face lit in a huge smile. "Hello, dears. What a joyous day it is to see you two planning a wedding. Come in, come in, Caleb is waiting for you."

Caleb Booker shook hands with Bull. "Ya'll have a seat."

He and Dipsey sat on the settee while the Bookers each took a chair.

Bull forged ahead. "We'd like to get married next Saturday, if that's agreeable with you."

Mrs. Booker raised her hands and fluttered them beside her head. "Wonderful. Folks will be so excited. Since it's cold out, I'll see if we can have your party in the town hall."

Pastor Booker glanced at his wife and smiled. "I think that would be perfect. It gives everyone a week to prepare."

She leaned over and patted Dipsey's hand. "Don't you worry about the reception. The ladies of this community are noted for providing a fine celebration. They'll be tickled to take care of everything."

"Really?" asked Dipsey. "I don't need to do a thing?"

"Just show up and be beautiful. By the way, I love your new hairstyle."

****

Dipsey laid her new wedding dress across the back of a chair so it wouldn't wrinkle. With it she'd wear the beautiful locket Bull had presented her with on Christmas Day. She ran a finger over the rose gold, circling the diamond in the center. She'd never owned anything so fine. Two more days and she'd be Mrs. Dawson. She sighed with contentment.

Bull could afford to provide her and Joshua with luxuries they'd never experienced before, but his love and caring meant far more. Her son adored the man. If Thomas could see them from heaven, he'd be smiling. He'd have liked Bull.

She and Joshua had been away a week. Bull hadn't wanted them to return home, but she needed to be in her own place, collect her thoughts, and do some packing. They'd decided to live in Bull's new home after the wedding and find renters for the farm. Plenty of folks would jump at an opportunity to work their land on a share basis.

Stephen must have left the area, as they'd not seen hide nor hair of him since that day in court. Joshua was happier than she'd seen him since before Thomas passed away. They both had much to be grateful for.

She went downstairs to finish supper. Joshua sat at the kitchen table with his lessons. He pushed his books aside when she set a plate down beside him. Tonight was cold ham, green beans she'd canned last summer, and bread.

Joshua finished and carried his plate to the sink to wash and dry. "I'll go feed the boys and the horses."

"No, I'll do it. You finish your studies."

"You sure? This essay is taking me longer than I thought."

"I'm sure." She ruffled his hair, and for once he didn't jerk away. She resisted leaning in to give him a hug; she didn't want to push her luck and lose the ground they'd gained since Bull had entered their lives. There'd be time for hugs later.

It was still plenty light outside, so she wouldn't need to light the house lantern. She slipped into Thomas's old coat, stepped outside, and strolled across the yard to the barn. Inside she scooped a portion of grain into a pail for each of the boys and then Joshua's paint and her Mazie. The animals munched away while she gave them each water. Suddenly the two mules snorted and rolled their eyes in agitation.

"What on earth?" She turned—and stared into Stephen's hate-filled eyes. Frantic, she darted to get around him. He laughed and caught her. She fought, and his slap to her face sent her reeling back into a wooden beam. She cried out from the pain in her back and slid to the ground, but struggled to scoot away from him as she sought a weapon of any kind.

"No one's here to save you this time. I'm going to take my pleasure with you, and then beat you senseless. We'll see how that fancy man of yours feels about marrying you then." He laughed as he unbuckled his gun belt, hung it over a stall, and loosened the buttons on his trousers. "He'll not want you then, all used and ugly."

Her body shook with fear and revulsion. "Please...please...don't do this. Somebody may be watching the place right now and catch you. They'll hang you, if they don't shoot you first."

"Nope. I scoured the place real good. Reardon's men all went home." He frowned. "Don't yell and bring the boy out. I'll shoot him, and you know it." He dropped to his knees before her. She shut her eyes against the sight of his leering face. He slapped her. "Open your eyes." She forced them open. Her mind snapped shut.

****

Dipsey lay curled into a ball on her side. The barn door creaked, jolting her from the misery. *Joshua. Nooo!*

"Ma. Are you all—"

Joshua's eyes widened when he saw Stephen, who stood grinning as he strapped on his gun belt. They darted to her as she pushed to sit up.

"I'm fine, son. Go back to the house."

"Yeah, boy. Mind your ma, now."

"You bastard!" He ran at Stephen, fists swinging, and caught him on the nose. Blood spurted as Joshua went for his shins, kicking him.

Stephen roared and grabbed Joshua by the hair. He hit him in the face over and over again. Dipsey screamed and clawed at Stephen's legs. "Stop, please, he's just a boy."

"He broke my nose. I'm going to kill him."

She grappled to get the gun in the holster at his hip. He backhanded her. Her head hit a post and stars danced in front of her eyes. She pulled herself up by the post and lunged for the pitchfork hanging on the back wall. It dropped easily into her hands. Fear for her son and revulsion at what Stephen had done to her fueled her strength as she plunged the tines into his back.

Chapter Eleven

Stephen screamed and reached back, trying to grab the fork handle. Dipsey held on, moving as he did, maneuvering him away from Joshua. If Stephen fell, the tines might pierce her son, who lay at his feet.

"Ahhhhh...you bitch...may you rot...in hell." He choked and blood spewed from his mouth.

Crying, sobs rising from her stomach in spasms, Dipsey shoved and sent Stephen tumbling forward onto the ground. He lay still, blood forming a pool beneath him. She fell to her knees and emptied her stomach on the dirt floor.

Shaking with fear and revulsion, she crawled to Joshua and cradled his head in her arms. His eyes were bruised and red, his nose crooked and bleeding, the flesh of his lips broken, but his chest rose and fell. Gratitude swelled in her chest. Tears fell on his face as she rocked him. "I'm so sorry. Oh, God, forgive me. I did this to my child. My past will never let me go."

He moaned. "Ma? Ma!" He tried to sit up, but she held him in place with the palm of her hand.

"It's all right, son. You're going to be okay. I'll get help." She laid him back against the hay and, on her knees, made her way to Stephen's side. Hand against his back, she waited to feel a rise. Nothing. Good. He deserved to die. She felt no remorse in having killed him. He'd taken her last chance of happiness, taken her dignity, and hurt her child.

She reached for his gun, pulled it from the holster, and with it clasped in her hands pulled herself up by one of the support beams. Outside, she turned toward the Reardons' place and fired three rounds into the air. They would hear it, as would Bull. She returned to her son and held him until they arrived.

****

Bull dropped to his knees by Dipsey. Tears blurred his vision at the wounded expression in her eyes. He knew from the pain he saw there that Stephen had violated her. His hand shook as he stroked her hair and murmured words of comfort, his voice thick with his own pain at seeing her so. Her grip on Joshua tightened when Turner tried to take him.

"Let me get him inside, so Doc can tend to him."

Bull stroked her hands. "Come on, darling, he's going to be okay."

Big tears trickled down her cheeks, but she nodded and turned loose.

Turner lifted the boy and carried him outside.

Bull sank to the straw and pulled Dipsey across his lap. Arms around her, he held her close and, words choked, whispered against her hair, "I'm so sorry, my love. I'd do anything to remove your pain."

She clutched at his shirt, her face hidden against his chest. Shudders raked her frame. He drew her nearer, trying to ease the shakes and also prevent her from seeing Cole jerk the rake from Stephen's body. Two of Turner's men lifted him onto a tarp and rolled it around him.

Cole approached and squatted down beside them. "Dipsey, listen to me now." She raised her head and stared at the next stall, refusing to make eye contact. "I think I know what happened here, and I'm sorry to have to do this, but I've got to know for sure. I'm going to ask some questions. Just nod yes or no. Can you do that?" She bit her lip and nodded.

He pushed his hat back on his head, giving them a full view of his eyes. Grooves of concern wrinkled his brow. "I need you to look at me, Dipsey."

She sucked in a deep breath and returned Cole's gaze.

"Now, Stephen attacked you? Is that right?"

She nodded.

"Joshua tried to protect you and Stephen beat him." She trembled but her head bobbed once.

"That's when you used the pitchfork on him."

"Ye...yes...and God forgive me...but I'm not sorry."

Cole stood. "Don't blame you one bit. The man deserved to die for what he did to you and the boy. It was clearly defense of your son. He might've killed Joshua if you hadn't stopped him."

Bull breathed a sigh of relief. He liked how the law worked in the old West. There'd be no waste of time on investigations, no squandering of money on a trial. Cut and dried law enforcement. Of course there were exceptions, but this situation was clear cut.

He moved Dipsey off his lap, stood, and helped her to stand. His fingers traced the broken skin on her face and lips. "Let's get you in the house so Ruby can help you clean up and treat these cuts."

"I don't think I'll ever be clean again."

****

Dipsey sank into the warm water Ruby and Bull

had poured into the round tin tub she kept on the back porch. Now Ruby bustled around her, talking as she placed clean towels and a gown on the back of a kitchen chair.

"Just 'cause you've got a few bruises don't mean you need to postpone the wedding. Folks will understand. Now, you just get all that crying out of your system and put this dirty business behind you."

Yeah, most people probably would, but there were still those in the community who hadn't accepted her. They'd say she'd asked for Stephen's attentions. She shuddered at the memory of his touch, the hate in his eyes and voice.

Dipsey soaped a rag and scrubbed at her skin. Would she ever feel clean again? No. Stephen had stolen what little dignity she'd regained in her life. She couldn't marry Bull. He deserved a clean woman. Her tainted past had been bad enough, but now this... "No, there will be no wedding."

"Well, if you want to put it off a week, folks will understand."

"No, Ruby. I'm not getting married this Saturday or next. Bull is a good man. He deserves better than the likes of me."

Ruby stood, hands fisted on her hips. "Now, you listen to me, missy. That man loves you. He don't care that a man's had you before him, else he'd not have courted you in the first place."

The truth stung. Perhaps what the older woman said was true, but Dipsey wasn't changing her mind. She loved Bull too much to saddle him with an unclean wife. Folks had begun to tolerate her. Now they'd recoil in revulsion and possibly avoid him too.

"Now, step out of that tub before you turn into a prune." Ruby shook open a towel, and with her head averted held it open for Dipsey to step into. Gentle arms wrapped the fabric around her and hugged her. "I know you're hurting, honey, but remember, you did nothing wrong. Stephen is the dirty one here. Don't let him spoil all the good in your life."

Dipsey sobbed against Ruby's shoulder as that dear older lady whispered words of comfort and patted her back. At last she was dried up. She kissed Ruby on the cheek. "You're a good woman, Aunt Ruby."

"Pshaw." She sniffed, and Dipsey caught the gleam of a tear on the wrinkled face before she turned away. "I'll clean this up while you slip into a gown and robe. Go on up and see your boy."

Dipsey swallowed a grimace of pain as she climbed the stairs. The area inside her thighs hurt from Stephen's brutal treatment, and bruises marked the pale flesh of her hips and legs. No matter. It was the invisible aches that wouldn't fade. Or would they, in time?

Bull sat beside Joshua's bed talking quietly. His bass voice blended with the higher tone of her son's. "I couldn't protect her, Bull." His voice broke. "I tried, but—"

"You tried, son. Stephen was a coward. No real man forces himself on a woman or beats up a boy." Bull grabbed Joshua's hand. "You did more than most boys your age." His chin wobbled. "I'm so glad you're going to be my son. I'll be the proudest father in the county."

Dipsey shoved a fist in her mouth to cover her cry, but they both looked up.

"Ma." Her son was a small boy again, and she rushed to his side.

She sat on the edge of his bed and smoothed the tears from his cheeks. "I'm so proud of you, even though I'd like to spank you for attacking Stephen like that. He could have killed you."

"I had to do something, Ma." His eyes searched her face. "I know what he did...did...to you." His voice broke. "Will you be all right?"

"Yes, I'll be fine." Her heart broke for him. He'd be so disappointed at her decision, had been disappointed so many times in his young life, but it couldn't be helped. "Do you think that since we're both all banged up I might be able to kiss you?"

He glanced at Bull, who grinned and nodded. "I guess so."

She leaned down and kissed both cheeks and then his forehead. His arms came around her and squeezed. It took all her strength to keep from wailing.

****

"What do you mean there'll be no wedding?" Bull stood before her in the parlor. His face paled, then quickly went beet red.

She turned away so he wouldn't see the pain in her eyes. "I can't marry you. I'm dirty. You deserve better."

He roared. "That's ridiculous. I love you. What Stephen did to you doesn't affect who you are or how I feel about you. Now, that said, we're getting married Saturday. Your bruises have healed." He paced the room. "I could understand you wanting to wait until they cleared up, but they're gone."

"I can't, Bull. I'm sorry, but I can't."

"Why? Don't you love me? Did you lie about that?"

She whirled. "No. You know I didn't."

He took her hands and brought them to his lips. "Then marry me Saturday."

"I can't." She croaked, "What if there is a child?"

"Oh, darling, any child of yours will be a child of mine. I'll love him or her as much as I do Joshua, as much as I'd love our child."

Her heart hurt. It threatened to climb up her throat and choke her. She shook her head. "That's what you say now, but in time you might come to resent such a babe."

"That's insulting, Dipsey. I'm a man of my word and I expect you to be a woman of yours." He dropped her hands. "You'd best be ready Saturday, because we're getting married."

"We're not, Bull."

He slammed his hat on his head. "We'll be seeing about that."

Chapter Twelve

Saturday morning Dipsey rose early, washed, dressed, and stepped quietly downstairs. She'd let Joshua sleep a little later this morning. At the kitchen window, she stared out at the barn as the sun rose and cast it in a yellow glow.

Today would have been the day she and Bull married, but there would be no wedding. She'd not seen or heard from him since he'd stomped from the house three days ago. A tear trickled down her cheek, and she brushed it aside. It was just as well. She feared she was pregnant, another blow against her reputation in this town, as her monthly was several days late. Palm protectively across her belly, she vowed to love the child.

Noise from Joshua's room startled her from her reverie. What was he doing up and about so early? She stirred the coals in the fire and put bacon in the pan.

Joshua stomped down the stairs, hitching up the straps on his overalls as he walked. He smiled. "Morning, Ma."

"Morning, son. What are you doing up so early on a Saturday?"

He shrugged. "Anxious to get my chores done." He slipped into his coat, grabbed the milk bucket and went outside.

She sighed. Maybe he'd forgiven her at last for not

marrying Bull. She'd tried to explain her reasons, but they made little sense to him.

They'd no sooner finished breakfast than a wagon arrived with Ruby, Charity, and Dessa, and loaded with parcels. She groaned. She did not need their fussing and interference in her life today. Misery didn't need any company as far as she was concerned.

She opened the door to the women. "What are ya'll doing out and about so early?"

Ruby set a bouquet of flowers, one that looked suspiciously like a wedding posy, on the table. "Why, getting you ready for your wedding, what else?"

"I'm not getting married today."

"Yes, you are," all three women piped.

Charity took her arm and led her into the parlor. "Sit down and listen to me." Dipsey did as she was told. Charity paced the room a minute and then sat down across from her. "My mother died when I was very young, and Daddy never married again, never loved another woman—until you. Now, I'm not saying he didn't have sex with women. He's a man, for heaven's sake, and in our time period people have sex before marriage, if they so choose."

Dipsey's mouth fell open. Did she mean all women were soiled doves?

Charity saw her expression and laughed. "No, not like that. If a couple is committed, but not ready to get married, they might even live together."

"And people accept this?"

"Not all. Some do more readily than others." Her grin sobered. "Now, Daddy knew you were a prostitute before, but he didn't think you became one because you liked the lifestyle. He figured you were forced into it to survive."

Dipsey nodded. "Few people see it that way, though."

"That's true, but what's important is how Daddy sees it, right?"

She had to admit Charity's words made sense. "Possibly."

"Don't you care what he thinks?"

"Of course I do."

"Then think about this. You are not any different in Daddy's eyes because of the rape. If anything, he loves you more than he did before." She dropped her palms to her thighs. Dipsey jumped at the clap. "Now, you can sit around and feel sorry for yourself, or make yourself, my daddy, and your son happy by getting married today."

****

Bull thought he'd faint from sheer joy when he saw Dipsey enter the church on Joshua's arm. They'd sent word she was coming, but until he saw her, he'd had doubts. What had the women said to convince her to show up today and go through with the ceremony?

The organist began the wedding march, and before he recovered from his elation, Dipsey was his wife.

"You may kiss your bride, Mr. Dawson."

He raised her veil and leaned close, their noses almost touching. His heart hammered with joy. "I love you, Mrs. Dawson."

Her smile was radiant. "I love you too, Bull Dawson."

It had been a while since they'd kissed. When his lips touched hers, he clasped her tightly, molding her body to his, as he stroked her mouth with his own.

Dipsey wrapped her arms around his neck and returned his kiss with equal ardor. At the hoots and cheers from the congregation, they broke apart.

Dipsey covered her red cheeks with her hands and then laughed.

As usual the ladies of Prairie had outdone themselves. Tables groaned under the weight of the food and decorations. A baseball diamond had been laid out, and Joshua, along with the other town boys, played baseball. A few of the men joined in. On another day, Bull would take part, but not today.

He slipped an arm around Dipsey's waist and squeezed. "Are you ready to go?"

"So early?"

His face must have shown his disappointment, because she grinned and winked. "Yes, let's say goodbye."

The goodbyes took too long, in his opinion. An hour later they were in the buggy, headed home. Dipsey scooted closer and laid her head on his shoulder.

He slipped his arm around her waist, enjoying their closeness and Dipsey's sweet fragrance. Though new at this buggy driving business, he dared to take his eyes from the road and kiss her. Fearing they'd end up off the road, he turned his attention back to the horse. "How did the women convince you to come today?"

She cuddled closer and placed her hand over the top of his, twining their fingers. "Well, Charity told me a tale about the future...how women have sex before marriage...how Stephen's attack didn't change who I was.... She was convincing."

"That's my girl. Charity always could argue a good case."

His adopted dog met them as they turned onto the property, trotting alongside as the buggy progressed. Belle tolerated his presence, and the mongrel had sense enough not to get in her way.

"Have you decided on a name for him yet?"

"No. I expect Joshua can help out with that. They'll probably be good buddies."

"He'll like that. His last dog didn't return one day. Probably a bobcat got him. I've been slow to replace him. If I had, maybe Stephen wouldn't have snuck up on me that night."

Belle stopped in front of the house. He placed two fingers on Dipsey's lips. "Let's not be dwelling on what we can't change, love."

He lifted Dipsey down from the buggy. "I'll be inside in a minute." She started for the door. "Wait...wait." He caught her on the porch and lifted her into his arms. "I almost forgot, darling."

She curled an arm around his neck. "I'm glad you remembered. I felt a little bereft there for a minute."

Her skirts hampered his ability to see the doorknob, and he bumped against the wood as he searched. She giggled. "Here, let me." Leaning toward the door, she turned the knob.

With his hip, he pushed the heavy wood away and walked into the main room. "Welcome to our home, Dipsey."

Cupping his cheek, she kissed him, a short but heady gesture that left him wanting more, but he was a patient man.

"I love this place, Bull."

He sat her on her feet. "I built it with you in mind, you know."

"You did not."

"Did too."

Feeling around on the table, he located the matches and then lit the hanging light over the kitchen table. It washed his bride in a warm glow.

"The day we met, I never saw you smile, but once..." He shook his head. "I can't remember what happened exactly, but your lips twitched, and I saw how pretty you'd be with a smile on your face." He tapped her nose. "I was interested then, but it was the day Turner and I rode out to see your land I made up my mind to marry you."

Eyes round, jaw dropped, she gaped at him in surprise.

His hands framed her face. "Ah, love, you are a beautiful woman." Anxious to get Belle settled and be back inside with his bride, he planted a quick kiss on her lips. "I'll be right back. There's brandy in the cupboard. I'd enjoy a glass, if you'll join me."

"I'd enjoy a glass, too."

It didn't take long to get Belle bedded down. When he entered through the back door, Dipsey had warm water ready for him to wash up. As he dried his hands, he couldn't take his eyes from her. She'd removed her bonnet and loosened her hair. It hung down her back in golden waves. The soft bangs brought out the blue of her eyes and the beauty of her creamy complexion. Why did she hide such a beautiful asset in a bun?

She handed him a glass. He touched his to hers. "To us."

"Yes, to us."

Their eyes locked over their glasses as they each took a sip. The heady beverage warmed a path down to his belly. He hoped it would calm Dipsey, help her relax tonight. With his hand at her back, he directed her to the sofa. "Let's sit for a while."

Dipsey pulled her feet up under her and leaned into his side. "You're barefoot. Aren't your feet cold?"

"A little, but my new shoes were pinching my toes."

He pulled the quilt from the back of the sofa and laid it across her skirt.

As they sipped their drinks, Bull worried, wondering if she dreaded going to bed with him, if Stephen's ghost would invade their coming together. With his free hand, he allowed his fingers to comb her silky hair.

She dropped her head into his hand. "Mmmm, that's nice." He massaged her scalp. "Are you trying to put me to sleep?"

He chuckled. "No, just want to make sure you're relaxed. I don't want you to fear me."

She drained her glass and handed it to him. He set both tumblers on the ottoman and pulled her onto his lap. Her arms circled his neck. "I don't fear you. The fact you don't find me distasteful after Stephen...makes me trust you more than I ever could have."

"Ah, darling, that makes me so happy." He nuzzled her neck as his hand stroked her back. Encouraged when she didn't stiffen, he allowed his hand to move up her ribcage to cup her breast. "Remember, if you're not ready, we don't have to make love tonight. I'll be content to hold you, to just touch you like this." He stroked her flesh through the cloth with his thumb. Her lids lowered and she moaned softly. "You like this?"

"Mmmm-hum. I do."

He moved her from his lap, stood, and pulled her to her feet. "Time for bed, don't you think?"

"Indeed I do."

****

Fredericksburg, Texas, November 2014

Jacob Reardon stood at the pond and surveyed the area in the semi-dark of early morning. Today a crew would arrive to dismantle the fireplace, and the rocks would be used elsewhere. It'd been a shame to destroy the cabin, but he'd promised to fulfill Granddad Dawson's wishes, and that's what he'd wanted. Something about not wanting more people to go missing, travel back in time, which had been Granddad's goal when he'd purchased the cabin and the land around it. Evidently he was successful, though Jacob didn't know how.

Another crew with graders would also be here soon to start clearing the land for the proposed lake. A shame they'd ruin so many trees.

He sat on a stump and opened the book, *Nineteenth-Century Life in Prairie, Texas,* Granddad had left with him. It fell open to the page he visited most often—the picture of Granddad and his family. He stood in front of a house, his arm around an attractive woman. A teenage boy held a little girl with blond curls. The caption read: Buford "Bull" Dawson, his wife Dipsey, son Joshua, and daughter Amy. It was dated September 1894. Bull had taken the bar exam in June of 1893 and gone into business with Jonas Bailey. No doubt about it, his granddad was a happy man.

Jacob closed the book and stuffed it back in his briefcase. He carried it to his rented truck and poured a cup of coffee from the thermos filled at a local café.

Leaning against the vehicle, he sipped the warm liquid and watched the sun rise over the trees and touch the sparkling water of the pond. A mist rose and inched over the glass surface and beyond, its tendrils seemingly alive.

He pushed away from the truck and stared. That was odd. He'd noticed the fog on other mornings, but it'd never been this thick or widespread. An eerie tingle touched his spine. He shuddered.

Hopefully it would burn off before his crew arrived.

Acknowledgements

For *A Law of Her Own*:

There are several references in history and literature to the custom of "marrying under the gallows."

1. *A Sharp Nose and a Thin Lip* Easton, MA *The Easton Gazette*, Saturday, June 21, 1862 (Salisbury University, Nabb Research Center)

2. Andrews, Andrew. *Old Church Lore* London: William Andrews & Co., The Hull Press; London, 1891

3. Hutchinson, Rev. H.N. *Marriage Customs in Many Lands* D. Appleton Co., *The New York Times Saturday Review of Books and Art*, November 27, 1897, Wednesday

Though the custom of saving a man or woman from the gallows referenced in the articles above occurs in England, France, and on the east coast of the United States, for my short story I've moved the concept to Texas. The mention of an ordinance or law is strictly a figment of my imagination.

I'd like to thank my editor, Eve Mallary, and Baylor Biology PHD student and junior college instructor, Michelle Rapier, for helping me with facts on forensic issues of collecting semen from fabric. Both have access to a font of knowledge on the subject. For facts on the price of land in 1888 and nineteenth-century medical advances, thank you to Google, Wikipedia, and the Texas State Historical Association's *The Handbook of Texas Online*.

Further Acknowledgements

For *A Marshal of Her Own*:
http://www.typewriter.be/remingtonstandard2.htm
http://typewriter.blogofstuff.com/typewriter108.html
http://www.ideafinder.com/history/inventions/typewriter.htm
http://www.ringpen.com/history.html
http://inventors.about.com/library/inventors/blwaterman.htm
http://inventors.about.com/library/weekly/aa100897.htm
http://www.officemuseum.com/pencil_history.htm

A word about the author...

Linda LaRoque is a Texas girl, but the first time she got on a horse, it tossed her in the road, dislocating her right shoulder. Forty years passed before she got on another, but it was older, slower, and she was wiser. Plus, her students looked on and it was important to save face.

A retired teacher who loves West Texas, its flora and fauna, and its people, Linda's stories paint pictures of life, love, and learning set against the raw landscape of ranches and rural communities in Texas and the Midwest. She is a member of RWA, her local chapter of HOTRWA, NTRWA and Texas Mountain Trail Writers.

Linda writes contemporary western romances, time travel romances and futuristic romances.

Visit Linda at these locations.

http://www.lindalaroqueauthor.blogspot.com

www.lindalaroque.com

https://www.facebook.com/linda.laroque

http://www.goodreads.com/author/show/649259.Linda_LaRoque

Linda's Amazon Page

Other Books by Linda LaRoque

Contemporary Suspense
A Stolen Chance

Time Travel

The Turquoise Legacy:
My Heart Will Find Yours
and *Flames on the Sky*
~*~
A Law of Her Own
A Marshal of Her Own
A Love of Her Own